Vets with Benefits

Angel Peaks

Sophie Penhaligon

Published by Sophie Penhaligon, 2022.

VETS WITH BENEFITS

First edition. May 13, 2022.

Written by Sophie Penhaligon.

Chapter 1
Maddie

The first week of January could be difficult for a lot of people and I was no exception. As I sat in The Heavenly Java coffee shop staring out at the icy sidewalks, I considered this fact. It was a dark month with the light fading at around four in the afternoon and coupled with big dumps of snow it was enough to make even the most seasoned snow bunny dream of hibernation.

Saying goodbye to Christmas revelries and taking down the decorations had left me feeling a little empty, coupled with the fact that Christmas had not been the greatest this year. With none of my friends in town I'd spent the week holed up in my parent's home enjoying a fun, old-fashioned family Christmas, which whilst pleasant enough, felt a little lonely without my friends around for support.

As usual, Angel Peaks was buzzing with seasonal ski visitors and the place was almost steaming from their damp ski gear as they tromped around in oversized boots getting snow everywhere, leaving their enormous jackets on the backs of their chairs for people to trip over. I knew the town relied on tourists to fuel the economy, but my mood was such that I just wanted my small town to go back to its sleepy summer days when you could shoot a cannon down Main Street and not hit anyone.

The bell on the door jangled, and I looked up hopefully, to see the elegant figure of my best friend, Kate McKenzie, dressed casually but still managing to look like she'd just come from a photo shoot.

"Kate!" I yelled, a little too enthusiastically as I jumped up and waved, and a couple of tourists who were taking their sweet time drinking their lattes turned to look at me. I watched as their eyes drifted from me to my friend as they followed her journey through the crowded coffee shop to get to me. It was something I'd seen a thousand times before and one of the downsides of having an ex-supermodel as your best friend.

Almost six feet tall with long, silky black hair and a dewy complexion, I could see that the guys on the next table were practically salivating, but she was already taken, and I knew she had no interest in the familiar chat up lines she'd heard a thousand times before. She evidently knew they were staring at her because she stared back with one of those ice-cold glares she was famous for, before her face changed back to an excited grin as she approached me.

"Maddie!" she squealed, hugging me. "I've missed you."

"I find that hard to believe," I said, dryly flopping back into my chair. "You've just spent ten days in Seattle with Mr. Sex God himself, so I don't suppose you were thinking about anything else."

"Oh, Maddie. Don't be so dramatic. Of course I was thinking about you. We weren't having sex all the time. Sam's still nursing that broken leg, although he's a lot better. He's hoping to go back to work this week, part-time at least."

But I could tell by her face that was exactly what they'd been doing most of the time. Since she'd hooked up with Sam Garrett back in October, she'd been wearing that serene glow, only seen on women who were getting it down on a regular basis, and if past experience was anything to go by, Sam and Kate had probably been at it like rabbits for the entire Christmas break. He was still nursing a broken leg after falling through the floor when he went after Kate, but I would take a bet that wasn't slowing him down in the bedroom department in the slightest and I enviously contemplated all the work arounds they'd figured out on how to remain sexually active whilst still in a walking cast.

Despite my post-Christmas blues, I was seriously happy for her. She'd had a pretty rough life at times and the chances of her getting together with the boy who once bullied her to near destruction seemed impossible, but miracles do happen, even in Angel Peaks. It was more that I wanted what she had. I wanted that loved-up glow, those heart eyes and that ache deep inside that only comes from an extremely active sex life, none of which I currently had.

Shrugging my melancholy aside I turned my attention to Kate who was telling me about their Christmas with her stepfather, Bob. "How did Bob and Sam get along?" I asked her, trying to engage my brain again.

"Really well," she said, enthusiastically. "I was a bit nervous, because of Sam's past, but they bonded over sport and Chinese food. It was a real family Christmas. We were missing Mom of course, but I think having us there really made the difference for Dad."

"That's great," I said, squeezing her hand. Sam had been the victim of a violent father who had been killed in a road accident. Both of them deserved all the happiness they could get, and they seemed to be getting it in spades.

"So, what about you Maddie? How was your Christmas?" she asked.

"It could have been better," I said, dismally.

She screwed up her nose. "Aww. What happened?"

"It was more what didn't happen. You and Sam were in Seattle. Scarlett went home to New York state and Ryan and Reece both went home to their families. That left me, my parents, and my three wonderful brothers. Can you even imagine how painful it is to spend Christmas with those three? No wonder I ate my weight in chocolate."

"Maddie, you love your family. They're not that bad," she said. I could tell she thought I was exaggerating.

"They're fine in small doses, or when there's only one of them, but being trapped with all of them over the holidays was torture."

Kate was very familiar with my family and, in particular, my three larger-than-life brothers. I could see she was trying to conceal a grin. "Okay, what was so bad about it?"

I looked at my watch. "How long do you have, exactly?" She raised her eyebrows and nodded as if she wanted me to continue. "Okay, let's cover the gifts first. Matteo bought me a pair of plaid slippers with pom-poms that have a zipper up the side. You know, the ones the seniors wear. It came with a card which read, *To my wonderful spinster sister. At least these will keep your feet warm.*"

Kate was trying to keep a straight face but failing miserably. "What about Josh?" she said through her giggles. "He's pretty sensible."

"Not really. He got me a singing cactus toy for my desk. His card said something about not being able to hug a cactus."

She looked perplexed. "What do you suppose he meant by that?"

"I know exactly what he meant. I'm the cactus – get it? He was implying I'm prickly and no one wants to hug me or do anything else with me come to that."

"Aw Maddie, it was just a joke. Well, I'm sure Ben probably got you something nice, eh?" she said hopefully.

"Well, actually, Ben's gift was pretty practical. A new vibrator with a 12-pack of AA batteries. My mom pretended to be shocked, but then I saw her trying out all the functions later, so she obviously wasn't that shocked." I paused for a moment and took a sip of my black coffee as she continued to chuckle at my misfortune. "Of course, you see what this means, don't you?"

She shook her head with a confused look. "What?"

"My family thinks I'm destined for the scrapheap. A lonely spinster who will end up knitting cat hair into tiny sweaters and collecting buttons in a tin. God, I hate that word. *Spinster.* How come men get to be bachelors, which sounds completely laddish, and we have to be spinsters? The word alone makes you sound like a dried-up old prune."

She shot me a sympathetic smile. "You still have Reece. Things were going okay between you two before I left."

I rolled my eyes. "Yeah, okay in a *best buds* kind of way. Not a *let's get dirty* kind of way. I don't want to be just another friend who he tells dirty jokes to and shoots pool with once in a while."

"You want more," she said, quietly.

"So much more," I said, trying not to feel sorry for myself. I'd met Reece Mackey three years ago when he first arrived in Angel Peaks to take over the veterinary practice, and I'd been instantly attracted to him. In fact, there wasn't a woman in the town who wasn't instantly attracted to him. Tall with floppy auburn hair that was constantly obscuring his beautifully expressive eyes. He made me want to drool just looking at him.

Unfortunately, we'd gotten off to a bad start with an argument over my parking space and we'd been sparring ever since, mostly in a good-natured way, but sometimes things got a little heated between us. The problem was that my social skills with men were notoriously bad. I just didn't seem to know how to behave around them. I blamed it, in part, for being brought up with three annoying older brothers. I was so used to using my tongue to strike them down, I defaulted to that behavior around all men, Reece included.

Kate sighed. "We just need to work on your interpersonal skills around the weaker sex," she said.

"And what does that mean in plain English?"

"It means you have to be nicer, Maddie. He won't know you like him if you keep telling him he has a face like a horse's ass. It sends out all the wrong signals. I think he's totally confused."

I rapidly shredded my napkin, feeling frustrated. "I don't know how to," I whined. "It's unnatural for me to be anything else."

She looked thoughtful for a moment and fluffed up my curls with her hand. "Maybe you don't need to change as such. Maybe we just need to play up your good points. You have a good heart, Maddie. You're beautiful inside and out. If you could just rein in the sarcasm and aggression a bit and let him see how much you like him, he'd be all over it. I know he really likes you."

"I'm not convinced he likes me in the way I want him to like me," I said, sadly. "He thinks I'm funny and cute and fun to hang out with. I'm just like one of the guys to him."

"Well, speak of the devil. Look who's just arrived," she whispered out of the side of her mouth. "Here's your chance to try out those new skills."

I swallowed hard as I saw the object of my affection enter The Heavenly Java. He was looking as drop-dead gorgeous as he always did; in fact, I think in his absence he had grown even more drool-worthy, if that was possible. Or perhaps it was just because I hadn't set eyes on him for two weeks and absence really did make the heart grow fonder. It had to be said my heart rate seemed to go into over-drive whenever he was around, not to mention that obscene feeling I got deep within my core. Yup, I had it bad for Dr. Reece Mackey.

I watched as he paid for a coffee and chatted amiably with the barista before he came sauntering over to our table in that lazy, re-laxed manner, as if he had all the time in the world. There was never anything hurried about Reece; his slow, sexy smile, that relaxed movement of his hand as he brushed the hair out of his eyes. It made me want to jump on him and lick him all over, like an over-enthusi-astic puppy.

Kate stood as he approached our table and he kissed her lightly on the cheek before he turned to me and ruffled my hair affection-ately as if I were one of his canine patients.

Kate made a big fuss of getting him to sit next to me and then she announced, "I'm glad you're here, Reece. Sam and I would like you both to come over tonight if you're free. Everyone's invited, Ryan and Scarlett as well. We thought that since we were apart at Christ-mas it would be nice to get together, now we're all back."

"Some of us didn't go anywhere," I said. "Besides, we got together before Christmas, at Ryan's place. Don't you remember he spent hours making all those fancy appies and Reece ate most of them in five minutes? They were supposed to last all evening." I gave Reece a withering look.

"Hey, I'd just come from surgery, and I was starving," he protested. "Anyway, they were tiny. He should have made something bigger. I'm a growing boy, you know."

I glanced across at him and wondered where he put all the food he consumed. He was tall and lean, and his tight, muscular body gave no indication that he could inhale a tray of canapes in thirty seconds flat. All that pastry went straight to my hips.

"So, can you both come?" Kate repeated, obviously keen to get a commitment out of us.

"I'll come if you're going to feed me," Reece told her. "Make sure it's big stuff. None of that airy-fairy stuff that Ryan makes. In fact, I could bring a few pizzas over if you want."

"Don't worry. I'll sort out the food," she told him. "You know how much Ryan hates store-bought pizza."

Our friend Ryan Carmichael was the local family doctor who was also a culinary wizard in his spare time. The thought of eating store-bought pizza brought him out in hives.

"I'll bring a veggie platter," I told her. "I'm trying to be good."

Reece snorted loudly beside me, and I kicked him, hard, under the table.

"What?" he said with an innocent look. "What did I do?"

"You don't have to *do* anything. Existing is enough." I said, narrowing my eyes at him.

"I exist only for you Maddie," he said, batting his eyelashes and causing an eye roll from me.

Kate got up from the table and Reece helped her with her jacket like a gentleman, even though we all knew nothing could be further from the truth. "Okay, I have an errand I have to run for Sam, but can you tell Scarlett about tonight, Maddie? I'll give Ryan a call as well. I'll catch you guys later." And with that, she gave me an exaggerated wink behind Reece's back and took off for the door.

He looked at my sad black coffee, which remained undrunk in my cup. "Not having one of those triple shot creamy latte things today, then?"

"Sad January," I replied.

"What the heck does that mean?" he said, the laughter dancing around his eyes and lighting them up like fireflies.

"I overindulged a bit over Christmas. I need to cut back." I said, scowling at my cup and contemplating the fact that I actually hated black coffee.

"Everyone overindulges at Christmas Maddie. That's what Christmas is for. There's no point in making January miserable to make up for it." He stared at me for a while with an uncharacteristically serious expression. "Is something else bothering you? You don't seem yourself."

"No. I'm just trying to be nice, and it's hard work."

His expression immediately changed; his eyes were shining with obvious amusement, and it was doing things to me that should carry a government health warning. He reached over and innocently took my hand. "Why were you trying to be nice? You're never nice to me."

I snatched it back, unwilling to allow him to get the upper hand. "I don't know. New Year's Resolution, I guess. Must be nicer to asshole vets."

"Ah, and there was me thinking you were starting to have feelings for me after all this time."

I put my head down, feeling the color rise to my cheeks. It obviously didn't go unnoticed as I heard him chuckling beside me. There was no doubt about it. Reece Mackey enjoyed torturing me, and I ended up feeling like an awkward teenager whenever I was around him. I wondered what he would do if I told him I did have feelings for him. Would he still be laughing then, or would that just make things supremely awkward between us? I would never know, because I had no intention of telling him and running that risk, whatever Kate might think.

"Well, as much as I would love to sit here with you all day, I have animal patients waiting for me," he said. "Shall I pick you up tonight? It'll save you driving."

"Oh... Okay, thanks," I said, uncertainly, waiting for the kicker that never arrived. He'd never offered to pick me up for one of our friend's nights before, so his thoughtfulness threw me a little.

"I'll see you at six. Do you think I should bring anything? Bottle of wine...maybe some condoms for later?" he added, under his breath.

I couldn't conceal a smirk. "No need. I always carry a good supply. Although I may not have any small enough to fit you," I said, waving my little finger at him.

He shook his head and laughed as if he knew I'd got one up on him, before he shrugged into his jacket and left with a cheeky wink. This was our familiar territory; a place where we both felt comfortable. Jokes and teasing. Him baiting me and me rising and taking the bait, and then hitting back harder. He loved it and, in a way, so did I, but I wanted to move beyond what we had, and I didn't know if we could. It seemed to be our default behavior, and we'd been in the frenemies zone for a long time. As that thought washed over me, it filled me with renewed melancholy, and I sighed heavily.

I stared angrily at my black coffee as if it were the cause of all my problems, and I thought about ordering a hot chocolate with extra whipped cream, but then I remembered how hard it had been to button my jeans that morning, and I resisted the urge.

I didn't have another client that afternoon. As the only CPA in Angel Peaks, January was always a slow month. There tended to be a bit of a lull before people rushed in like headless chickens in February, worried about tax season. It was a good month to catch up on paperwork and clean out files on my computer system, but I was in no mood to go back to my office.

In the circumstances, there was only one thing to do, and that was visit Scarlett. If anyone could cheer me up, she could. As I walked down Fourth Street towards her bakery, the sinful sweet smells filled my nostrils and I realized visiting Scarlett may have been a big mistake. The chances of staying on the straight and narrow in a bakery full of her decadent treats seemed slim.

I smiled to myself as I saw the pretty sign above her door announcing *Scarlett's Sweet Seductions*. Scarlett O'Brien's arrival in Angel Peaks had caused a bit of a stir, mostly because she was unconventional, to say the least. Not many people wandered around the town wearing a pirate hat and a ballet tutu over her snow boots, but she was an artist, and people forgave her rather zany behavior when they sampled her amazing, sweet goods.

As well as that, she did an awesome range of X-rated cakes which would make even a porn queen blush. I'd spent many happy hours staring at her catalog of dick cakes that she made for bachelorette parties.

She'd modeled her bakery on a traditional French patisserie, and she had used her artistic talents to decorate the interior to include beautiful glass cabinets and pastel colors that brightened the gray, wintry weather. Walking through her door was like stepping inside one of those pretty little macaroons that look almost too good to eat.

As I breezed through the door, the tiny bell tinkled to alert her she had a customer. I was a little surprised to find my friend with her forehead on the counter, moaning.

I rushed over with concern. "Scarlett, are you okay? Are you hurt?"

She didn't stand up but instead chose to talk to me from where she was. "Bored, bored, bored," she whined, repeatedly banging her head on the counter.

"Oh God, you scared me for a moment. I thought you were hurt. What's going on?" I asked.

"I have no fucking customers, that's what's going on. Everyone goes on a diet in January and my sales go down the toilet. I haven't even got any orders for cakes. I don't know how I'm going to make my bank loan this month if this goes on." She looked up at me, her face pink and creased from having laid on the counter for too long. She was a pretty girl with auburn curls piled on top of her head and an elfin face. She looked a little like one of those old-fashioned porcelain dolls and she had plenty of admirers around the town, but no man was brave enough to take on her slightly eccentric side.

"It's early days yet," I told her. "It'll pick up, you'll see. Valentine's Day is just around the corner and will be great for business." I tried to reassure her, but I knew how close she sailed to the wind with her finances, and the stress of running a business single-handed was no simple task for anyone. "Anyway, how was your Christmas?" I asked, trying to get her on to a lighter subject.

"It was good to see everyone. I haven't seen my nephews for almost a year, and they've grown so much," she said.

"Your mom and dad must have been happy to see you."

"Yeah, I guess," she nodded, artfully rearranging a tray of chocolate chip cookies that were making my mouth water just looking at them. "They always fuss, though. You know what I mean. There are always questions."

"Questions?"

"*Are you eating enough, Scarlett? Are you sleeping enough?* And then there's the worst one. *Are you seeing anyone, Scarlett?* It drives me crazy!"

"It's just because they love you. I think because I've always lived close to my family, the nosiness is just second nature. *You* live without it for fifty weeks of the year, so it annoys you. If it was a constant stream of questions, you wouldn't think anything of it."

She looked confused. "I'm sure there was logic in there somewhere, but it completely passed me by."

"You must miss your family, Scarlett," I said. I knew it couldn't be easy being on the other side of the country with no family around you, but it was her choice, after all.

"Sometimes," she said. "But it was hard to be myself living back there. There were always ... expectations."

I nodded. She was ten years younger than her brother and she had been what they described as a surprise baby. Because of the way she looked and the fact she wasn't much taller than most of the middle school kids, her family treated her like she wasn't capable of anything. When her grandmother passed and left her a sizeable inheritance, she upped and left and bought the bakery in Angel Peaks, a town on the other side of the country that she'd never even visited. It was a pretty foolhardy move, but if anyone had the balls to pull it off, it was Scarlett.

"Anyway, let me get to the point," I said. "Kate asked me to invite you over to Sam's place tonight for a get-together. Can you come?"

She put a finger to one of the cute dimples in her chin as if she were thinking about it. "Now, let me just consult my social calendar. I may be double-booked." She pretended to flick through an imaginary book before she looked up at me. "Well, would you look at that. I appear to be free for the next fifteen fucking years, so I think I can squeeze it in, yes." She unclipped her hair before winding it around and re-pinning it, high on her head. "Are Reece and Ryan coming as well?" she asked.

"Reece is definitely coming. In fact, he said he'd pick me up." I frowned for a moment. "I wonder if he was joking, and he won't actually turn up. That's just the kind of thing he'd do. Leave me waiting there, fuming. He'd find that really funny."

"Ah. Dr. Mackey is making his move at last. About freaking time. He's been mooning over you for as long as I've been here."

I laughed. "He does not moon over me. He might moon *at* me on occasion but that's just because he's a rude pig."

Scarlett laughed and slapped the counter with her hand. "Hey, that's given me a great idea for a new line of cakes. Mooning cakes for when someone has offended you. You could send them an ass cake to show them how you feel."

"Do you think you could model asses as well as you can other body parts?" I asked.

"I can model anything," she said confidently. "Give me a body part and I'll recreate it out of fondant."

I didn't doubt her for one second. She was a talented artist and when she wasn't modeling fondant into rude body parts, she was creating beautiful paintings that she tried to sell in the local gift stores.

"I'll drive tonight because I have to be up unspeakably early tomorrow, as usual. Perhaps I'll give Ryan a call and see if he wants a ride."

I giggled. "He might not come with you. You scare him."

She rolled her eyes and swept her hands down her oversized apron. "Look at me. I'm an itsy-bitsy cutie pie. How could anyone be scared of me?"

"Scarlett, you drove your Fiat into a snowbank the last time you had him in the car. He was white when you arrived at Reece's house. Ryan scares easily. You have to be gentler with him."

She laughed like an evil villain. "I know, but it's so much fun to wind him up. I just can't help myself."

"And try not to get into a culinary argument with him tonight," I reminded her.

"We do not argue," she said huffily. "We just discuss who makes the best treats. He gives his treats away for free, Maddie. That's taking away my business."

"He's just a sweet guy. He loves to cook, and he loves to share his stuff with people. You can't blame him for that."

"I just wish he wasn't so good at it," she said. "Why can't he just stick to being a doctor? I don't go into his office and do minor surgery on people," she said, pretending to brandish a scalpel.

"Maybe you should just date him, Scarlett. You could exhaust him in the bedroom and then he wouldn't have any energy left for baking. He just needs a good woman."

She snorted. "And believe me, I am *not* that woman. Ryan needs someone sweet and mild. I'd scare the living daylights out of him, in and out of the bedroom."

I had to agree with her on that count. She was the only person I knew who'd dated a fire eater, and even he hadn't even been able to cope with her.

"Okay," I said, turning to go. "I'll see you later then."

"You going to make out with Reece in the car?" she asked with a wink.

"Nah, I think that's highly unlikely. I'm more likely to castrate him before we arrive."

Chapter 2
Reece

The office was busy that afternoon with a whole assortment of animals, but I hadn't been able to take my mind off Maddie. I was reminiscing about the day I met her almost three years ago. I had been new in town, and I'd pulled in close to her office building to dash to the bank, not realizing I'd taken her personal parking spot.

I had just been strolling back to my vehicle when I spotted her. Petite and curvy, with long blonde curls, and headed in my direction. She hit all my buttons instantly, but the look she gave me could have frozen hell over. Without breaking stride, she had immediately launched into a tirade of abuse.

"This is *my* parking spot," she spat, her chocolate eyes flashing with fire. "It is very clearly marked, and I need you to move your vehicle right now!"

I tried a charming smile, which worked with most people, particularly women. "I'm so sorry. You see, I'm new in town and I didn't see a sign."

She was evidently immune to the charm because the rant continued. "Are you blind? If you are, you certainly shouldn't be driving. It's right there!" she said, jabbing her finger in the direction of the tiny sign I'd obviously missed. "I suppose you're one of these out of towners who comes up from Denver and buys up all our property so local people can't afford to live here anymore," she continued, not stopping for breath.

I was frankly stunned. I always thought small-town people were friendly, but this girl would have given Attila the Hun a run for his money. I was frozen to the spot as she went off on me, feeling both bewildered and bewitched. Then an elderly gentleman with a small dog approached me. He ignored her completely as she ranted on, then he turned to me, saying, "That's Maddie Moreno. She's crazy. Don't piss her off."

Maddie Moreno. Even the sound of her name stirred something deep within me, although I failed to see how I could be so turned on by this little hell kitten. I don't think she'd realized at the time that I was the new veterinarian who'd come to replace Dr. Graham when he retired, but she soon found out.

Maddie was the proud owner of a whole menagerie of weird and wonderful animals and when I found her records in my file cabinet, I knew she was going to be needing my services, eventually; I just had to wait it out. About a month after our minor altercation, I saw her name on my appointment schedule to bring her cat in for her annual shots, and I was hoping I'd be able to have some fun with her. I came out to the waiting room to introduce myself and I watched as her face changed from shock to concern. The waiting room was full of clients with their respective pets, but I didn't bother lowering my voice.

"Oh dear, Ms. Moreno," I said, with a serious look. "I'm not sure I can take you on as a client. You see, I have a strict bullying and harassment policy and I'm not convinced you'll be able to adhere to it." The waiting room fell into stunned silence, and then I stood back and watched her squirm; it was absolutely delicious.

"But there are no other vets in Angel Peaks," she protested. "I'd have to go to Havenridge, and that's an hour's drive and poor Willow hates the car. And then there's Henry and Sylvie and Bunnicula to consider. And who's going to come from Havenridge to see my donkey and my goats? It'll cost me a fortune."

I raised my eyebrows at her, not giving an inch, because she was totally adorable, and I was enjoying this far too much. I knew if I just waited it out, I'd probably get the apology I was waiting for.

"That day I found you in my parking spot, I was late for a meeting with a client and I'm not normally like that at all," she said, coolly.

"On the contrary, Ms. Moreno," I said with a poker face. "I have it on good authority that's exactly what you're like. Apparently, you have quite the reputation as a bit of a hothead."

"Who told you that?" she snapped.

"Half the town," I replied. "Mind you, that was the polite half. The rest of them said you were totally crazy, and I should avoid you like the plague."

Her face turned a delicious shade of pink and she fidgeted in her seat, stroking poor Willow so energetically I thought all her fur would fall out. "I'm sorry, Dr. Mackey," she said, almost too quietly for me to hear.

"I didn't quite hear that," I said with my hand to my ear. "Would you mind repeating it?"

And then she looked up at me, fixing me with those beautiful brown eyes, and I knew I was done for. She wasn't at all embarrassed and she knew exactly what I was doing. "I'm sorry Dr. Mackey. I can assure you I will never be rude to you in your office. Now, could you please see Willow? She gets anxious with all this hanging around." And with that, she rose to her feet, and, with her head held high, she strode past me into my treatment room.

It was an apology on her own terms, and she'd stuck to her word. She'd never been rude to me in my office, just everywhere else in town. Our interactions ranged from flirty banter to full-on slanging matches, but there was one thing in common in all of this; with every exchange, she set me on fire just a little bit more. There was something about Maddie Moreno that was like a drug to me, and I could never get enough.

Although we'd known each other casually for about three years, we'd only started moving in the same friendship circle about six months ago. We'd bumped into each other at Ray's Bar over the years and exchanged a few words, and more often than not, she was with some guy. I soon learned that Maddie's dating partners never lasted more than a few weeks and I took to observing how she interacted with the guys she was with.

I was never much of a people watcher, but she fascinated the hell out of me. She seemed to swing from hanging all over them like a piece of Velcro to being completely abusive to them, and I think most of them gave up from downright confusion. She was a puzzle for sure, and Maddie-watching soon became one of my favorite occupations. I'd find a quiet spot and sit with a beer so I could watch what was going on at the pool table or at the bar with Maddie and her date for the night. It was like watching a train wreck in slow motion, and I'd gotten to the stage where I could almost predict exactly what was going to happen next.

Usually the guy stormed off, having had enough, and she would just shrug her shoulders and order herself another drink as if it didn't concern her in the least. Sometimes the sight of her departing suitor would be met by a cheer from some of the locals and she would calmly extend her middle finger to the assembled onlookers. One night I'd watched all this happen and after a few minutes she approached my table in the corner of the bar.

"Hi Reece," she said sweetly, as if butter wouldn't melt in her mouth. "Wanna shoot some pool with me."

It was the summer, and she was dressed in a pair of skin-tight cut-off jean shorts and a white tank that showed off all her beautiful curves. Her skin was bronzed from the sun and there was a smattering of freckles on her nose, making her look adorably cute. She stood in front of me leaning on her pool cue, and it was all I could do not to salivate.

"I'm not sure it's safe to play pool with you Maddie," I teased. "I've seen what happens to your dates."

She narrowed her eyes at me and then looked casually around the bar at the other guys who were drinking there. "Well, if you're scared, I guess I'll just find someone else."

I was out of my seat before she could finish her sentence. "You don't scare me, Maddie Moreno. Even though I think you'd like to."

I heard her husky laugh as she walked in front of me to the pool table and watched the gentle sway of her hips. I knew then I was in serious trouble. She might as well have threaded a ring through my nose and led me around.

She thrashed me at pool that night, although I put that down to the fact that I couldn't take my eyes off her leaning over that table. It's hard to focus on your game when a thousand filthy thoughts are filling your head.

Since then, it had almost become a regular thing. We drank beer, we played pool, and bit by bit she told me a little more about herself. She was the baby of the Moreno family, and she grew up with three older brothers. I asked her one night how that was for her. She looked thoughtful for a minute before she answered me.

"I think my parents thought they were getting a little princess when they had me, but I just wanted to be like my brothers. To be one of them. They taught me how to catch snakes and fish and stuff like that. I was never like the other girls. How could I be? A lot of guys don't like that."

It was unusual for her to be quite so honest. Usually, she deflected that kind of question, but I seemed to catch her in a reflective moment. And then seconds later she was back to insulting me about the way I held my cue or something, as if she didn't feel comfortable revealing that side of herself.

And so we kind of got into this pattern of behavior. We sparred, we flirted, we even fought, but it was as if we never really scratched the surface of what was going on in the depths, for either of us. Sometimes it was hard to know where to stop with it all and at times, we both pushed the boundaries a little too far. I'd ended up hurting her feelings just before Thanksgiving last year. I hadn't meant to hurt her, but I'd made some off-the-cuff remark I thought she would find funny, but she didn't. Since then, I'd felt a lot more guarded around her. The last thing I wanted to do was hurt her, but we always walked such a fine line, and she sure knew how to push my buttons in more ways than one.

Having spent the Christmas holidays with my family, I was surprised at how much I'd missed her. On several occasions, I had to stop myself from calling her, which was something we never did. I missed her snarky voice and those beautiful eyes that she was forever rolling at my cheesy remarks.

That morning she'd told me she'd made a new year's resolution, but what she didn't know was that I'd made one as well. As the clock struck twelve on New Year's Eve, I realized that the only person I wanted to be with was miles away, so I made myself a promise. I would stop all this dicking around and I would make an effort to move forward with our relationship. I knew it wasn't going to be easy because she was a challenge. That was one of the things I enjoyed about her; just when I thought I had her figured out, she would do something completely out of the blue. Like that night she almost decapitated me with her pool cue because I'd insulted her musical tastes. It was a good job I ducked when I did.

The problem was that she was so damn sexy when she was annoyed. Her blonde curls took on a mind of their own and sprang all over the place, and her face got all flushed and pink. Seeing her like that always sent my mind straight to the gutter and fantasizing about Maddie in my bed, in my shower, on my kitchen table and every other flat surface in my house took up far too many of my waking hours.

She surprised me a little that morning because something was definitely off about her. Although she'd done her best to joke with me, there seemed to be an underlying sadness that I'd not seen in her before. Maybe that's why I'd jumped in with both feet and offered to drive her to Sam's place. I'd half expected her to blow me off with some insult, but she just accepted my ride almost graciously. It was weird.

I knocked on her door at six sharp and she threw it open with unnecessary force in a very Maddie-like way. Maybe it was just because I'd missed her over Christmas, but I thought she looked even more beautiful than usual. She'd tamed her wild hair into a pretty up-do, and she was wearing light makeup and a tightly fitting blue wrap sweater which showed off her best assets. I realized I must have been staring at her breasts because she snapped her fingers sharply in my face before saying, "Hey, bozo! My eyes are up here."

"Sorry, Mads," I said, laughing. "You know me. I'm easily distracted. I know you're probably going to hit me, but I have to say the girls look particularly wonderful tonight."

She snorted dismissively, before grabbing her purse from her hallstand. "They're too big. I'm going to save up for a reduction."

"No, no!" I said, with a look of horror. "There will be no reducing on my watch."

"It's okay for you. You don't have to live with them, getting in the way all the time. I reached across my desk to grab my paperclips yesterday and I knocked over my coffee."

"Well, I have a huge appendage that's always getting in the way, but you don't hear me talking about having it reduced."

She shot me a withering look. "In your dreams, Reece Mackey."

I looked around nervously as we headed for the car. "Where's Dave? He's not loose, is he?"

She laughed wickedly. "I can't believe you're afraid of my llama. He's a sweetheart. Why are you scared of him? You're a vet, for fuck's sake."

I looked at her incredulously, scarcely believing that she didn't remember the last episode with her goddamn llama. "He bit my ass," I said indignantly. "His teeth went through my jeans and broke the skin."

I could hear her giggling as she climbed into my Jeep. "That's not possible. He only has bottom teeth. The worst he could have done is give you a nasty suck."

"I'm telling you, he bit me," I insisted. "I couldn't sit comfortably for a week. I should have sued you."

"Oh, poor baby. Did it leave a mark? Would you like me to kiss it better?"

I was glad she seemed a bit more upbeat than she had that morning, so I played along a little, since I knew she would expect it. "It's the very least compensation I would expect from the owner of a rabid llama. Ass kissing. While you're down there, you can kiss something else as well."

"Filthy bastard," she growled, but she was grinning, so I knew she found it funny. "Anyway, he's not rabid. You scared him."

"I tell you, Mads, that llama has it in for me. I've been around animals for years and I could see it in his eyes."

"Dave is a very good judge of character," she said. "He obviously doesn't trust you." She looked across at me with that flirty look. "Maybe I shouldn't trust you either. Dave's never wrong about people."

I shot her a sly wink. "He's right on that one. You should definitely not trust me."

Chapter 3
Maddie

When we pulled up outside Sam and Kate's place, I could see that Scarlett's little Fiat 500 was already there, parked in her usual haphazard way. Scarlett's philosophy on parking was why only take up one space when you could have three. I wondered if she managed to get Ryan there without him having a panic attack. Reece was being unusually chivalrous, and he helped me down from his Jeep before taking my arm and walking me up the path to the house.

Sam had a lovely little heritage house in the older part of Angel Peaks, and he'd done a really nice job of renovating it. My dad owned the biggest construction company in the area and even he was impressed by the quality of Sam's workmanship. For someone who was a physical therapist, it was good to see he had other talents with his hands. Of course, Kate would argue he had many talents with his hands, but I wasn't sure I wanted to hear about that.

I could hear Scarlett's sing-song voice as we walked through the door, and it sounded like she was already giving Ryan a hard time about something.

"Ryan, I am *not* giving you the recipe for my Secret Kiss Cookies. If I do that, you'll make them, and then you'll give them away free to all your patients and I won't have any trade at all. If this month gets any worse, I'll be selling my body on the streets of Angel Peaks and it's too damn cold to give outdoor blowjobs in this weather."

I could see Ryan's flustered face from the doorway as he tried to pacify her. "Scarlett, you know I would never want you to do something like that. I just thought in the true spirit of baking comrades we could share some of our secrets."

Scarlett stood on her toes and tried to get in Ryan's face, but she was still too short and ended up talking to his chest. "No can do, Dr. Carmichael. My secret kisses will remain just that. Secret."

I could hear Reece chuckling behind me. "Hey, Ryan. Are you aggravating that little redhead again? I've warned you about that before."

Scarlett spun around with her hands on her hips. "Hey, Mackey. Not so much of the little redhead, if you don't mind! I don't call you the big, ugly dimwit."

"I think you do actually, Scarlett," he responded. "But I know that it comes from a place of love."

Scarlett snorted incredulously and turned back to her stand-off with Ryan. I could tell it was going to be a lively evening as usual, and I glanced over to see Sam and Kate in the kitchen sucking each other's faces off. I walked in and loudly deposited my veggie platter on the island. "Excuse me, you two. Can't you keep that for later? We do have to eat in here, you know."

"Sorry Maddie," Sam said, grinning like a lovestruck idiot. "I can't control myself when I'm around her."

He was still hobbling around, but he had a walking cast on now and he was doing a lot better. He'd broken his leg back in November when he'd fallen through the floor of a disused building trying to get to Kate. I think it was then that she realized just how much he loved her, and they'd been a disgustingly sweet item ever since.

I looked at the array of amazing food already laid out on the island, and I could see Ryan had a hand in most of it. Reece's arm snaked in behind me as he tried to snaffle a cranberry brie pastry off one of the plates and I slapped his hand.

"You need to wait for everyone else," I hissed, spinning around and coming dangerously close to his face. He pinned me to the island with one arm while he stuffed the treat in his mouth with a grin, before grabbing another one and repeating the process. "Reece Mackey, you are a pig," I whispered. "There's no other word for it."

He laughed and grabbed the entire plate and took off with them into the living room. "I'm comfort eating," he shouted over his shoulder. "It's because I'm not getting any affection in other areas of my life."

Ryan called over to me with a sympathetic look. "It's okay, Maddie, I made extra this time after he ate them all last time. I've hidden the second tray."

"You shouldn't have to make more. He's an outrage. He must cost you a fortune in baking supplies." I glanced into the living room to see Reece totally unaffected by my words, happily scoffing his spoils of war.

I turned back to Sam and Kate and found them filling glasses with what looked like champagne. "Come and grab a drink, everyone," Sam yelled. "Kate and I have an announcement to make."

I gave Kate a questioning look as I snagged a glass of champagne, but she just gave me a serene smile in return. The others joined me and grabbed a glass and we all stood around, waiting.

"We have some news," Sam said, clearly bubbling over with excitement. "While we were in Seattle at Christmas, I asked Kate to marry me. And she said yes. We're getting married!"

We all stood there for a moment with our mouths open before Scarlett broke the silence in her own indomitable way. "That's fucking brilliant!" she yelled. "I'll make the cake, but there will be no bridezilla demands. I'll say what you're getting, and you *will* be happy with it."

"I can help," Ryan added. "Maybe I can do some of the catering. I suggest finger food rather than a sit-down meal. People will be able to mingle better."

Kate was looking at me for my reaction, but I didn't know what to say. My head was swimming with all this information, and it was hard for me to take in. I really wanted to feel happy for her because I could see how thrilled she was, but the history between Sam, Kate, and myself went deep and it was painful just thinking about it. I threw my arms around her and held her close but, in reality, I felt like such a fraud standing there with the tears pricking in my eyes.

All the time, I was aware of Reece watching me because he never missed a trick. He stepped forward and pulled Sam in for a hug. "That's great, man. I'm really happy for the two of you, although I still don't know how you managed to snag this beautiful woman. She must be crazy."

Sam was looking quite emotional, and I knew how much he loved Kate. She'd forgiven him for what he did to her all those years ago, but I wasn't sure that I had. I didn't know if I even could. It wasn't just her life he'd wrecked. It was mine too.

"I'm going to need a best man," he told Reece. "And there's no way I can decide between you and Ryan, so I'm going to have both of you."

Reece looked thrilled, but then Ryan interjected. "Oh no. I'll be a groomsman and help you with the catering. I'm not very good at public speaking and stuff like that. Let Reece do that for you. He'll be great at it."

"Really? Reece said, looking genuinely excited. "No one's ever wanted me to be best man before, not even my brother. I promise I won't let you down, Sam."

"And I'm hoping Maddie will be my maid of honor," Kate said, smiling at me affectionately. "And maybe Scarlett could be my bridesmaid."

"No, no. Sorry, Kate. I don't do the bridesmaid thing," Scarlett said. "But I'm happy to be a groom's person with Ryan. We could wear matching tuxedos. It'll be great. Have you set a date yet?"

Sam and Kate looked at each other lovingly before Sam said. "It would be tomorrow if I had my way, but we've decided on Easter weekend at the beginning of April. It should be a bit warmer by then."

The room descended into an excited buzz of chatter, with everyone talking at once. Ryan and Scarlett were interested in what venues they were thinking of and what kind of food they wanted, and Kate was asking Scarlett and me to go to Havenridge with her to pick out a dress. I hoped I was nodding and smiling in all the right places because it felt as if my mouth and my brain weren't actually connected, and I couldn't say anything useful at that moment in time.

I was aware that Reece had sidled up behind me and felt his warm hand on my shoulder as he leant forward to whisper into my hair. "You okay, Mads? You're awfully quiet."

"Hmm," I said, grabbing the bottle of champagne and pouring myself another large glass. "I'm good. Everything's good."

"Liar," he said, quietly enough for only me to hear.

I offered him the bottle to see if he wanted another glass, but he shook his head. "No, I need to get you home safely. I just had half a glass. I'm not having any more."

I felt his hand run down my arm and grab my fingers. "Don't worry. We'll talk later when I get you home."

"I don't need to talk. I'm fine." I spat, pulling my hand away from him roughly.

"Okay, have it your own way," he said through gritted teeth, and then he sauntered off to speak to Sam.

I stared down at my glass of bubbly filled with regret at my behavior. This was exactly why I had no one in my life, because I expended a lot of energy pushing people away. What I really wanted to do was go home, get into my comfortable pj's, and cuddle up with my cat Willow, but I didn't want to appear rude by leaving early. I looked around at my friends and the excitement and happiness on everyone's faces and I felt like a freak. Why couldn't I just feel happy for them?

I nibbled on a carrot from my veggie tray and then realized I was consuming a gazillion calories in the copious amounts of champagne I was knocking back, so I helped myself to a couple of Ryan's delicious-looking pastries. The bubbles were starting to go to my head and the lights on Sam's Christmas tree were dancing in front of my eyes like a psychedelic light show.

Although Reece seemed to be engaged with Sam, I could see him glancing up at me from time to time. He bent down and said something to Sam and then he came over. "Do you want me to take you home?"

"It would seem rude," I said flatly.

"You don't look that well, Maddie. I think I should take you home," he said, ignoring my previous remark. "Come on. I'll grab your jacket and we'll get you out of here."

He came back with my jacket and slung it around my shoulders. "I'm taking Mads home," he announced to the others. "She's got a bit of a headache."

Kate came rushing over, full of concern, but I waved her away. "I probably just sank the bubbles too fast," I assured her, pulling her in for a hug. "I'm so happy for you," I told her. "I'll call you tomorrow," I said, heading for the door.

January was always the coldest month in Angel Peaks and tonight was no exception. You could almost feel the frostiness crackling in the surrounding air, and it immediately chilled my face as we stepped outside. I climbed into Reece's Jeep and rested my head against the window, staring out at the blackness of the night.

We drove home in silence, and the atmosphere between us was heavy with unspoken words. I didn't dare sneak a glance at him as we drove, but instead kept my eyes averted out of the side window, preferring to lock myself away in my own little bubble of denial. The sadness that seemed to engulf me twisted in my gut and I was desperate to get home to my personal haven, where I could lick my wounds.

I was gutted that I didn't have it in me to feel happy for my best friend, and I was devastated that I continued to push away the person beside me who had grown to mean so much to me. I pondered that there must be something lacking in me in some way that made me unable to accept the hand that others offered me. Why did I have to consider it a weakness to embrace the comfort I so desperately craved?

We pulled up outside my house, and we stared at each other for a moment without speaking. I realized if I was going to redeem this situation, I needed to make the first move. "Thanks for the ride. Do you want to come in for coffee?" I asked.

His brow creased in confusion. "You want me to come in? Are you sure?"

"Only if you want to. I'm not twisting your arm or anything." I said, trying not to snap.

He obviously didn't need asking twice because he was already clambering out of the car and headed for my front door. I followed along behind him, aware of that floaty feeling you get when you've chugged down an entire bottle of champagne in twenty minutes flat. Once we were inside, I added a couple of logs to my woodstove and opened up the damper to get the fire going again.

I looked down fondly at my ancient cat, Willow, and gently stroked her head as she lay curled up in her basket next to the stove. She opened one eye and yawned, observing me with affectionate indifference. She was eighteen years old and spent most of her time sleeping and she reminded me of Grizabella in the musical *Cats*. She was the first pet I'd ever had and had been a gift from my parents for my eighth birthday. Pets are like kids, you're not supposed to have favorites, but Willow and I went way back, so she was pretty special to me.

I looked across at Reece to see he was looking around the room appreciatively. "You do realize this is the first time you've allowed me inside your home?" he said.

I shook my head with a frown. "No, that can't be right. I'm sure you've been in here before."

"Nope. I would remember. Closest I've gotten is your barn. You've never asked me in."

I glanced at him sadly, silently acknowledging just how crap my social skills were. "I only moved in just over a year ago," I said pathetically, as if it were an excuse.

He grinned good-naturedly, setting my heart alight. "Still unpacking then, I guess."

"Do you want coffee?" I asked.

"Sure. I also want a tour of your entire house now I've actually gotten inside."

"Why don't you just poke around yourself while I make the coffee," I told him. "Don't even think about going in my underwear drawer, though."

I could hear him chuckling to himself as he went upstairs. My house was an original farmstead from the early 1900s and I'd had my eye on it for years, often popping in to see the elderly couple who lived there. I'd watched sadly as it fell further and further into disrepair as they weren't able to cope with it anymore and eventually, they moved into assisted living.

I'd bought it at a bargain price because it needed to be completely renovated and it was a lot more than most people would take on. I'd always been good at saving money, and I was happily mortgage-free. Of course, having a family who owned a construction company didn't hurt either, and my dad and my three brothers had completely gutted the place and turned it into a beautiful home for me. It came with a couple of acres of land and a big barn, so I could keep all my animals, which was a huge plus.

I could hear the floorboards creaking as he moved around from room to room. Upstairs, I had three bedrooms and a bathroom with a huge cast iron tub. My brother Josh was the architect in the family and when he drew up the designs, I'd asked him to keep it as close to the original as possible and he'd sourced the tub for me. He loved old buildings as much as I did, and he'd actually bought himself a penthouse apartment when Moreno Construction renovated the old warehouse building.

My eldest brother Matteo was a master carpenter and spent a lot of his time constructing high-end timber frame properties in Haven-ridge, but he'd really embraced restoring the original features of this house, including the original fireplace and the beautiful sash win-dows.

Ben was the closest in age to me, only eighteen months older, and he seemed to be able to turn his hand to anything: plumbing, electri-cals, you name it, and Ben could do it. He also ran the business side of the construction company and dealt with schmoozing the clients and contracts and such.

The coffee was rhythmically dripping through the machine, and I heard Reece's footsteps coming back down the stairs. "Your place is just beautiful, Maddie. It's so tidy. I thought you might have left some bras and panties lying around, but there was nothing."

"Sorry to disappoint you," I said dryly.

"What's this room?" he asked from across the hallway.

"Oh, it's supposed to be a dining room, but I use it as my pet room. Henry's in there with Sylvie and Bunnicula. It's okay, Henry's covered up, so he shouldn't be too abusive."

I could hear him laughing as he opened the door. Like most of my friends, he was very familiar with the stories of my potty-mouthed African Gray parrot, Henry. He hadn't started life swearing like a sailor, but I'd had to attend an accounting conference in Den-ver about a year ago and I had made the stupid mistake of leaving my brother Ben in charge of my animals. Having spent two years trying to get him to say, "pretty boy", I returned from Denver to find he had a vocabulary of about five hundred words, none of which were appropriate in polite company. I had to stop asking my elderly grandmother over for visits.

"Can I uncover him?" he called.

"Sure, but I take no responsibility for what he might say to you. He's more vulgar than you." I poured out the coffee and carried it into the living room with some cream and sugar. My head was swimming after all the champagne I'd consumed with very little food to soak it up, so I sat on my couch and rested my head on the arm, listening to what was going on in the next room.

"Hi, Henry. You are one beautiful bird," I heard Reece say in a soft voice.

"Big mistake," I murmured sleepily, as Henry launched into a foul-mouthed tirade. I could hear Reece laughing hysterically as Henry's language grew edgier by the minute. "Reece, you're winding him up," I said, trying to stop the room from spinning.

Suddenly he came striding in, with Henry perched on his shoulder. "I fucking love this bird. You're going to have to let me borrow him." He must have noticed I was slumped on the couch because his voice changed to one of concern. "Maddie, are you okay? You don't look so good; you're really pale."

"I feel a bit weird," I said.

"Weird like you're going to pass out, or weird like you're going to throw up on my shoes, because there is a difference."

"Your coffee's on the table," I told him. "I think I'll just sleep here tonight. It's cozy by the fire."

"No, we should get you to bed, or you'll wake up with a stiff neck," he said.

"Definitely not as good as waking up with a stiff man," I said, clearly finding my own joke hilariously funny because I started to giggle, and then found I couldn't stop.

"Okay," he said firmly. "You are going to bed before you puke in my coffee. Come on, let's go."

He helped me into a sitting position and the spinning got much worse. "Oh no!" I whined. "Not good. Not good! Let me lie down again. I just want to die here in front of my fire with my cat and my parrot."

"Fuck off!" Henry shouted, sounding just like my brother, Ben. "Maddie loves dick! Maddie loves dick!"

"Reece," I mumbled.

"Yeah?"

"If I do die, can you please kill Ben for me? I'm leaving you the parrot in my will."

I could hear him laughing, but it sounded all echoey, as if he were in a tunnel. Then I heard the sounds of his footsteps on the stairs before he returned, clutching a pillow and a blanket. He gently lifted my head and tucked the pillow under me before covering me up with the blanket.

"Perhaps I should undress you," he said with a thoughtful expression.

"Try it and you're not leaving this house with your balls," I slurred.

"Some things never change," he said, smoothing my hair away from my face with a smile. "We never got a chance to talk about what was going on with you tonight."

"Nothing's wrong. I'm just not a nice person," I said, with my eyes firmly closed. The alcohol was starting to make me feel maudlin and that was never a good sign.

"Horse shit," Reece said, dismissively. "We'll talk tomorrow. I'll bring you breakfast and some Tylenol because I have a sneaky suspicion you might need some."

"Reece."

"Yeah?"

"I really like you," I mumbled, almost inaudibly.

"Hmm. Now it's getting interesting," he said. "Sounds like confessional Maddie is making an appearance. Perhaps I should stay."

I didn't answer because I could feel myself falling into a heavy sleep. My legs felt like lead weights, and I don't think I could have moved if I tried. The last thing I was aware of was Reece bending forward and kissing me gently on the forehead. I heard the front door close quietly and allowed myself to drift away.

Chapter 4

Reece

I pulled up at Maddie's at 8 a.m. the next morning, knowing she would already be up. Although it was Saturday, she would always be up to attend to her animals, whatever state she was in. She could have double pneumonia, and she'd still drag her sorry ass out of bed to make sure they were okay.

I parked the Jeep next to the barn with the attached paddock and sure enough, Maddie was in there with the four occupants. There was Dave, her crazed llama, Richard, the sweet donkey she'd taken on when the local petting farm closed, and then there were Glenda and Gordon, the fainting goats.

I watched her struggling to lift a bale of hay down from her storage area next to the barn, so I tiptoed over and grabbed it above her outstretched hands. She startled for a moment as if she didn't know I was there, but then she muttered a thanks as she grabbed the bale from me and manhandled it over the fence to the waiting hungry beasts.

"I didn't think I'd see you this morning," she called from the paddock.

"I told you I'd bring you breakfast and some Tylenol," I said.

She looked over her shoulder at me with a puzzled frown. "You did? I don't remember that."

"Well, I brought you a breakfast sandwich from Heavenly's and some orange juice, so get those animals fed and get your butt inside."

She fussed around with the animals for a bit, cooing to them softly and making sure they had everything they needed before she came through the gate and secured it carefully.

She looked different this morning, and I couldn't remember ever seeing her this way before. Her face was scrubbed clean, and she wore no makeup. She was bundled up against the cold in old work clothes that she probably kept for mucking out the animals, and she had secured her hair on top of her head with a chunky hair clasp. It was as if she was laid bare for me to see. She had nothing to hide behind and I got the impression it made her feel vulnerable, or perhaps I was just reading too much into the situation.

There was a distinct uncertainty about her. I could see it in the way she moved, in the way she kept her head down and didn't make eye contact with me. I was carrying a brown paper bag with her breakfast, and I followed behind her as she led me into the house. I could smell the coffee immediately as we walked through to the kitchen, and I would hazard a guess that it was the first thing she'd reached for when she woke up and found herself fully dressed on the couch instead of in her warm cozy bed.

She disappeared upstairs, and I heard the water running briefly. In a few moments, she appeared again in fresh clothes with her hair around her shoulders. She hadn't bothered with makeup, and she looked younger than she normally did. I think perhaps that was adding to her air of naivety, but I knew it was fleeting, and that as soon as she found her feet, she'd be back to her usual sassy self.

Wordlessly, she grabbed a plate from the cabinet and placed it on the table along with glasses for the juice I'd brought. I rummaged around in my pocket and pulled out the Tylenol I'd picked up earlier. "Need these?" I asked.

She nodded and tore into the package, popping two red pills in her mouth and swallowing them down. "That champagne really did a number on me last night," she finally said.

"Well, you were knocking it back, Maddie," I said. "I don't think you're supposed to drink it that fast."

"I guess," she said, looking a little embarrassed. She opened her mouth and hesitated for a moment before she continued. "Last night. Did I say anything I shouldn't have?"

It was apparent she was suffering from morning-after memory loss, and I wondered how much mileage I could get out of this situation. I knew it was a little cruel, but I couldn't resist. I didn't get this opportunity very often and I was going to make the most of it.

I smiled serenely, saying nothing because I knew if I waited it out, she would continue to talk. If there was one thing Maddie hated, it was silence.

"Sometimes, when I've had too much to drink, I say things, and then I can't remember I've said them the next day." She blinked across at me as if she was expecting me to fill in the gaps.

"Well, you definitely said things, Maddie," I said without elaborating.

"Oh shit," she said, covering her face with her hands. "Just how bad was it exactly, Reece?"

I unwrapped her sandwich and placed it on the plate she'd put out. "Eat your breakfast." I told her. "You'll feel a lot better with some food inside you.'

She picked up her sandwich as if she was going to eat it, but then she put it down again with an angry huff. "You need to tell me what I said, Reece. You're deliberating winding me up."

"I'm just a bit disappointed you don't remember an evening I thought was pretty memorable," I said, trying to put on my best hurt expression. I could see her frustration was growing, although she was doing her best to keep a lid on it. For one rare moment, I was holding all the cards, and I was reluctant to give them up. "So, you're telling me you don't remember declaring your undying love for me?" I asked.

She moaned and clapped her hand over her eyes with a look of horror. "I really said that?"

I exhaled deeply, wondering how much longer I could keep this going, but then I took pity on her. "No, actually you told me I wasn't going to leave your house with my balls intact, if I remember correctly."

She narrowed her eyes at me, and I waited for the retribution. "You lied!" she said menacingly.

"There were no lies told. I just asked you if you remembered declaring your undying love for me. Anyway, you did tell me you really liked me."

"Huh. Hardly a declaration of undying love, though, is it? And in my defense, I was completely wasted. If old Mr. Jenkins, who feeds the ducks in the park, had been here, I would have said the same thing to him."

"Feeling a little better?" I asked her, watching her chug down the rest of her juice.

"Getting there," she said. "Thanks for bringing me breakfast. You didn't need to do that. I would have been okay."

"But it gave me an excuse to get inside your house again. I wanted to see Henry really badly. We had such a nice chat last night; he's my new best friend."

She laughed. "I assume he gave you a mouthful of abuse."

"He did. His potty mouth is worse than yours."

"Hey, I've been putting in an effort to tone my language down a bit. I thought you would have noticed."

I watched her as she took her plate to the sink and waved a cup at me to see if I wanted coffee. "Maddie, I notice everything about you, which brings me on to why I'm here. What upset you so much last night that you felt the need to sink an entire bottle of champagne in the space of about thirty minutes? I saw your face when Sam announced their engagement. You didn't exactly look thrilled. Do you and Sam have a history or something?"

She ignored my question and pulled her boots back on. "Do you fancy a walk? I'm going to take Dave and Richard for a walk. They need the exercise."

"Maddie, your llama hates me. He'll probably try to bite my ass again."

"Which will be hysterically funny, and it will cheer me up, which is, after all, why you're here."

"I am not getting my ass bitten for your amusement," I said, but she obviously had other ideas, as she was already shrugging into her winter jacket and heading for the door.

We walked out to the stable and Maddie attached a leading rein to Richard and Dave. "Okay, you take Richard," she said, handing me the donkey's leash. He was a sweet old thing, and I had no problem taking him. I was more concerned about the evil-minded camelid who already had his ears back and was eyeing me with obvious disdain.

"You take that thing in front then," I told her, pointing at Dave. "He's not walking behind me. I'll be a moving target, or rather, my ass will be."

I could hear her having a conversation with Dave about what an idiot I was, and Dave was nodding his head amiably as if he agreed with her.

There was a track that snaked around behind Maddie's property used by local dog walkers and the occasional cross-country skiers, so it was fairly easy walking. "Are you going to talk to me, or is this just one of your avoidance tactics?" I asked.

She turned and looked at me and unfortunately Dave turned too and abruptly spat a big green gob of undigested breakfast at me. Luckily, I was too fast for him, and I ducked just in time, but Maddie was thrilled and congratulated him on his aim. "Just shoot a little lower next time, buddy," she told him. "Then you'll definitely get him." I was beginning to think she would be more interested in me if I was a llama.

"I'll talk," she said. "I just needed to clear my head first."

She strode off in front and I was amazed at how fast she moved for someone with such short legs. Dave trotted along happily beside her, and it sounded like she was singing to him. I'm not sure what it was, but it sounded suspiciously like *The Pina Colada Song*. Anyway, whatever it was, Dave looked like he was enjoying it. *Who the hell sings to a freaking llama?* I thought, and then I felt guilty because I wondered if Richard was feeling left out, but there was no way I was going to sing to him. Serenading animals was not something we covered at veterinary school and besides, I had some self-respect.

After about twenty minutes, we'd completed the loop, and she secured the animals back in the paddock to join the two goats. She wandered over to her chicken house with a basket and came back with a handful of eggs. "Not many in the winter," she said, showing me her haul.

We headed back into the house, and I noticed her cheeks were pink from the cold. I was learning a lot about Maddie just by spending some time with her at home. I already knew she loved her animals, but she clearly also loved being outdoors. She was twenty-six years old, and she was set up with a beautiful little house with land. I knew she had help from her family to get it renovated, but I couldn't help but admire her. I was older than her by four years, but I was still renting my place and although I always meant to buy a property and put down roots, I never seemed to get round to it. She just seemed so together with everything.

We left our boots at the door and stripped out of our outdoor clothes, and she brought some coffee into the living room, throwing a couple of logs in the woodstove before she settled down. She'd obviously tidied up from the previous night, and there were no signs she'd spent the night camped out on her couch. "You sit there," she said in a bossy tone, pointing to a squishy armchair.

"What if I want to sit over there?" I teased, pointing to the spot next to where she was going to sit.

She shook her head at me and pursed her lips. Obviously, the seating arrangements were non-negotiable, so I flopped down in the chair while she took the couch and folded her legs up beside her.

"How much do you know about Sam Garrett?" she asked me.

It seemed odd to me that she used his full name. He was just Sam, our friend, an all-around good guy, and now engaged to Kate. "I think I know most of what happened," I said. "He confessed it all to Ryan and me last year when Kate came on the scene. He told us how he'd bullied Kate mercilessly for four years during middle school and he also told us why."

She sighed heavily. "I know. He had a terrible upbringing. I had no idea his dad was beating him like that. In fact, I didn't know the full extent of it until he fessed up to Kate." She paused for a minute as if she were gathering her thoughts. "Did he tell you anything about me?"

"Oh yeah. He said you were a fucking warrior, Maddie. Fought for Kate when no one else did. Tore a strip off the principal of your school. I was well impressed."

I watched as she added extra sugar and cream to her coffee. Clearly, sad January was already over for Maddie, or perhaps she needed a bit of a lift. She was certainly looking gloomier than usual.

"It was the end of eighth grade and Kate was a mess; like a suicidal mess. She couldn't take his shit any longer. Her mom took her off to Seattle and they started a new life, which I guess was the best thing that could have happened to her. She saw counselors, her mom married Bob, and Kate had a new dad, which was amazing."

Her face was grief-stricken, as if she was reliving it all over again. I desperately wanted to move over next to her and hold her, but I knew she would have none of that. Maddie liked to give the impression she was as hard as nails and she needed no one, but I knew that wasn't true. I'd seen glimpses of the sorrow that resided beneath all that bravado, and it broke my heart.

She looked up at me, and I could see the tears sparkling in her eyes. "It shredded me when she left," she said. "She'd been my only friend from preschool, more like a sister, really. She practically lived at our house because her mom was always working. When she left, there was this big hole in my life; a big hole in my heart." She paused for a moment and gulped, as if she was trying to collect her thoughts. "I hated Sam so much I wanted to kill him. He drove her away. I never told anyone how I felt."

"Why not?" I asked.

A tear had escaped from her overflowing eyes, and she scrubbed at it angrily as if it had no right to be there. "I grew up with three older brothers. I learned to keep stuff in. *Don't cry, Maddie. Don't tell Mom, Maddie, she'll give us shit. Keep your mouth shut, Maddie.*"

I could imagine what it must have been like. Hell, I had a twin brother, and I was always the black sheep myself. I could remember saying similar things to him when I'd done something I didn't want my parents to find out about. But she was just a little girl who wanted to be like her big brothers.

"After Kate left, I never made another friend. People avoided me in high school because I had a bit of a reputation. I think people were scared of me, but I was so lonely. It wasn't until Scarlett moved to Angel Peaks last year that I actually had someone else in my life."

Things were starting to slot into place for me. I had been around when Kate turned up in Angel Peaks the previous October. Hell, I'd actually been in Ray's Bar when she was reunited with Maddie. I remember it distinctly because Maddie thought I was hitting on Kate, and she gave me a mouthful of abuse. At the time, I had no clue about the history between them all, because Sam had never told me. I just figured Kate was a friend of Maddie's from out of town who'd come for a visit.

Of course, the ironic thing was that not even Sam knew who Kate was. He hadn't seen her since eighth grade and I guess she'd changed a heck of a lot since then, embarking on a modeling career at the tender age of sixteen. Once he found out she was actually the girl he'd bullied mercilessly all those years ago, he was in a right old state, especially since he'd already fallen for her in a big way.

I knew Maddie had been involved in all this mess, but I didn't realize the extent to which she was still hurting. Now she'd explained it to me, I could understand why it was so hard for her to feel good about their engagement.

"I feel like such a bitch," she whispered. "I love Kate, and if anyone deserves happiness it's her. I should be happy for her, and I know in my heart Sam's a good man, but there's a part of me that still feels that pain. It feels like betrayal," she said. "She's marrying the boy who tore her away from me." She laughed bitterly, "Christ, would you listen to me. I sound like a fucking twelve-year-old!"

She obviously couldn't hold her emotions in check any longer because she put her face in her hands and started to sob. I moved off the chair to approach her, but she held her hand up to me. "Don't you dare feel sorry for me! I don't want your pity."

I ignored her and sat down next to her on the couch, pulling her into my arms, despite the fact that she started pummelling me with her fists. Eventually, she stopped fighting me, her body deflating as if she had no fight left in her.

"I probably smell like llama," she choked through her tears.

"That's okay, I'm a vet. I smell like animals all the time." I said, pulling her closer and stroking her back. It was a rare treat to be that close to Maddie. She reminded me of the cats that came into my office that desperately wanted to be petted but then would lash out at the last minute out of fear or mistrust. She'd never allowed me that close before and now that she was in my arms, I didn't want to let her go.

Despite her misgivings that she smelled like Dave, she didn't. She actually smelled of vanilla and jasmine, probably her shampoo. I stroked her hair and found that it was as soft as silk. Her curls were always springy, and she always complained that the humidity made her hair do wild things, but between my fingers, it felt far from wild.

I noticed that she'd stopped crying, and she lay very still against my chest, her breathing slightly labored.

"You okay?" I asked.

"Hmm. I feel like an idiot," she said, pulling away from me. "So now you know. I am a bitter and twisted individual."

"You're nothing of the sort," I told her. "Do you think it would help if you talked to Sam and Kate, or maybe just to Sam? Just to let him know how you feel."

She looked at me as if I were mad. "Absolutely not!" she said. "I don't want to put the damper on their wedding. That would be cruel. No. I shall bite my tongue and be the stupid maid of honor and everything will be fine. I just need to get over myself."

"*Stupid* maid of honor," I said, unable to hide my amusement at her indignation.

"Yes. Stupid maid of honor. Sounds like old maid, doesn't it? Did you play that game when you were a kid? No one wanted to be left holding the old maid. Fucking ironic, really. I think they call it life imitating art."

"And I think someone's feeling sorry for themselves," I said.

"Patronizing prick," she mumbled under her breath.

"There's my girl," I laughed. "I knew she was in there somewhere. Okay, why don't we just give you a new title? You could be the hot girl of honor. That sounds better, doesn't it?"

"Yeah," she said with a grin. "Hot kick-ass bitch girl of honor."

"That's too long, Maddie," I told her. "No one will remember that. Let's just stick to hot girl." She seemed much happier with her new title, so I continued while luck was on my side. "I'm going to be the best man, and I believe it is tradition for the best man to get off with the hot girl of honor."

She curled her lip at me, looking like a cross between Dave the llama and a Muppet. I guess people do start to look like their animals after a while. Then she launched into one of the rants she was famous for.

"Why would Sam even choose you as his best man when he could have chosen Ryan? You have the attention span of a goldfish. It'll be a disaster! You'll forget the rings and turn up at the wrong church. God, you'll probably get the date wrong."

I smiled at her with a smug expression, completely ignoring her best attempts to insult me. "That, my little chipmunk, is where you are completely wrong. I am going to be the best, best man ever."

She snorted with what I think was intended to be disbelief, but what sounded more like a demented pig. I almost sprayed coffee across the room with laughter. "Perhaps chipmunk was a bit of a misnomer. Perhaps I should have gone with—"

She put her hand up like a traffic cop at an intersection to stop me. "Don't even go there, Reece Mackey, or I might be tempted to relieve you of your manhood."

This was good, I thought. She was back on fighting form, so perhaps she was feeling better.

"So, what makes you think you're going to be able to overcome years of ineptitude and suddenly become a person responsible enough to be Sam's best man?" she asked me.

"Ryan gave me this!" I pulled out a small paperback from my back pocket, holding it up so she could read the cover. *The Best, Best Man: The Ultimate Guide.*

"Reece, a book can't reverse years of not giving a shit."

"That's where you are quite wrong," I said. "I sat up last night reading this book, and I have already learned so much about my duties. It's going to be a breeze. I'm going to read to you from the book. I'll change the words to suit your sensitivities..."

The best man and the maid... sorry, hot girl of honor, both have a very important role to play in supporting the bride and groom, and it's usually a good idea if the two of them work together to coordinate their support efforts.

"You just made that up," she said with a dubious look.

"No. It's here in black and white. Look." I said, waving the book under her nose.

"And your point is?"

"My point is, I think you and I need to make a concerted effort to get to know each other better and to be nice to one another."

"Why?"

"Because it wouldn't be appropriate for you to call me a fuckwit during the ceremony," I said with a serious expression.

"I have never called you a fuckwit. Although, come to think of it, that is a good one and I will file that insult away for later use." I could almost see her making a mental note.

"You see, that's my point exactly. Maddie, you and I have this weird dynamic. It's like an offensive form of foreplay."

She sniggered a little at that before she said, "I know. But we get along okay, don't we? I always thought you enjoyed our dynamic."

"I do, but I want more. And I sense you do too."

I noticed that her sad expression had returned, and I thought for a moment I'd made a serious misjudgment about her feelings for me because she was silent for a few seconds. Then she said, "You're right. I do want more, and I do really like you, but I am terrible at relationships. Come on, Reece, you've seen me in action. I get through more guys than Taylor Swift. I don't want that to happen to us."

"What do you mean?" I asked her.

"Well, just say we started dating and I screwed it up, just like I have so many times before. I'd be losing a really good friend. I'm afraid to go there. As much as I hate to say this, it's probably safer for us to stay in the friendzone. Then I can't ruin anything."

She wasn't looking at me when she said any of this. She was staring into her woodstove, watching the flames flickering away behind the glass door, her face was full of sadness, which was so unlike her. I wasn't going to give up that easily. I knew we could be great together, but I understood her reservations. I didn't exactly have a great dating record myself, so I tried to think of a solution that would work for her.

"What if we just kind of expanded our friendship a bit? You know, spend more time together doing things without the others, and making an effort not to fight or insult each other."

"What kind of things?" she said, her curiosity clearly piqued. "Not just playing pool, I hope. I think I've had enough of that."

I was surprised to hear her say that because I thought she loved it, but I didn't let it deter me. "No, we can do different stuff. Let me plan something for next Saturday. I promise it will be fun and exciting. What do you think?"

She still looked uncertain. "So, like enhanced friends?" she said.

"Exactly! Enhanced friends."

"Secret, enhanced friends," she added. "I don't want the others to know about this. They'll just read too much into it."

"So, you're not going to tell Kate and Scarlett?" I watched as she shook her head with a determined look. "Okay, then I won't tell Sam or Ryan. It's going to be fun."

I wondered how far she would allow this new "friendship" to go and whether it would become friends with benefits, but I realized I was getting ahead of myself. It was going to be a case of slowly does it with Maddie, I could see that.

I stood up to leave but I was keen to test our new friendship before I left. Just holding Maddie in my arms had left me wanting more. "I'd like to kiss you goodbye now," I told her.

"You would?" she said, her voice a little higher than normal. "You mean like a friendly peck on the cheek?"

"No. We are *enhanced* friends after all. So, this would be an enhanced friends type of kiss."

She laughed. "You are full of bullshit, Reece Mackey."

"I know, and you love it. So come here and kiss me, then I promise I'll go."

She approached me a little shyly, like she wasn't sure what to do. Maddie was no shrinking violet with guys, and I'd seen her plant a lip lock on guys that made her look like a dementor sucking out their very soul; I'd been consumed with jealousy on more than one occasion. But this was new territory for both of us, moving from one way of being to another. It was unchartered waters that felt more than a little illicit, and it was making me as horny as hell.

I took her hands and placed them around my neck, putting mine around her waist and pulling her closer. "Should I get you something to stand on?" I joked, considering our height discrepancy.

"You are a rude pig," she hissed, removing her hands from my neck and taking a step back. "Why would I kiss a rude pig?"

"I'm sorry, you're right," I blurted, remembering that she was a bit sensitive about her height. "That was uncalled for. I have to unlearn my bad behavior with you. I'm just so used to sparring with you Maddie, and you are so delicious to spar with." She looked at me with disbelief, clearly not used to me apologizing for my insults right out of the gate like that. "Let's try that again without my smartass comment."

I grabbed both her hands and pulled her towards me, this time just placing her hands on my shoulders. "Do something for me," I whispered.

"What?" she said, looking up at me with those chocolatey eyes.

"Let me take the lead. I know it might be tough for you, but humor me." I was desperate to show her there was another way than the one she was used to, but first I had to get her to let go of the reins for a while. I knew it wasn't comfortable for her to do that, but I hoped she'd give it a shot.

She nodded as if she understood, and I stared down at the pretty pink lips that I'd craved for so long. Her cheeks were a little flushed from sitting in front of the fire, and she was looking up at me with curiosity, as if she didn't know what I was going to do next. I gently swept my thumb across her lips before bending my head and placing my mouth on hers. She was used to giving assault-style kisses, but I wanted this one to be gentle and sweet. I wanted it to be a journey of discovery for both of us, and I wanted to have that moment indelibly printed in my memory, because there would never be another first kiss with Maddie Moreno.

She tasted sweet and creamy from her recent caffeine indulgence, and I gently explored her bottom lip with my teeth, nibbling and teasing, trying to elicit a reaction from her. I moved my hands from the sides of her waist and up her back, painting swirls with my fingers, happy as I felt her body soften into me with a small groan. It was turning into the kind of kiss that destroyed all sense of control as she moved her hands to the back of my head, her fingers twisting in my hair.

I knew I had to be the one to pull away from this or we would go further than I had intended. It had been a great taster for both of us, but I knew it was important to leave her wanting more. As I pulled away, she gave a disappointed sigh, and I couldn't help but smile.

"Was that friendly enough for you?" I asked.

Her eyes had grown dark and needy, and it was all I could do not to sweep her up in my arms and carry her to her couch, especially since I felt like I was bursting out the front of my jeans.

"That was..." she looked down at the floor and shook her head as if she didn't have the words to describe it.

"That was amazing," I said, providing the words for her. "And a perfect introduction to our enhanced friend's status. I'm going to go now. I'll call you during the week and let you know when I'm going to pick you up on Saturday."

After grabbing my jacket, I escaped into the cold air before I could weaken. Dave was in the paddock as I climbed into my Jeep, so I couldn't help but give him a parting shot. "You might think you have the upper hand, my friend, but she's mine now. You wait and see."

Chapter 5
Maddie

I was sitting in my office on Monday morning trying to focus on the computer screen in front of me, but nothing was making sense. I'd been in la-la land since Reece had kissed me on Saturday, and I was finding it very difficult to concentrate on anything other than how it felt to have his lips sealed against mine. I'd fantasized many times about what that moment would feel like, but never in a million years had I thought that he could actually take my breath away with just one kiss.

As much as I told myself it was just a goddamn kiss, I didn't seem to be able to pull my mind away from the feel of his hair between my fingers, or the sensation of my heart racing deep in my chest. And then he'd left. Just as I was feeling I'd reached the point of no return, he'd left, as if the whole thing had meant nothing to him. I wondered if he was in fact just pushing my buttons like he usually did, but it didn't feel like that. It felt like he was falling right along with me.

I was also thinking about the fact that he'd promised to take me out on Saturday and if he would change his mind. Maybe that kiss had made him feel differently. I'd told him I didn't want to get involved with him, and I regretted that. In fact, there was nothing I wanted more than to be involved with Reece Mackey; I was just afraid of all the potential outcomes. What if things went wrong? What if I ended up falling in love with him and he didn't feel the same way? What if, what if, what if...?

I was still beating myself up about all this when I heard my friend's unmistakable footsteps clip-clopping up the staircase outside my office. Although we all gave her a hard time about it, Kate still insisted on dressing as if she was still in the Seattle business district, and that often included sky-high heels. How she didn't kill herself on the snowy sidewalks I really don't know.

When she'd relocated to Angel Peaks in November and moved in with Sam, she'd rented an office space in one of my dad's buildings across the street from me, so I was thrilled to have her so close after being apart for so many years.

She knocked on my door before opening it and peering around to check I wasn't with a client.

"It's okay," I told her. "I haven't got anyone coming in until the end of the week. I think everyone's still recovering from Christmas."

I noticed she was clutching a couple of brown paper bags and steaming coffee cups. "I thought we could have lunch here today," she said. "Is that okay?"

I told her that was fine by me. My office was also in one of my dad's buildings and, as usual, I'd had preferential treatment when it came to fitting it out, including a beautiful gas fireplace and a couple of comfy chairs, so it was a like a home away from home.

She'd brought a delicious mushroom soup from Heavenly's, as well as a couple of sandwiches and my favorite double shot vanilla latte. I'd spoken to her over the weekend, but only briefly so I figured this would be a good time to catch up on her wedding plans.

"I was worried about you on Saturday," she said with a frown, as she laid everything out on the coffee table. "You didn't look good. Are you okay?"

"Yeah, I told you. I just chugged my champagne too fast. You announcing your engagement like that came as a bit of a shock. I just wasn't expecting it," I said.

"I thought maybe you weren't too happy about it," she said, quietly.

I immediately felt guilty that she'd clued in on my reservations. "Kate, I'm thrilled for you," I told her. "Like I said, it was just a shock."

"Maddie, Sam's not the same boy from eighth grade that bullied me, you know that don't you? He's amazing and I love him so much. I never thought I'd find someone who would love me the way he does, and the fact that it turned out to be Sam Garrett makes it even more unlikely."

I grabbed her hand. "I know. Really, I can't tell you how happy I am that you've found all this, it's just that there's been so much change in the past few months. First, you came back to Angel Peaks to help him sort out his business while wanting to secretly murder him, then you fell in love with him, then you moved here, and now you're marrying him. I suppose it just all takes a bit of getting used to."

"Not just for you. For me too," she said quietly. "I feel like I'm on some crazy roller coaster ride and it keeps getting faster and faster." She stopped and looked thoughtful for a moment. "But then, when I'm with him, everything makes sense. He gives me the kind of peace I've never had in my life. I can totally see us growing old together."

I could relate to that because, at the end of the day, it was exactly what I wanted for myself. I'd dated so many men who were completely wrong for me in the past. But I didn't want to date the one who I really wanted to be with in case it destroyed our friendship.

"Love is so damn complicated," I said sadly. "I think the fact that you've found someone who loves you as much as you love him is nothing short of a miracle."

She laughed. "I know. I keep pinching myself. Dad was concerned that it was happening fast as well. He thought I was coming here for a month on business and then I turn up with a guy on crutches who wants to marry me. It was all good when he got to know Sam, though. He's thrilled for us."

"And so am I," I said emphatically. "Now, I need to know what I can help you with to get this wedding arranged. I'm taking my duties very seriously and so is Reece, by the way."

"Yeah, Reece is being pretty sweet at the moment," she said with a wink. "Is there something you're not telling me?"

I had to think fast because there was no way I was going to tell her about the kiss. "He wants us to call a truce and work together for your wedding. He turned up on my doorstep with a book of instructions on how to be the best, best man. He's actually taking something seriously for once in his life."

"Aww, that's so sweet," she said, with her hand to her heart. "I know he and Sam have always been close."

"Yeah, he was afraid I'd call him a fuckwit in the middle of the ceremony and hit him with my bouquet or something. I promise you I won't." I added, quickly.

"It might liven things up a bit," she said with a giggle.

"Nope, we will both be mature and well-behaved. You can count on us."

"Good, because I want you to come with me to choose my wedding dress in Havenridge next Monday. Do you think Scarlett would like to come? Her bakery isn't open on Mondays, is it?"

"I don't think Scarlett would pass up on a road trip to Havenridge," I said. "Where are you getting your dress from?"

"Probably *Tying the Knot*," she said. "I've booked an appointment for ten if you can make it. I thought we could have a spot of lunch after. We'll try to get your dress at the same time."

"And do *Tying the Knot* know they're going to be providing the dress for an ex-supermodel?" I asked.

Kate waved her hand and looked a little embarrassed. "Oh Maddie, that was years ago. I don't suppose they'd be very interested in that."

"I know someone who will be interested, and that's Harry Connors from The Gazette. He's going to find out you're getting married. You know that don't you?"

She looked concerned. "I don't want our wedding to turn into a media circus," she said. "We just want a small, quiet affair. Maybe we should get married somewhere else."

"Absolutely not," I said, a little annoyed that she would be bullied into submission by that bunch of vultures. "You need to make sure that your expectations are clear beforehand. Maybe Reece and I could go and talk to Harry on your behalf. I know you've been steering clear of him since that last incident. You could offer him an exclusive on the wedding pics if he keeps his mouth shut. What do you think?"

"Well, I guess it would be a scoop for him, although I'm not convinced anyone would be still interested in me."

"Believe me. There are still people out there who are interested."

I noticed that she'd laid out lunch beautifully on the table and my mouth watered. My attempt to diet since my recent Christmas splurge was not going well, but at least this all looked reasonably healthy, and she hadn't brought anything sweet with her, which was a good sign.

"Have you settled back into work?" I asked her, interested to know how things were going since her move from Seattle. Kate ran a company called *Angel on Your Shoulder* with her business partner Lloyd. They specialized in troubleshooting businesses that were in danger of going under, and that was why she'd come back to Angel Peaks the previous year when one of Sam's physical therapy offices was going through some challenges.

"I'm trying to settle back to work," she said. "But I'm a little distracted since Sam proposed. I don't want to let Lloyd down by slouching off. I do have a couple of jobs in Denver, which is great. We never really stretched ourselves into Denver because we were always so busy in the Seattle area, so if it goes well, this could be an expansion for us."

"And is that what you want?" I asked.

She looked uncertain. "If you'd asked me last year, I would have said absolutely. You know how ambitious I was. I was all business. And now..." she stopped as if she was considering what to say.

"And now you've found someone who fills that gap in your life," I said, completing her thought.

She laughed, seemingly a little embarrassed. "God Maddie, you know me better than I know myself. I've lost that competitive edge since I met Sam. Is that a bad thing, do you think? I don't want to lose my own identity."

"How can it be a bad thing if you're happy?" I asked. "When you meet someone special, I guess things change. It's not necessarily a bad thing. Just different."

We chatted for a while about the wedding preparations. She'd already decided on a local florist, and they were going for a church wedding in the pretty little white chapel in the center of town. They'd been discussing the venue for the wedding reception, and she told me what options they'd narrowed it down to.

"We've got three on the list. The Celestial, Loon Lodge and..." She paused and gave me a mischievous grin. "Drumroll please."

"Why do I need to do a drumroll?" I said, rolling my eyes.

"Our third option is the Evergreen Senior Center," she said with a hoot of laughter.

I was halfway through my coffee, and I almost choked on it. "The Evergreen Senior Center? For your wedding reception? You have got to be kidding me."

Her lips tightened, and she shook her head. "Nope. I'm deadly serious. It's an enormous space, and it has sentimental value. It's where Sam and I first danced together."

"Yup, and The Celestial is the first place you slept together. So, I think that holds far more sentimental value than the seniors' center. I am officially vetoing The Evergreen."

Her mouth dropped open to argue. "But think how much the seniors would love it, Maddie. It would make their year."

I put down my coffee and looked at her seriously. "Kate, this is your wedding day. With any luck, it will be your only wedding day."

"Huh. It had better be my only wedding day," she said.

"Exactly. It is not an occasion to be thinking about others, like how happy the seniors would be. This is your day, Kate. Be selfish. Make it about you and Sam; you guys deserve it."

She held her hand to her heart. "Aww. Thanks, Maddie. You're right. I think The Celestial would be the best choice. They could probably beef up their security there as well, in case we think the press might be a problem."

I clapped my hands. "It'll be amazing! Their ballroom has that stained glass dome with the stars. I can't wait." I surprised myself at how excited I felt about all this. On Friday when I'd left their place, I'd felt all doom and gloom, but now I was listening to her plans I was starting to get carried away by it all.

She looked at her watch. "I have to run. I have a Zoom conference with a new client in half an hour. I want to make sure I'm prepared for it. I'll just leave all the food here for you."

I looked around at what she'd brought to see she'd barely touched her soup or her coffee. Given her history of an eating disorder the sight concerned me. "Kate. You've hardly eaten anything. Don't do this to yourself."

She looked a little embarrassed. "It's okay. Sam's making sure I eat properly at home. I'm just really excited about everything."

I nodded, but I replaced the lid on her soup and packed it back into the brown bag before handing it to her. "Take this with you and promise me you'll eat it while you're getting ready for your meeting."

She rolled her eyes but shot me a cute smile. "Yes, Mom. I promise. Okay, I'll call you about Monday, and then maybe you can let Scarlett know we're having a girls' day out!"

She took off out the door like a whirlwind, and I listened as her heels clip-clopped down my stairs until she was out of earshot.

Chapter 6
Reece

I was home late from work on Thursday. It had been a hell of a day with an emergency surgery on a dog who'd been hit by a car, but I'd managed to save him, and the owners were super grateful. Things like that made my job worth doing, and I was on a bit of a high despite my exhaustion.

I put my key in the lock and entered my modern townhouse. My friends always joked that it looked like I'd just moved in, and I suppose in a way it did. There were no pictures on the walls and the place just had that kind of unlived-in feel to it, despite the fact I'd lived there since I moved to Angel Peaks almost three years ago.

I'd always been pretty pragmatic about living quarters. As long as I had a comfortable bed and food in the freezer I could warm up in the microwave to fill my belly, I was happy. At least I thought I was happy. Since I'd been hanging out with Maddie in her cute little house, coming back to this place left me feeling kind of flat. I wasn't sure whether it was the pull of her cozy woodstove and her enormous tub or whether it was just the lure of Maddie Moreno herself, but whatever the reason, it made me sigh as I glanced around at my rather character-less home.

Tonight was the night I'd decided to call her about our Saturday date. Well, I was labeling it a date to myself, but I knew I would have to be careful to reframe it to her in a different format. I'd already had everything planned by Tuesday, but I wanted to keep her on ice for a couple of days, hoping that it would fuel the fire a bit.

It was a gamble waiting to call her, and I was concerned she might lose interest in the meantime and make other arrangements, but I was determined to stick to the plan I'd made. After our kiss on Saturday, I'd gone home with a throbbing erection and a desperate need to move things along with her. She'd made her reservations clear, so I knew I had to develop some ground rules for myself, otherwise I would screw things up and I'd be back to square one.

When I got home, I'd pulled out a pad of paper and wrote my rules down so I would have something to refer back to. Rule number one was that us being together had to be her idea. Or at least she had to think it was her idea. If there was one thing I knew about Maddie it was that she liked to lead the show and one way I was going to let her lead was by initiating our relationship. If I pushed her or tried to convince her in any way, she was guaranteed to dig her heels in. I realized I would have to employ a bit of reverse psychology here, and that was one of the reasons I'd delayed in calling her. If she thought I was too keen, I'd be out the door before I even knew what had happened.

Second, although I wanted her to think it was her idea, I knew damn well I had to be in control of the situation. That would mean reining myself in a little and not letting things get hot and dirty too quickly. I snorted in disgust when I wrote that one down, because nothing would make me happier than getting hot and dirty with Maddie, like yesterday. That was one of the reasons I'd pulled out of our kiss before things could get out of hand. I had to leave her wanting more. I had to leave her wanting me. If I handed over control to her, she'd grab the reins and take off like a wild stallion, and I'd be in the Maddie Moreno discard pile in the blink of an eye.

Lastly, I knew I needed to bring my A-game; nothing less would change her mind about this stupid 'friends only' arrangement she seemed to be insisting on. That meant coming up with some great dates that she would love and just generally spoiling her rotten. I was pretty sure men hadn't done that for her in the past and I would have the distinct advantage. When I finished writing all this down, I looked at it and frowned in frustration. It seemed like an impossible task. I'd had the advantage of watching Maddie with her failed dates over the years, so I knew what didn't work. Now, I just had to figure out what *did* work.

I went to the fridge and poured myself a beer. It wasn't like I could even talk to any of my friends about this dilemma because I'd been sworn to secrecy. And if she thought I'd gone behind her back and talked to Sam or Ryan, all bets would be off.

I grabbed my beer and flopped down on my leather couch. Pulling out my phone, I stared down at it for several minutes, rehearsing what I was going to say to her. I laughed when I realized how much effort I was putting into all this. Normally, I wouldn't have thought twice about calling a woman up on the fly and asking her out. But this wasn't just any woman, this was Maddie, and she could sniff out bullshit at 100 yards.

I called her up on my contacts and punched the dial button, listening as her phone rang several times. Just when I thought it was going to go to voicemail, she picked up.

"Hi, Reece," she said in her lazy drawl. "I wasn't sure if I was going to hear from you."

I sensed a slight edge of irritation in her voice and figured that it had to be a good thing. It meant she'd been waiting for my call, and she was pissed I hadn't called her earlier.

"Hey, Mads," I said, trying to keep it light and breezy. "You still on for Saturday?"

She hesitated for what felt like minutes, but what was actually probably only a couple of seconds. "Yeah, I guess. If you still want to do something."

Yup, definitely pissed, I thought with a smile. "I would have called you earlier, but it's been a hell of a week. Emergency surgery for a poor dog who was hit by a car today."

The tone of her voice softened abruptly. "Oh no! Was he okay?"

"Yeah, he's going to be fine. He'll be in a cast for a while, but he'll recover."

"God, Reece," she stammered, and I could hear the emotion in her voice. "I don't know how you do what you do. I couldn't do it. I'd be in tears all the time."

And there it was. That brief glimmer of how vulnerable she really was. Maddie tried to be rough and tough, but inside was a soft center, particularly where animals were concerned. She'd revealed a fair bit of that soft side just recently, which was interesting because she was normally a lot more guarded.

"It goes with the territory," I told her. "I can't let it affect me, otherwise I wouldn't be able to do my job properly." Of course, that wasn't strictly true. I did get affected by it, especially when it involved cruelty to animals. I'd punched a guy out a couple of years ago when I found out he'd been abusing his horses, and strangely enough, my status in the town had gone up after that, particularly with a certain lady I now had on the end of the phone.

"Okay, Saturday," I said, changing the subject. "Can you be ready by nine?" I asked her.

"Of course," she said, dryly.

"Right. Make sure you're dressed to be outside. You'll need snow pants, a hat, gloves, all the usual stuff. And bring a day pack with some water and a snack."

"Are we going skiing?" she asked.

I smiled to myself. "Nope. But that's all I'm telling you. Nine o'clock, Maddie. I'll see you then."

I hung up before she could try to wheedle my secret out of me. She had that power over me, and she was really good at getting information out of people. I guess that's why she was a CPA.

Chapter 7
Maddie

I was ready to leave at nine on Saturday, just as Reece had said. I'd bundled up and was getting hot inside the house. I thought about waiting for him outside, but then I decided that would look far too keen, and I definitely didn't want to give that impression.

I didn't have to sweat for too long because just before nine I heard the unmistakable sound of his Jeep pulling into my driveway and I went to the window to watch. I heard Dave giving out his distinctive warning sound, which sounded like a horse playing the trumpet. He obviously knew it was Reece and was warning me he was here. I have no clue why Dave disliked Reece so much, but it was embarrassingly obvious. Dave set Richard off, and all the hee-hawing caused one of the goats to faint, so there was basically chaos going on out there. Anyway, I had a qualified vet on the property, so I wasn't concerned.

I let Reece knock on the door because I didn't want him to think I'd been standing there waiting for him, and then I took my own sweet time to answer. I flung open the door and found him standing there with a big grin and a fair-isle beanie. Somehow, he still managed to look sexy. Damn him.

"What the heck's going on outside," he laughed.

"It's what you call a domino effect," I told him, pulling on my jacket. "Dave gave the alarm, Richard backed him up, and Glenda promptly fainted. Not sure where Gordon is. He's probably asleep in the barn. Just think yourself lucky Henry wasn't out there at the time, or you would have gotten a mouthful of abuse as well."

He was looking suitably impressed. "It was amazing. I'm going to film it next time and put it up on YouTube."

I tucked my hair up into my pink beanie. "You are not putting my animals up on YouTube so they can be mocked by the foolish masses."

"But they'd be stars!" he protested. "You might get free llama food for life or something."

"Don't care," I said. "Now, where are we going?"

He waggled his eyebrows at me. "It's a surprise, and I'm not telling you because I know it will kill you not to know."

I narrowed my eyes. "Ha! That just goes to show how little you know about me."

"I know more than you think, my little chipmunk," he said with a dramatic wink, so I rolled my eyes equally dramatically.

"Do you have to call me that?" I said huffily. "Is it because I have fat cheeks?"

"Face cheeks or butt cheeks," he said with an innocent expression, holding open the passenger door for me.

"Face cheeks, you dork! As far as I know, chipmunks are not known for having fat asses."

"There's always the exception to the rule," he said, loading my daypack into the back of his Jeep. "There might be plenty of fat-assed chipmunks running around. You just haven't seen them. They're probably at home on their little chipmunk treadmills trying to shed those extra Christmas pounds."

He finally climbed into the driver's seat and grinned across at my somewhat vexed face. "And in answer to your question, neither. Your cheeks aren't fat, and your butt is curvaceously perfect, so don't you go thinking about having fat sucked out of that either. Kiss?"

"What?" I said with a creased brow, confused by the last word in that sentence.

"Do I get a kiss?" he intoned, as if I were hard of hearing.

I frowned. "I'm not sure. I'm still annoyed about the chipmunk conversation."

He threw back his head and laughed. "How can you be annoyed about the chipmunk conversation? It was just a little fooling around." He grabbed my jacket and pulled my face closer to his. I could smell the mint of his toothpaste along with that unmistakable Reece smell that seemed to get my pulse racing whenever I was within olfactory distance of him.

"An enhanced friend's kiss," I said, a little huskily.

"Exactly," he said with one of those slow, sexy smiles. "An enhanced friend..."

I didn't let him finish his sentence, grabbing him and planting my lips firmly on his instead. He made a startled sound as if I'd caught him unawares, but I was damn sure I wasn't going to let him take the lead this time. I needed to gain back some control, and this was the way I was going to do it.

Keeping a firm hold on his jacket, I knelt up on the bench seat before transferring my grip to the sides of his head. My kiss was a lot more demanding than his had been, and I worked his lips with mine, teasing the seam with my tongue. He opened his mouth with a groan, and I slipped my tongue inside as I felt him tighten his hold on me. We were making out like hormone-crazed teens, but I wanted to be the one to end the interaction, so I gently pulled away.

"Was that friendly enough for you?" I said with raised brows, feeling eminently pleased with myself.

He looked at me for a couple of moments, evidently stunned, as if he was trying to gather his thoughts. His breathing was ragged and, for once, he didn't have that characteristic cockiness about him. "Yeah, holy crap. That was really—friendly."

He started the engine, and I looked away out of the side window with a smirk. It was the first time since I'd met him that I'd seen Reece Mackey lost for words, and it was a powerful feeling. Of course, now I had to deal with that lustful feeling deep within my core, which wouldn't be going anywhere for the next few hours, but I figured it was worth it.

We drove along in silence for a while, and I wondered what the hell we were doing. Our attraction to one another was indisputable. It had always been there, simmering away in the background, like a slow, sexy tango that built-in passion and then diminished again, never quite reaching a crescendo.

I wondered if we could be lovers without having it affect our friendship. If the others didn't know about it, perhaps we could maintain a clandestine relationship and still be friends. I was just pondering whether it was a workable solution when he spoke, and I realized we'd been driving for a good twenty minutes.

"We're here," he said. He'd obviously recovered from my assault on his lips and his sexy, easy-going attitude seemed to have returned. I looked out of the windshield as he drove carefully down a narrow track and we traversed a steep curve. Suddenly I realized where we were as I saw the sign mounted to the fence, *Howling at the Moon Dog Sledding Tours*. I gave a little squeal of delight. "We're going dog sledding?"

Reece was wearing a huge grin, clearly pleased with himself. "Yup. I come out here to check out the dogs from time to time, and I thought you might enjoy it."

I couldn't contain my excitement. There was no playing it cool with this one and I grabbed his arm. "I've always wanted to go dog sledding."

I jumped down from the Jeep and he held his arm out to me, which I took, excited to meet the dogs. The sound of the howling increased as we approached the kennels, and I could see in the distance about twenty huskies milling around in the pen outside.

There were a couple of people in the pen with the dogs, and Reece raised his arm in greeting as we approached. "Erik, how are you?"

A tall blond man walked toward us. "Hey, Reece. Good to see you, man. Is this Maddie?"

I nodded and stepped forward to shake his hand. Erik had long blond locks and blue eyes and wouldn't have looked out of place on a Viking longship. He had a gruff manner about him, but he seemed to love the dogs and he talked to them gently as we wandered amongst them.

"They're not pets," he told me with a brusque tone. "So I ask people not to pet them. They're working dogs."

I was fascinated to see some of them had dug out holes in the snow and were laying partially buried, curled around in a tight circle, and I pointed it out to Reece.

"Yeah, they do it to keep warm when they're outside. Smart, aren't they?"

I was worried about their well-being, and I frowned. "They're not outside all the time, are they?" I tried to keep the bite out of my tone, but where animals were concerned, I was always ready to fight their corner.

Reece and Erik both laughed at the same time. "She's a tiger, Reece. I don't think you can handle her." He turned to me with a smirk. "They're in a warm kennel at night; you don't need to worry. Reece does regular welfare checks on them. They like being outside during the day. They'd go crazy if you kept them holed up. Okay, come on Maddie, help me harness up these dogs."

I nodded and followed him to the sled. "We're just friends," I told him as I picked up the harness from the ground. "Reece and me. Just friends." Erik looked up at me, and for the first time, his tanned face crinkled into a full grin. "You keep telling yourself that, Maddie. Just keep telling yourself that. If you want my advice, which you probably don't, it's easier just to give in to it."

"Total crap," I muttered, and grabbed a harness and a wriggling husky and copied Erik's movements as he strapped the dog into the contraption.

Pretty soon, we had a team of eight dogs in their harnesses, and I glanced over to see Reece working with a pretty Asian girl with a silky black bob cut. They were harnessing up a second team, and they seemed to be chatting amiably and laughing together like old friends. I instinctively felt a pang of jealousy and Erik followed my eyes and grinned as if he knew what I was thinking.

"That's my wife, Sakura," he said.

I felt awkward because he'd seen the flash of jealousy on my face. So much for protesting my "just friends" status with Reece. "She's very pretty," I said, stating the obvious.

He smiled. "Thank you. I think so too."

With both teams assembled, Erik told us that he would go out in front with the first team, and Reece and I would follow behind with the second.

"The dogs know what they're doing, so don't worry," he assured us. "We have an uphill section to start off, so you're going to have to get off and help the dogs out until we get to the flat part."

Reece and I took a place on either side of the sled and our team followed Erik's team out onto the track. Sakura was going to stay behind with the dogs who weren't coming, and I have to say, they did not look happy about being left behind. Erik assured us he would take them out later, but I looked sadly over my shoulder as we left them behind us, howling in indignation.

He was right about the uphill section because no sooner were we on the track than it started to climb quite significantly. We watched Erik hop off his sled and push from behind, so we did the same. I was obviously a lot more out of shape than I realized because, after a few minutes of pushing the sled uphill, I broke out in a very unsexy sweat, and I ripped off my hat and unzipped my jacket.

I was pretty sure my face was beet red, and I could feel my curls sticking to my head in a hot mess. I could hear Reece chuckling beside me, and much to my annoyance, he didn't seem out of breath at all. "You okay there Maddie?" he grinned, obviously enjoying the sight of me sweating my ass off.

"I'm fine," I huffed. "I'm just a little overdressed, that's all."

After what seemed like a lifetime, we finally reached the top of the hill, and my lungs felt they were going to explode. Reece was clearly unable to hide his amusement. "I didn't know you suffered from asthma," he said. "Did you bring your inhaler?"

"I am not asthmatic," I growled. "Kindly shut the fuck up. I've got shorter legs than you. It's not fair."

I watched as Erik hopped on the sled and he shouted behind him. "You two will need to balance each other out. Make sure you work as a team to keep your sled stabilized."

The dogs set out on the track, pulling us along at quite a pace, and it was absolutely magical. It was bitterly cold, but the air was still, and the frost crystals that were suspended in the air sparkled like diamonds in the sun. The snow hung heavy on the trees, making them look like huge snow-covered statues, and I quickly re-zipped my jacket and replaced my hat because I'd turned from being boiling hot to suddenly freezing.

Reece grinned across at me. "Having fun?" he asked.

I beamed back at him, totally enamored with this activity. "It's amazing!" I said, unable to hide my excitement.

We'd been traveling for about thirty minutes when Erik stopped up ahead of us, and our team of dogs stopped automatically. They were obviously used to the routine. He walked back toward us, checking on all the dogs as he made his way back.

"Okay, in about ten minutes, we're going to get to a downhill section, followed by a steep curve as we make our way back. As you go round the bend, the sled is going to keel over a little, so make sure you counterbalance it with your weight. It's just like riding a motorcycle," he said.

"But I've never ridden a motorcycle," I said, a little concerned about this maneuver. "What happens if I get it wrong?"

Erik grinned. "If you get it wrong, one or both of you will end up in the snow. You'll be fine. Just stay on the sled."

Reece narrowed his eyes and looked at me. "Did you get that? Because I don't want to end up in the snow."

"Don't be such a baby," I scoffed. "It's just snow. It's not going to kill you. Anyway, I've got this. You don't have to worry."

I sounded confident, but as we started our descent and the dogs sped up, I saw the curve Erik had been referring to and my confidence flew out the window. It wasn't so much a curve as a hairpin bend. "Holy shit," I muttered.

"You'll be fine," Reece assured me. "You're just going to need to lean out on your side a bit to make up for the weight difference. Whatever you do, stay on the sled."

I nodded but was filled with uncertainty. I just didn't see how we would make it around the curve in one piece. As we started to turn the bend, I felt the sled tip a little; I panicked and shrieked.

"Lean out, Maddie," Reece yelled, but just at the last minute, I lost my nerve and jumped off the sled at the side.

It was the worst thing I could have done, and I watched in horror at the train wreck, or rather sled wreck, that ensued. Without my weight to balance it, the sled tipped over precariously to the side and Reece was unable to right it. I gasped as it jettisoned him off into the deep snow at the side of the track. Then the sled tipped over completely, and the dogs came to a standstill, looking behind them in disgust. This was obviously not the first time this had happened, and they knew what to do.

Reece had completely disappeared into the deep snow, and I hurried across to him as quickly as I could in heavy snow boots to try and help him out. Erik had stopped up ahead and was looking back in amusement, so he obviously wasn't concerned about it.

As I got to the place where he'd disappeared, I could just see his figure in the snow. It looked like he was trying to make a snow angel in snow that was far too deep, and his legs and arms were spread out wide. His face was covered in snow, but his eyes were open with frost edging his eyelashes.

I bit my lip hard because I wanted to laugh, but I was really struggling to keep it in. "Are you okay?" I said, trying to sound concerned but failing miserably.

He blew out air, clearing the snow from his face. "Which bit about staying on the sled did you not get?" he growled.

"Well, I thought the sled was going to tip over, so I jumped off," I said, getting closer to him.

"So, you saved yourself and let me fend for myself," he said.

"Not exactly," I said, my mind scrambling for something to say. "You're fit and strong and I knew you'd be okay," I said, hoping flattery would win him over. "Here, let me help you up."

I leaned forward and extended my hand to him with the intent of pulling him up, but he grabbed my hand and pulled me into the snow before rolling on top of me. He was covered in snow, and it was like being assaulted by the abominable snowman. "Get off me, you big oaf!" I yelled. "You're making me cold!"

"I'm making *you* cold," he said incredulously, looking down on me with lumps of snow hanging from his hair. "Do you think I might be a bit cold?" And with that, he grabbed a handful of snow and shoved it down the back of my jacket before I could stop him. It was just the kind of thing one of my brothers would have done and I immediately saw red.

"You complete bastard," I yelled. "I'm going to kill you!" Although he had me pinned to the ground, I managed to grab a handful of snow, which I intended to smoosh in his face, but he was too fast for me, and he grabbed my wrist and pinned it above my head.

Then he began to laugh. It was a full belly laugh, and it echoed around the snowy landscape. "What the heck are we doing, Maddie?" he said, looking down on me with a warmth that could have melted the surrounding snow.

"We're fighting, just like we always do," I said, sad that we'd defaulted back to our regular behavior. "I guess being friends is just too hard." I was still clutching the snow in my pinned wrist with the hope that he would release me, and I could go in for the kill.

"Drop your weapon," he said softly. "Let's stop this."

I was mesmerized by the softness in his eyes that had replaced the frustration that had resided there only seconds earlier. I opened my hand and let the snow fall out, effectively disarming myself, but he didn't release me. Instead, he covered my lips with his and kissed me with an intensity that had been missing from our first kiss. His kiss told a story of longing and desire and it echoed what I was feeling. As his tongue dove into my mouth, I groaned with a yearning hunger, not caring what we were risking or why this was a bad idea. I wanted him and he wanted me, and had we not been dressed in fifteen layers of clothing, it would have happened there and then.

A gruff voice interrupted us. "What the heck are you two doing? You can't make out in the snow. You'll freeze to death. Believe me, I've tried it and it doesn't work. Frostbite is not sexy."

I opened my eyes and looked up at Erik's somewhat bemused face. "Just friends, hey?' he muttered. "You two are the friendliest damn friends I've ever seen. Come on, help me right the sled and we'll head for home."

Reece rolled off me and extended his hand to pull me up, and we wordlessly brushed the snow off each other before helping Erik with the sled.

As we rode back, I stood in front of Reece, and he caged me with his arms from behind. I felt warm and secure, and I wondered why the hell we hadn't ridden like that from the get-go. Sakura was waiting for us back at the kennel and she laughed when she saw the remnants of snow still clinging to Reece and me.

"Didn't make it round that curve, huh?" she said. "I've told Erik so many times not to take people on that route. He thinks it's funny."

Both Reece and I turned at glared at Erik and he held his hands out in surrender. "Hey! I've got to have some fun. Besides, that kiss was worth it, wasn't it?"

Reece shook his head and laughed before stepping forward to shake Erik's hand. "Thanks, man. We had a lot of fun. Didn't we, Mads?"

I thanked them both and watched Erik put food and water out for the dogs before we made our way back to Reece's Jeep. I looked across at Reece and noticed he was quite red in the face. "Are you okay?" I asked him. "You're really flushed."

"Yeah, I've just got a bit of a headache. Probably brain freeze," he said.

"Sorry," I whispered, looking at my hands. I knew it was my fault he ended up freezing to death, but I couldn't regret what happened and the heat from that kiss was still lingering deep within my core, igniting a longing for more. More kisses, more fooling around, more everything.

He grabbed my hand and gave it a squeeze. "It's fine. I'll just drop in at your place and grab some of those Tylenol, if you don't mind. I don't think I have any at home."

"I have soup!" I blurted out.

He looked at me questioningly. "You have soup?"

"Yeah, I made chicken soup before you picked me up this morning. You can have some hot soup. It'll warm you up." I didn't want this day to come to an end, and I knew Reece was ruled by his stomach.

He smiled across at me as he started the engine. "Soup sounds great."

Chapter 8

Maddie

As we pulled up outside my house, I realized that Reece was not looking good. His cheeks were still flushed, and he was shivering slightly. We got inside the door and shed our damp jackets and snow pants and I saw he was wearing sweatpants and a long-sleeved t-shirt underneath.

"Is that wet as well?" I asked him, as I watched his teeth chatter.

He nodded. "Yeah, it's all wet. I feel so cold."

I quickly threw a couple of logs on the fire and pulled the chair closer to the woodstove. "Okay, you sit there," I said, throwing a blanket over him. "I'm going to run you a hot bath. First, I'll bring you some Tylenol; I think you're running a fever."

He chugged the pills and glass of water I gave him. "Did you say you're running me a bath?"

"Yes," I said, heading for the door. "And consider yourself honored. No one uses that tub, and I mean no one, apart from me. I make Ben use the shower room when he stays over. I figure this is a medical emergency, so you're lucky."

He was laughing quietly as I took the stairs, but I could tell he wasn't himself. There was no witty backchat like there normally would be, and he was shivering like a leaf. In the bathroom, I turned both taps on full and filled the enormous tub with hot water, adding a few drops of essential oil. The steam soon filled the room, and the scent of clove and thyme oil wafted in the air.

Once the bath was full, I headed back down to the kitchen, where I'd already turned on a pot of chicken soup. I ladled some into a bowl and put it on a tray with a bread bun. As I walked back into the living room, I found Reece with his head back, looking like he was sleeping.

"How are you feeling?" I asked him.

"Not great. My head is pounding, and I can't seem to get warm," he said, wearily.

I sat down beside him with the tray. "Here, eat this, and then you can have a hot bath. It might make you feel better."

He tucked into the soup before he looked up. "This is great Maddie. Aren't you having any?"

"I'll have some later. First, I want to get you sorted out." I looked at him sadly. "I made you sick. I'm worried about you."

"You did not make me sick. Maybe I got a virus or something from someone at work. It happens."

I watched as he ate half his soup and then he set it aside. "Sorry, Mads. It's really good. I just don't feel like eating it."

"Oh my God!" I exclaimed. "I've never known you refuse food. You must be dying."

I noticed he was shivering again, but when I felt his forehead, he was burning up. "Why don't you take a quick bath and then you can have a sleep in my spare room. You might feel better then."

Despite the fact he looked terrible he still managed to laugh. "I've been trying to get in your bed for three years. If only I'd known how easy it would be. I just had to get sick."

He tried to stand but he was decidedly wobbly, so I grabbed his arm and helped him up the stairs. When we got to the bathroom, I sat him on a chair in the corner of the room. "Okay, leave your clothes outside the door. I'll wash them and dry them, and I'll find you something to wear. I'm pretty sure Ben left some stuff here. He usually does."

He looked up at me with an amused expression. "You're a good nurse, Maddie. Perhaps you should have done that instead of being a CPA."

I snorted. "Are you kidding? I'd probably end up murdering my patients if they annoyed me."

I headed out of the room and left him to it, hoping he wouldn't pass out and hit his head, or worse still drown. I went back downstairs and disposed of his half-eaten soup before fixing myself a bowl and putting some coffee on.

I was just cleaning up when he shouted down the stairs. "Maddie, I'm done, but you didn't leave me any clothes."

I tore back up the stairs and into the spare room and rooted through the closets. Sure enough, I found Ben had left t-shirts, boxers, sweatpants, and other stuff. My brother was notoriously bad at remembering to take stuff home and left things wherever he went, which was in Reece's favor. "Do you want some boxers and a t-shirt?" I called to him.

There was a silent pause. "I think wearing Ben's boxers would be weird," he said.

I rolled my eyes, even though I knew he couldn't see. "They are clean, Reece. I'm not expecting you to wear Ben's used boxers. How about some sweatpants then?" He was quiet for a while, and I continued to rummage. "Hey, I've just found a bathrobe. Would that be more acceptable?"

"Yeah, at least it's not been on his crotch," he said. "You haven't got anything that's been on your crotch, I suppose?" he added hopefully.

I opened the bathroom door a crack and extended my arm inside, clutching the robe. "You're lucky you're sick after that remark," I told him. "Put this on. Get in bed and then I'll come up and see how you are."

I grabbed his clothes that were lying in a pile outside on the floor and headed back downstairs to load them into the washing machine. When I came back up with a glass of water for him, I walked into the spare room, but he wasn't there. I was concerned he'd passed out in the bathroom, but when I went to look, he wasn't there either. "Reece, where the heck are you?" I called.

"I'm in bed," he said sleepily. "Where you told me to go."

I walked into my own bedroom and there he was, stretched out in the middle of my bed like a starfish. I'd allowed no one to sleep in my bed before and it was a bit of a shock. "That's the wrong bed!" I spluttered. "This is my room."

"I didn't know," he said, not opening his eyes. "It's a very nice bed. Comfy. Cozy. Room for two."

I sighed heavily, realizing there would be no moving him at this point. He looked absolutely terrible and moving him to the other room would have been cruel, so I put the water down on the nightstand and drew the drapes over. "Get some sleep," I told him. "Maybe you'll feel a little better later. You can't go home to that empty shell of a house you live in feeling like shit with no one to look after you."

He opened his eyes and looked at me sadly. "I know. It's awful. I never used to think it was awful, but now I do. Sit with me, Mads," he said, straightening his body so I could join him on the bed.

It felt weird being on my bed with someone else in it. I'd never had a man in this bed before; I always made other arrangements for my sexual exploits. In fact, I'd never even invited a man back to my place before, preferring to keep it as my own little personal space. Thinking about it now, I realized it was one of the ways I shut people out. I'd been doing it for so long that it had become a habit, but now Reece was wheedling his way into my private little bubble, one long leg at a time. And here he was in my bed, enjoying my 800 thread count Egyptian sheets and my goose down duvet.

Strangely I didn't resent it at all, not one little bit. Maybe it was because it was Reece, but it felt good to have him in my bed, as if he was meant to be there. I didn't want to dwell on such thoughts, so I questioned him about his own living situation.

"Why do you stay there if you don't like it?" I asked. "You rent the place, don't you?"

He sighed heavily and closed his eyes and I thought he was going to drift off to sleep, but then he answered, "I thought it was all I wanted. All I needed really. Then I came here. I really like it here."

He wasn't sounding very coherent, and I wondered if he was a bit delirious. I felt his forehead again and he was pretty warm. "I wonder if I should call Ryan," I said, more to myself than to him.

"No, don't call Ryan. He's probably busy. I'll be fine once I sleep it off."

"Then get some rest," I said to him, making to stand up.

"No, I want to talk to you," he whined, sounding like a petulant teenager, and making me laugh. "You can cook," he said, which seemed like a strange statement for him to suddenly come out with.

"Yes, I can cook. I'm a Moreno, we can all cook. My mom wouldn't let us leave home until we could cook Thanksgiving dinner. It's one of her rules."

He smiled. "It's a good rule. Even Ben?"

I giggled to myself. "Hmm. That was the Thanksgiving we had to call the fire department because he set fire to the turkey. Who the heck sets fire to a turkey?"

"So how did he get to leave home?" he asked, sounding drowsier by the minute. I knew it wouldn't be long before he drifted off.

"I think Mom tore up the rule book with Ben. She knew she had to, or he'd still be living there now, driving her crazy."

Reece's face had relaxed, and his breathing became more even. I took a moment to soak in the sight of his peaceful face. He was so beautiful, all I wanted to do was to reach out and touch him. Even slightly flushed from his fever, he took my breath away. I'd never been able to spend time just looking at him in the past for fear of him laughing at me, or one of our friends reading too much into it, but now I could spend as long as I wanted gazing at him and not feel guilty about it.

I thought about what I would do if he were mine. I would probably climb in beside him and snuggle up to him, just to be close to him. It didn't matter that it was the middle of the afternoon; if he were mine, that's where I would want to be. But he wasn't mine. I wasn't really sure what he was. He'd offered me more, and I'd refused, choosing instead to preserve the friendship we had, because if I lost that I'd be left with nothing, and that was too much to bear. Using one gentle finger, I brushed some of the hair away from his eyes, trying not to disturb him, and then I got off the bed as quietly as I could before turning off the sidelight and heading downstairs.

I tried to keep myself busy for the rest of the afternoon. With that many animals, there was always something to do, so I busied myself with feeding and brushing and cleaning. Every hour or so, I would check on Reece, and he was still sleeping soundly, so I just left him to it.

I told myself that he would need to stay overnight, because there was no way he was in any fit state to drive home. Besides that, I enjoyed having him there, asleep in my bed. Even though he was out for the count, and we weren't interacting, it just felt good to have him there. I could almost pretend we were in an actual relationship and not this weird no-man's-land we seemed to have found ourselves in.

When I checked on him in the early evening, he seemed to be stirring, so I sat on the side of the bed and hung around to see if he would wake. His eyes fluttered opened, and he attempted a smile. "Maddie, what time is it?"

"It's just after seven," I said. "How are you feeling?"

"A bit better. Hungry, I think, but I'm not sure," he said, huskily.

I leaned over and put my hand on his forehead. He was still hot, but not quite as bad as he had been earlier in the day.

"I think you should take some more Tylenol and have something to drink," I told him. "Do you want to try some food? I could bring you up a sandwich or some soup."

He looked up at me with exhaustion etched on his face. "I don't want to eat in your bed. Maybe I'll try to get up."

I heaved a sigh of disbelief. "You look terrible; you're not going anywhere. I'm going to have to wash the sheets anyway, so it makes no difference. Just tell me what you want."

He smiled at that. "If I told you what I really wanted, you'd probably hit me."

"I don't hit the infirm," I retorted. "Okay, I'll just get you something to eat and you can see how you feel."

I got up to walk to the door, but he called after me.

"Maddie,"

"Yeah," I said, turning back to face him.

"You're pretty special, you know that, don't you?" he said from his prone position.

"Yeah, yeah. Tell me that when you're sober," I shouted over my shoulder as I headed down the stairs.

⌇

HE MANAGED TO EAT SOME soup and half a sandwich, but he certainly didn't look in any fit state to get up. He trundled off to the bathroom to wash up, and he looked a little better when he came back.

We hung out for the evening, and I plugged in my laptop so we could watch a movie, but I'm not sure how much of it he actually took in. He may have been drifting in and out of sleep the whole time, but it felt good to just hang out with him without any of our regular snarky remarks.

Once the movie had finished, I told him I was going to take a shower before bed.

"Where are you going to sleep?" he asked.

"In the spare room, I guess," I said with a huff. "As you seem to have taken over my room."

"There's plenty of room," he said, throwing back the duvet to show me the unused side of the bed. "We can share."

I raised my eyebrows. "That would be weird, and I'm pretty sure it goes way beyond the boundaries of enhanced friends."

"You've been lying on the bed with me all evening," he said. "You'd just be under the covers. What's the difference?"

"Seriously? I'd be under the covers with a semi-naked Reece. That's the difference."

"A semi-naked Reece, who is totally incapable of doing anything other than sleeping," he argued. "Come on, Maddie. I might get really sick and need you in the night. I might die. You'd come in and find my stiff body in the morning and feel really guilty about it."

"It's one particular stiff *part* of your body I'm concerned about," I said, clutching my pajamas and heading for the stairs before he could respond.

It felt good to stand in the shower and let the hot water consume me. So much seemed to have changed in a day, and I felt like I was steering a boat on stormy seas with no idea where the tiller was. Watching Reece, spending time with Reece, it was all addictive. Before this weekend, we had confined our interactions to evenings with friends and games of pool at Ray's. This was completely different because it had felt more like a relationship. It was the kind of thing you did for people when you were with them, cared for them, loved them even. That last thought hit me like a shovel in the face. It was the very thing I hadn't wanted. The thing I had tried to avoid, so it didn't complicate things.

And then there were those kisses to consider. Admittedly, the kiss I'd given him in the Jeep was a case of me trying to gain the upper hand, although it had been enjoyable all the same. But that kiss in the snow had been a different beast altogether.

I shampooed my hair and massaged my head aggressively, as if I was trying to sort out all the confusing thoughts that were flying around in there. Unfortunately, it didn't work, and I just ended up with a sore scalp. Once I'd dried my hair and tried to tame its usual craziness, I climbed into my favorite pj's, which were actually a Christmas gift from my parents. They were pale gray and covered in little white llamas that looked just like Dave, and I adored them. Mom had been so pleased that I'd liked them that she'd said she'd buy me a pair in every color, which would be fine by me. She said she'd keep her eyes peeled for llama slippers as well. I giggled to myself when I thought about that because it sounded like the kind of thing that would give Reece nightmares.

I wandered into my pets' room to say goodnight to everyone. Henry did actually say goodnight, but then he added a mouthful of abuse that totally spoiled the effect. Bunnicula was my lop-eared bunny and the sweetest little guy you could ever imagine. I named him after one of my favorite book characters from my childhood, but he was nothing like a vampire bunny; he was far too cute. We rubbed noses, as was our way, before he hopped into his little house.

Finally, I went past Sylvie's terrarium. She was the most beautiful corn snake, and she was quite an impressive size. Her markings were the most amazing autumnal shades of orange and gold, and she really was quite affectionate when she was in the right frame of mind. She was actually my easiest pet to care for since she only needed to be fed every couple of weeks. She scored extra points because she freaked out my eldest brother Matteo, who was terrified of snakes. Matteo was a huge guy who could lift things that were twice his weight, but if I approached him with Sylvie, he went totally batshit crazy and ran around the place screaming like a 5-year-old. It was hilarious and a great payback for some of the things he'd done to me over the years.

I shut off the light and made my way into my living room to say goodnight to my old favorite, Willow. She was already snuggled in her basket, and I don't think she even noticed as I bent down to gently stroke her head. "Goodnight, old girl," I whispered. I looked down at her tiny body and sighed. She seemed to be thinner than usual, and I knew that there would come a time in the not-too-distant future when she wouldn't be around anymore. My mom had tried to talk to me about it a couple of times, and I know she was trying to prepare me for the inevitable, but I didn't want to think about it. She'd been with me for so long, I just couldn't imagine my life without Willow in it. But I knew that the time would come. When we take pets on, we have to accept the fact they don't live as long as we do. I just wasn't ready to accept that brutal truth just yet.

I stoked up the wood stove and turned down the damper so it would hopefully keep going all night and keep the house warm. I had other means of heat as well, but I preferred just to keep the stove running, because it did a good job of keeping the house warm.

It was just after ten, and I tiptoed up the stairs, thinking that Reece had probably fallen back to sleep again. I decided to check on him before I turned in for the night and, as I walked into my room, I saw that he was laying on his side. I approached him and cautiously felt his forehead, relieved to find that he was a lot cooler. My guess was that his fever had broken and that whatever had afflicted him was on its way out.

I glanced over at the empty side of the bed longingly. I really didn't want to spend the night in the spare room, and I figured he was asleep anyway. I may as well be comfortable in my own bed, and then I could sneak out early in the morning before he even woke up. I was always up early anyway to feed the crew, so it was no big deal.

I crept around to the other side of the bed and slipped under the covers as stealthily as I could. As I lay there in the dark, I thought about whether he'd make my life hell after this. "Hey, Maddie, remember the night you slept with me." Somehow, I didn't think that would happen. Not this time. There had been a definite shift between us, like we'd moved into a different way of being. I just wasn't sure what that was or what it was supposed to be.

I was annoyed with myself for overthinking this and I huffed angrily and puffed up my pillow. The movement made Reece stir from his slumber. "Maddie?" he said, huskily.

"Hmm. You okay?" I whispered.

"Yeah. What time is it?" he asked.

"It's probably about ten-thirty."

"Okay," he said, sounding as if he was going to fall back to sleep, but then he spoke again. "Maddie, what's your name?"

Oh God, he's lost the plot completely, I thought, wondering if I'd be safer in the other room. "Reece, what are you talking about?" I said, a little rattled.

"Maddie is short for something, isn't it?"

Of all the times to ask about my name, I thought, holding back a laugh because it suddenly seemed funny.

"It's Madeleine if you must know," I told him. "Madeleine Rose Moreno."

"That's beautiful," he murmured. "It suits you. Beautiful."

"Thanks," I whispered with uncertainty. With Reece, I was always waiting for the stinger that came after the compliment, but this time it never came. We'd crossed an invisible boundary, and now the reality was blurred. I didn't know what we were anymore, and the thought terrified me. I had to let go of one way of being in order to cross into another, and I wasn't sure if I was ready to take that step.

What I did know was that I wanted to be closer to him. Being beside him was no longer enough, and my arms longed to wrap around him. I shuffled towards him and gently let my hand rest on his upper arm, our bodies now touching.

He was warm, but not burning up like he was earlier. He let out a long sigh, and I felt his body relax as if he'd been waiting for my touch.

For a while, I listened to his steady breathing before finally, I too succumbed to sleep.

Chapter 9
Reece

I woke the next morning to bright sunlight streaming through the gap in the drapes, and I was immediately aware of how much better I felt. I rolled over in bed to find I was alone, but I was pretty sure Maddie had been there last night. The slight indentation on the other side of the bed told me I was right, but when I put my hand on the empty space it was cold, so she'd obviously been up for a while.

I grabbed my watch off the nightstand and saw that it was already nine-thirty. Judging by previous experience, I knew she'd probably been up for a couple of hours. My head was a little woozy as I sat up in bed, but nothing like how I was feeling the previous day.

Glancing at the bottom of the bed, I noticed my clothes had been laundered and neatly folded and were now sitting on top of an antique chest. I desperately needed a shower and to brush my teeth, and I was also ravenously hungry. I swung my legs to the edge of the bed, hesitating for a moment while I got my head together, and then I glanced down at what I was wearing and sniggered. In a gray, hooded bathrobe, I was hardly the height of sartorial elegance, but then I remembered turning down Maddie's offer of a selection of her brother's clothing, opting instead to go for this.

I wandered over to the window and opened the drapes, looking out over Maddie's barn and paddock. I could see that crazed llama munching away on his breakfast, with Richard there right beside him, but there was no sign of Maddie.

As tempting as that big tub was, what I really needed was a shower, which I knew was downstairs. I grabbed my pile of clothes and headed cautiously down the hallway. I figured I would feel a lot stronger after a shower and something in my belly and, as I reached the bottom of the stairs, I looked to see if Maddie was in the kitchen, but I couldn't find her there or in the living room.

Figuring she was out working in the yard somewhere, I headed for her shower room, planning to shower and dress before she got back. But, as I swung open the door, I realized I'd made a serious error of judgment because, standing in front of me naked and dripping wet from the shower, was the most beautiful sight I'd ever seen. I thought she would grab a towel to cover herself or hurl every swear word under the sun at me, but she just stood there stunned, her mouth slightly open and her eyes wide.

If I thought she was beautiful fully clothed, nothing could have prepared me for this. Although I knew I should apologize and close the door, I couldn't look away. Every filthy dream I'd had about Maddie was nothing compared to the sight of her standing in front of me now. She was perfect from her full, soft breasts all the way down to her small, delicate feet.

I don't know whether it was that I was still wobbly on my feet or if it was the fact that my blood had rushed from my brain straight to my dick, but I suddenly felt decidedly dizzy and I grabbed the side of the door frame for support as my knees gave way.

"Shit, Reece," she said, throwing on her robe and grabbing my arm. "What the heck are you doing?"

"I wanted to take a shower," I mumbled, feeling pretty stupid. "I stink."

She giggled as she helped me into her living room and deposited me on the couch. She stared down at me as I tried to get my head together, the image of her beautiful naked form still etched on my brain.

"Well, you've seen it all now," she muttered, evidently coming to terms with what had just happened.

I put my head back and closed my eyes. "Yeah, and it was fucking beautiful."

"Yeah, yeah," she said, with that disbelieving tone that was so familiar.

I opened my eyes and looked at her. "Why do you never believe me?"

"Because you're full of bullshit, Reece. Who knows what the truth is? I'm not even sure you do."

I reached up and grabbed her hand. "Look at me Maddie," I said. She looked down at me, and I noticed for the first time that her cheeks were pink. Perhaps she was embarrassed that she'd just shown off a full-frontal. I wanted her to hear what I had to say. "You are beautiful. I could tear open this robe and show you just what you do to me, but I'm not going to."

She wrinkled her nose and grinned, and I knew there was a kicker coming. "Yeah, because I don't have my microscope on hand right now." And then she threw back her head and laughed, and I knew we were okay. The problem was that I wanted her to see what she did to me, since she obviously had no clue what an effect she had on me or how I felt about her.

Then she got all businesslike again, as if the moment had passed. "Okay. If you want to take a shower, I think you should eat first because then you'll feel a bit stronger. I pulled some bacon out of the freezer this morning, so if you hang tight there for a minute I'll get dressed and fix you some breakfast."

"Maddie," I shouted after her, because I wanted her to stay around and talk to me, but it was too late. She was already out the door. The sound of the hairdryer running in her shower room was followed by her light footsteps on the stairs as she headed up to get dressed

I looked down at Willow, who was in her favorite spot by the woodstove. She opened one eye and looked at me somewhat disdainfully. "What do you think I should do, Willow?" I asked her. "She doesn't believe me."

Willow tossed her head as if dismissing me, before closing her eyes and going back to sleep. It served me right for asking a cat for romantic advice. I'd probably get a better response from Henry, although it might not be the one I wanted.

Pretty soon I could hear activity in the kitchen, followed by the aroma of something wonderful. I was feeling a little better again, so I headed off in that direction, aware I was still wearing the rather stinky bathrobe which hadn't left my body since the previous afternoon.

I walked in to find Maddie at the stove cooking up a storm with a pan full of hashbrowns, bacon, and scrambled eggs. "Can I help you?" I asked, feeling the need to be useful, but in reality, not knowing where to start.

"Nope, you sit there," she said in her usual bossy manner, pointing to her kitchen table.

I sat down and poured myself some orange juice, which was a treat for my dry mouth. I watched in wonder as she rapidly plated two breakfasts and came to join me at the table. I noticed that her plate contained about half of what mine did.

"Aren't you hungry?" I asked.

She huffed. "If I ate that quantity of food I'd never get into my jeans," she said. "Men are so lucky. They just burn it off."

I stared at her appreciatively. "From recent experience, I can assure you that you have nothing to worry about."

She muttered something unintelligible that sounded like it contained a few curse words and then started to delicately pick at her breakfast while I demolished mine. Once I started eating, I realized I was famished, and I finished off the contents of my plate in no time at all, staring at its emptiness with a certain sadness.

She'd barely started, but she looked over at me. "You're still hungry, aren't you?"

I nodded. "How did you know?"

"Reece, I have three brothers. I've seen that look before. It's good though; it means you're feeling better."

She got out of her chair as if to fix me something, but I protested. "Maddie, sit down and eat your breakfast. I can wait a few minutes." She sat down a little unwillingly. "Do you always look after other people like this?" I asked her.

She chewed for a moment before she answered. "It's what we do in our family. We look after each other. I think it just happens that way when you're from a large family. I was the baby, but I seemed to be the one who always looked after the others. Especially Ben. He really needs looking after."

I laughed. Although Maddie was the youngest, it often never felt that way because Ben was the one who was the neediest in that family. It was strange because, in business, he was capable and very thorough. It was just all the other areas of his life where he didn't seem to have a clue.

"What do you normally have for breakfast?" she asked.

I thought for a moment as I poured myself some more juice. "I don't know. Something quick usually. Toast, cereal, Pop-Tarts, leftover pizza."

She pulled a face. "You can't eat like that. It's terrible. It's like someone's put a child in charge of a man's body."

"I'm always busy," I whined. "Sometimes I get called in for an emergency. Food just kind of takes second place."

She was up from the table and back at the stove. "That is no excuse," she said flatly. "Look at Ryan. He's busy as well at his office or at the hospital and he always cooks for himself. And for everyone else, come to think of it."

"Yeah, well that's Ryan," I grumbled. "I'm not Ryan. I just don't enjoy all that domestic shit."

"But you like eating good food," she said, countering my argument, and placing another heaping plate of food in front of me.

"Okay, get that down you, and then you'll be strong enough to have a shower. Now, what about tomorrow? Are you going to be well enough to work, or do you need to get a locum in?"

I hadn't even considered the fact that I might not be well enough to work the following day. In the three years I'd had my own practice, it wasn't something I'd ever had to consider because I'd never been sick. I frowned as I thought about it. It seemed like a lot of work to get someone else in to cover for me, and I was pretty sure I would be okay. "I think I'll be okay," I said.

"Give it some thought," she said as she grabbed my plate. "You've been out of commission for two days. You need to give yourself time to recover."

I stood up from the table and felt a lot steadier now that I'd eaten something. I tried to help her clear the dishes, but she batted me away with a kitchen towel as if I was an annoying fly. "Have a shower," she said.

I had to admit she was a lot more efficient than I was in the kitchen, and she zipped through the dishes in record time as I wandered off to the shower, feeling like a complete slouch.

Her shower room was just as immaculate as the rest of her house, tiled in white subway tiles with a huge rainfall showerhead. As I walked through the door, I got a vivid flashback of Maddie's naked body coupled with that lingering fragrance from her shower gel, and my seemingly permanent erection got a little uncomfortable. I pondered that I could sort out that minor problem while I was in the shower as long as I was quiet about it, since there didn't seem to be any chance of furthering my pursuit of Maddie today. I didn't think I was up to my "A" game anyways, and nothing less would do for Maddie. That was all I was prepared to give her, and I would not settle for anything less. She deserved my best, and that was what she was going to get. At least she was if I could persuade her it was what she wanted.

After a hot shower and a quick hand job, I felt almost human again, and I was happy to get out of Ben's bathrobe and dress in my own clothes. I had two days' worth of stubble on my chin, but aside from that, I looked like myself again. My fever had gone, and I was feeling decidedly stronger than I had been.

As much as I was reluctant to leave Maddie, I thought I'd taken up enough of her time and her house for the weekend, and I didn't want to overstay my welcome. I figured she might appreciate some alone time after having played nursemaid for me for the past 48 hours.

She wasn't in the house, but I found her out in the yard splitting up logs for the fire with an enormous ax. I was impressed at how she wielded that thing for such a petite person, and she was certainly putting her all into it. I made a mental note not to get in the way of Maddie when she was wielding an ax.

"I'm going to go now, Mads," I called over to her. "I think you've probably had enough of me by now."

Her face fell a little, and she looked disappointed before she quickly recovered. "You can stay as long as you like. I was just getting some firewood ready." She threw the ax on the pile of wood, and I walked over to her.

"You've done enough for me already. I'll let you enjoy the rest of your weekend in peace." I thought of how I might pay her back for everything she'd done. "Hey, I could take you out for dinner tomorrow if you like. My treat."

She looked down at her feet. "No. Someone might see us and jump to conclusions that we're dating or something."

I felt a little miffed, and I couldn't keep that out of my voice. "No. That would never do, would it?"

She looked a little exasperated. "We agreed to keep it quiet. At least for now. Please."

"Don't friends have meals out together?" I asked.

"We don't. We play pool and drink beer and tell dirty jokes," she said sadly, as if that could sum up everything we were. Except it wasn't what we were any longer. Neither of us wanted that. We'd outgrown that relationship like an old pair of shoes that pinched your feet. "Anyway, I'm going to Havenridge with Kate and Scarlett tomorrow to get Kate's wedding dress," she added.

I smiled, annoyed with myself that I'd gotten irritated with her. "Well, that'll be fun. You three will probably cause a riot."

She laughed. "Scarlett will probably cause a riot. She seems to do that wherever she goes. Anyway, I hope she reins it in a bit tomorrow. This is Kate's special day."

"I think you'll find Scarlett is a lot savvier about her behavior than she lets on. She is very capable of behaving herself."

"You think it's an act?" she said with a puzzled look.

"Not an act so much as a convenience. It suits her to be that way and it amuses people, so she plays to the crowd."

She nodded, clearly not convinced. "Anyway, if you're sick, go home and get Janet to rearrange your appointments. Do you need to take some Tylenol with you?"

I shook my head. "Nope. I think I'm good, thanks to you."

"Well, if it wasn't for me, you probably wouldn't have been sick in the first place. And I never thanked you properly for taking me dog sledding yesterday. I really enjoyed it, even if I did wreck it."

I grabbed her shoulders with a sigh. "You have to be the most frustrating woman in the universe," I said, roughly. "Firstly, I did not get sick because I fell in the snow. I had some kind of virus. Got that?" She nodded but didn't speak. "Secondly, you didn't wreck our day. It was a lot of fun, and it was Erik's fault I ended up in the snow, not yours. Got that?"

"I guess," she said.

"And I think it should be me thanking you, not the other way around. But if you insist, you can thank me properly now," I said huskily, pulling her into my arms.

There was no hesitation from her this time, and she didn't hold herself back. I braced myself for one of Maddie's full-on dementor kisses, but she took me by surprise, kissing me with an unfamiliar tenderness. It felt like she was pouring herself into this kiss and, if I didn't know any better, I would have said she was trying to convey a message with her lips. The problem was that I didn't understand what she was trying to express, and I needed her to translate for me with her words, but that was something Maddie never did. Committing her feelings to spoken words was just too hard for her, and she would never put herself out there like that.

She pulled away from the kiss, holding my face in her hands and looking up at me with a sad smile. "You take care of yourself," she breathed. And then she turned and walked towards the house without a backward glance.

Chapter 10
Maddie

Monday was another cold but beautiful day, and we were all excited about our trip to Havenridge. Kate had an appointment at *Tying the Knot* for 10 a.m., so by nine we were all cozy in the new SUV she'd bought when she moved here last year.

She was getting more familiar with driving in our snowy conditions, having spent several years in Seattle, but I offered to drive, if only for the opportunity to drive her swanky car.

"No, I should be fine," she said. "It's sunny and the roads are clear. You can drive home if you want to."

"I don't know why we didn't go in my Fiat," Scarlett complained from the back. "She's much more economical."

"You and I would have been okay," I told her. "But poor Kate would have been sitting with her knees up to her nose. Your car is great for small journeys, but this is luxury," I said, caressing the heated leather seats with a sigh. I closed my eyes and relaxed into the warmth of the seat. Scarlett was jabbering on in the back seat about nothing in particular. She'd obviously overdone the coffee again, or she was just really excited because her conversation seemed like a stream of random thoughts that weren't directed at anyone in particular.

As she didn't seem to need much in the way of a response, I allowed myself to drift back to my rather unusual weekend with Reece. Whenever I closed my eyes, I had flashbacks of those kisses we'd shared. Just thinking about them set me on fire. Coupled with that, I kept thinking about the shower room incident, as I was calling it. I don't know why I'd frozen like that when he'd opened the door. My natural reaction should have been to cover myself up and kick him out, but something in his eyes had prevented me from doing that.

At first, I had been stunned to see him standing there, but the look he had given me had mesmerized me. I'd seen lustful eyes before on guys I'd dated, but that had been something different, more like a burning hunger, and it had gone straight to my core. As I'd stood there for what seemed like an eternity, I'd willed him to make a move, to reach out to me, to touch me, but then he'd crumpled, and I'd had to shoot into action in a different way. If it hadn't been for the fact that he was still suffering the effects of a virus, I think the outcome of the incident would have been very different. I must have been smiling to myself, because Kate interrupted my lustful thoughts.

"What are you grinning about?" she said. "It looks like you're having a dirty dream."

I hastily tried to cover my tracks. "Oh, I was just thinking about Ms. Scarlett here and if Havenridge was actually ready for her certain brand of joie de vivre." I turned around in my seat and stared at Scarlett. "Are you going to cause havoc in the dress shop?"

She tried to look offended, although I knew she wasn't. It took a lot more than that to offend Scarlett. "As if I would. I will be like a little mouse. You won't even know I'm there."

Both Kate and I cracked up at that because the thought of Scarlett being in a room and people not knowing she was there seemed so far from reality that it was a joke. She always managed to fill a room wherever she went, and what she lacked in size she made up for in personality.

"Well, we have an appointment," Kate told us. "So it'll only be us in the store. If they can't cope with Scarlett, we will take our business elsewhere."

"Yeah, right on!" Scarlett yelled, making a victory salute.

Kate turned to me. "Have you thought about what kind of dress you'd like to wear? Colors, style anything like that?"

I scrunched up my nose. "You know me, Kate, I'm not really a pretty dress kind of girl. I'm happier in a pair of rubber boots." I thought for a minute. "Just something that doesn't make me look stupid. I don't want to look like a cupcake."

Kate tried to conceal a smile, very aware of my tomboy tendencies. "I think we can do better than cupcake."

"You want something to show off those magnificent boobies, you lucky wench," Scarlett added from the back. "I have none at all. I think you have my share. You can probably pick things up with them. Now, that's useful, isn't it?"

"Believe me, they're more of an encumbrance than anything else," I told her. "If you had them, you wouldn't want them."

"I bet men love them, though," Scarlett said thoughtfully. "Whenever I make booby cakes for bachelor parties, they always ask for big ones. No one ever wants small ones. One guy asked for boobies big enough to bury his face in, and apparently, he did just that. They sent me the photos afterward. I thought it was a bit of a waste of cake, but they probably ate it, anyway. Men are pigs like that."

Kate looked at me slyly. "Yeah, I bet Reece Mackey would like to bury his face in those."

I immediately blushed and tried to cover it with indignation. "Kate McKenzie! That fiancé of yours is a terrible influence on you."

I was saved from any further embarrassment as we pulled into the parking lot in the main square in Havenridge and Scarlett bounced up and down in her seat excitedly. "Yay, we're here!"

It was a million miles away from Angel Peak's downtown core. Here the Gucci store rubbed shoulders with exclusive hotels and day spas, and even just coming here for a shopping trip meant dressing up a little.

I was very familiar with Havenridge, and my dad had built several multi-million-dollar homes on the ski hill, some of them for celebrities. My brother Matteo had bought himself an apartment in Havenridge several years ago when prices weren't quite so crazy, and he'd tripled his money in that time. It made sense for him to have a base there because he did a lot of the timber framing in some of the more exclusive homes.

The bridal salon was located downtown next door to one of the day spas, and we all stared at the beautiful window display for a few minutes before Kate rang the bell on the door, which was currently locked. Apparently, it was exclusive enough to only sell by appointment, and we had a two-hour slot allotted to us.

A tall, elegant woman with gray hair came over and unlocked the door, greeting us with a warm smile. "Come on in, ladies. I'm Caroline; I'm so pleased to meet you. Now, which one of you is Kate?"

"That's me," Kate said, a little shyly.

Caroline regarded her with a smile. "Well, I don't think I've ever had such a beautiful bride to work with. You're tall and beautifully slim and you could wear anything and look wonderful."

"Well, duh," Scarlett chimed in. "She is a supermodel."

"Scarlett!" Kate chided.

Scarlett at least had the good grace to look remorseful. "Sorry. Was I not supposed to say anything? I'll just sit here and keep my mouth shut."

Caroline was looking at Kate with renewed interest. "I thought I knew you from somewhere. You're the girl who slapped that lowlife Rory Laverne, aren't you?"

Despite Scarlett's vow to keep her mouth shut, she clearly couldn't contain herself. "Yeah! That was her. She sent that motherfucker packing."

"She did indeed," Caroline said with a smile. "My friends and I watched it on Channel 7. We all cheered when you did that. He totally deserved it. Oh gosh! You're not marrying *him,* are you?" She looked concerned that she'd spoken out of turn.

"No, no. Absolutely not." Kate said. "I'm marrying Sam Garrett. He owns Garrett Total Health. He has a couple of offices here in Havenridge and one in Angel Peaks."

Caroline nodded as if she recognized his name. "Oh yes. He's very handsome. Much nicer than Rory Laverne," she added quietly. "So, you were McKenzie and now you're just Kate."

"Yes," Kate said. "And going forward, I will be Kate Garrett, so the McKenzie name will be retired forever."

Until that point, I hadn't even thought about Kate changing her name to Garrett. When I'd known her at school, she had been Kathryn Trollop. Then she had moved to Seattle and her mom had married Bob, and she'd become Kate McKenzie. While she was modeling, she was just known as McKenzie, and now she would be Kate Garrett.

"You've had more names than any of us," I joked.

"Yes, and this will my very last name change," she said with a determined look.

Caroline was obviously keen to get started. "Okay Kate, we'll get your dress and accessories sorted out first, and then we can take a look at your lovely bridesmaids."

"Oh, not me," Scarlett chimed in. "I'm a groom's person. I'll be needing a tux."

Caroline was evidently a consummate professional, and she didn't miss a beat. "We can absolutely arrange a tux for you. No problem at all."

I found it hard to believe they'd have a tux in Scarlett's size, but maybe Caroline was thinking about using something from the kid's section, because for sure, none of the men's stuff would fit her.

Scarlett and I sat together on a plush blue sofa sipping orange juice, provided by Caroline's assistant, while Kate emerged from the change room in a variety of beautiful dresses. I have to confess I felt a pang of jealousy since everything seemed to look so amazing on her. I could see it was going to be a tough decision.

After trying on about five gowns, she suddenly emerged wearing something that knocked everything else out of the park and I gasped. "Oh my God," I murmured.

"Holy hell!" Scarlett shrieked. "That's got to be the one."

Caroline smiled serenely. "Well, I think from the reaction of your friends, you might have found your dress. What do you think?"

The dress was intricate lace over a nude underlayer, which took away the stark whiteness of the dress. It was fitted, with a deep V at the front, but the back was what made it stand out, dipping into a low V with a sexy tassel to hold the whole thing together.

"Do you think I'll be warm enough?" Kate said, studying herself in the mirror.

Scarlett laughed. "I think that's the least of your problems. I would be more worried about whether Sam will be able to control his erection with you in that dress."

Caroline's eyes shone with amusement. "Usually, the groom is too nervous to be upstanding in the church, although I make no promises for later. I've seen some first dances that can get quite edgy." She turned to Kate. "Some brides have a cashmere wrap in case it's chilly. You don't have to use it, but it's good to have it at hand. Just make sure they turn up the heating in the church."

Kate grinned and gave a model twirl and Scarlett stuck her fingers in her mouth and gave a loud whistle. "I think this is the one," she said, brimming over with happiness.

Caroline helped her pick out a beautiful seed pearl headpiece, which looked amazing in her black hair together with a veil, which tucked in the back of her hair and covered her back for the church service. Being tall, she didn't need to have the dress shortened and could get away with just a small heel.

Once everything was in place, I snapped away with my phone, assuring Kate I wouldn't show anyone, as she wanted to keep her dress a secret from everyone, even her dad.

Then it came to the moment I'd been dreading. It was my turn to find a dress. Having seen my elegant friend parade in all those glorious gowns, I felt decidedly dumpy and didn't hold out much hope for finding something that made me look even a fraction as elegant as she did.

Caroline asked me to stand up and looked me over with a critical eye. "You have beautiful coloring and a figure to be proud of. We want to make sure we showcase it. Do you have any preference for colors?" she asked, looking between Kate and myself.

I shook my head. "To be honest, I'm not usually a very dressy person. I spend my time in my barn with my animals."

That wasn't strictly true. I did like to dress up on occasion, and I always made sure I was wearing something businesslike for work, particularly when I was meeting clients. It was just that pretty dresses weren't usually my thing.

Caroline grabbed a swath of fabrics and held them up to my face. "Hmm. I think you would look beautiful in rose gold," she said showing me a square of material. "What do you think?"

I looked at the sample she was holding up and was immediately fascinated. It was a deep dusky pink, but when you moved it in the light there was a gold sheen that ran through it. "That's amazing," I murmured.

"And it will look even more amazing on you," she said with enthusiasm.

Once I got over my self-consciousness and started to try on the beautiful gowns, I actually quite enjoyed it. In the end, we went for something quite simple with a higher neckline and an elegant slit to the thigh that could remain covered during the service. Although the dress was simple, the fabric elevated it into something stunning, and I'd never felt quite so elegant as I did standing in front of that mirror.

"I suggest a higher heel for you Maddie," Caroline said. "And we will bring out the rose gold accents for the other members of the bridal party." She clapped her hands like an excited child. "It's going to be wonderful!"

Once everything was arranged, we left the shop in a bubble of excitement, details for fittings and an appointment for the men in hand.

Kate wanted to go to the upmarket lingerie shop, which was a couple of doors down from the bridal salon, but I desperately needed a coffee, so I sent her off with Scarlett while I ducked into one of Havenridge's many coffee shops. Once I'd armed myself with a double shot latte, I pulled out my phone to check my messages. As I stared down at it, my mind immediately went to Reece, and I wondered how he was feeling.

My fingers hovered over the keypad uncertainly before I plucked up the courage to send him a message.

Hi. How are you feeling?

I didn't expect an immediate response, as I knew how busy he usually was during the day, so I put my phone down on the table while I inhaled my caffeine fix. It surprised me when my phone buzzed after a few seconds with a response.

Wasn't expecting to hear from you. Thought you three would be locked in a police cell by now. Not feeling great, but a quiet day.

I smiled when I saw he was well enough to make a joke, but I was still concerned about him after he'd been so sick over the weekend. I was also missing him, which seemed pathetic. It wasn't an ailment I normally suffered from, missing men, and it concerned me because it was an indication of just how hard I'd fallen for him. I quickly texted back.

Enjoying coffee on my own. Sent Scarlett and Kate off to buy underwear.

I was unsurprised by his response.

Did you not need underwear?

Smirking to myself, I composed a suitable response that I knew would get a rise out of him.

No need. I don't wear any.

There was a pause, and I watched the dots on the screen to show he was typing.

Thanks for that imagery, Chippy. Now what am I going to do with this erection before my next patient comes in?

I didn't really know how to respond to that, so I just sent a series of appropriate emojis.

Eggplant. Banana. Hotdog.

I grinned, thoroughly enjoying this brief diversion, and waited to see what he would come back with.

Hey Chippy. What I'm packing looks like none of those, but I could always use a second opinion.

I looked up to see my friends coming through the door armed with expensive-looking bags from the lingerie store, so I quickly texted back.

Have to go. My friends are back laden with panties. Speak to you later.

He texted back a chipmunk emoji followed by kissy lips and a taco, which was pretty disgusting. Kate and Scarlett approached my table full of pink cheeks and giggles, so I knew they'd been up to something.

"Hello, girls," I drawled. "Looks like you were successful."

Kate laughed. "Oh, my God. You should have come with us. Scarlett was a riot in that store."

Scarlett tried to look indignant. "I was not! I was just asking about crotchless panties. They're very practical in the summer months. They didn't have any. I couldn't believe it!" She sat down with a grin. "Anyway. As you were boring, and you didn't come with us, we got you a little something." She held up a beautiful cream bag with gold script and ribbon handles.

I eyed it suspiciously. "Okay, Scarlett. Is this something I want to be getting out in a crowded coffee shop, or should I wait until we're in the car?"

Kate and Scarlett looked at each other, and I thought they were going to burst. "You should definitely open it now," Scarlett said, clearly trying to keep a straight face.

We were tucked away in the corner of the coffee shop, and I looked around at the other customers, who all seemed too busy with their conversations to notice what we were doing. I put my hand into the bag and pulled out a tissue-covered package secured with a gold foil seal. If this was a joke gift, it was obviously a very expensive one.

Carefully peeling back the seal, I unwrapped the tissue paper, trying not to tear it, and revealed a very classy-looking black, lacy baby doll chemise, complete with a matching black thong.

"Hold it up!" Scarlett insisted. "Hold it against yourself."

Not wanting to disappoint my friends, I stood up and held the black chemise next to my body. A couple of older women at another table gave me the thumbs up, so it obviously met their approval.

"It's beautiful," I told them. "But when in God's name am I going to wear it? When I'm in the barn maybe, to compliment my rubber boots?"

Kate looked at me with a gentle smile. "Just put it away for a special occasion. It'll come. You just wait and see."

After a little more shopping we headed off for lunch. Kate was keen to go to the hotel she had stayed in with Sam when they'd been stranded there during a snowstorm. We managed to secure the same booth they'd sat in, and she went through what had happened, adding all the dramatic details. Although we'd all heard the story before, it seemed like she needed to relive it. It was a journey that had brought her to where she was today.

She stopped and took a gulp of her water, as if the emotion was almost too much for her, and I looked at her fondly. "And now you're going to marry him," I said softly. "Who'd have thought it."

Chapter 11

Reece

Thankfully Monday was a fairly quiet day for me because I don't think I would have been up to much else. My assistant Janet and I looked through the rest of my week and we agreed she wouldn't book any more appointments until I was feeling fit and well again. I just had to hope there wouldn't be any emergencies in the meantime.

It may have been a calm day, but I was still exhausted by the time I headed through my door just after five. I made myself a drink but, aside from that, I really didn't feel like doing anything. Although I was starving.

I sat there for close to an hour, staring into space aimlessly, when there was a knock on my door. Grumbling and hauling my ass off the couch, I headed over to open it and found the woman of my dreams standing on the other side, clutching what looked like a casserole.

Maddie narrowed her eyes and looked me up and down critically. "You look terrible. Have you eaten?"

I shook my head, too stunned by her sudden appearance and the aroma coming from her crockpot to elicit an answer. She bustled into my kitchen and plugged in her magical appliance before removing the lid and giving the contents a stir. "I made a beef stew before I left for Havenridge this morning. Do you want some?"

"Well, yeah. I'm starving," I said.

"Thought so," she said with a satisfied smirk. "And I'll take a bet you've only got crap in your freezer."

"I wouldn't call it crap as such," I said, watching her serve up a heaping bowl of steaming stew. Just the smell of it was making my mouth water so much that I thought I would start drooling like one of those Pavlovian dogs.

She opened my freezer and dug around for a bit, as if she wanted to confirm her suspicions. "Yup. Just as I thought. All crap," she said dismissively before slamming the door shut with a huff and placing the bowl of culinary wonder in front of me, together with an enormous slab of bread.

"Are you going to eat with me?" I asked.

She told me she'd had a big lunch at Havenridge and sat down next to me with a small portion of food. I groaned in pleasure as I tasted the first bite of the piping hot food. There was something about homemade stew that warmed you from the inside out, and I felt myself revive a little just from eating it. Not only was it delicious, but it looked really healthy, with a ton of vegetables. I had been thinking about warming up a pizza, but this was infinitely better.

"So how did your girls' day go?" I asked her. "It sounded pretty interesting from your texts. Are the good people of Havenridge still shaking in their boots?"

Maddie laughed. "Scarlett was reasonably well behaved, so it went well. Kate got an amazing dress. She's going to knock Sam for six. He is one lucky bastard," she said, blowing on her hot food.

I looked up from my plate. "And what about you? Did you get your dress?"

She smiled at me. "I did, and I'm actually quite pleased with it. I know I could never look as spectacular as Kate, but all in all, I didn't look too bad. Dresses aren't my thing normally."

It made me sad that she seemed to shred her own self-esteem at every opportunity she got, and I wondered why that was. This self-deprecating behavior seemed to be a habit with her, and I could never understand it. I sometimes thought it might be because she'd grown up with three brothers who were constantly throwing insults at each other. I was pretty sure she got caught in the crossfire at times, and I could see how that would affect an impressionable teenage girl who had little in the way of self-esteem to start with.

I put down my spoon and grabbed her hand. "Maddie, you're beautiful. Why can't you see that?"

She snorted derisively and pulled her hand away. "I just like to be realistic. There's no point in pretending to be something I'm not. I know what I am, and I don't like to kid myself that I'm more than that. It just leads to disappointment."

I didn't know how to respond to that, and I ate my food silently for a few moments, contemplating how I could make her see herself as I saw her. I wondered exactly what it was she saw when she looked in the mirror. Did she not see those beautiful brown eyes staring back at her or that cute little freckled nose? Did she not see a body that was so soft and curvaceous that it practically drove me to the edge of sanity?

"You have to stop comparing yourself to others," I said quietly, feeling more than a little frustrated. "I tell you I think you're beautiful and you don't listen to me. I don't know why."

She bit her lip as if what I said was genuinely affecting her. "Perhaps because I'm so used to you talking 95 percent bullshit that when you actually get serious, I don't recognize it."

She stood up suddenly, as if she wanted to get away from the conversation and busied herself in the kitchen with the plates.

"The problem is, you run away when things get serious. You're scared of something," I said.

She spun around angrily, her eyes flashing in the light. "I'm not afraid of anything."

Rising out of my seat, I approached her, caging her to the countertop with my arms. "Everyone's afraid of something, Maddie. Snakes, spiders, llamas. Admitting it can be tough sometimes. My question is, what are you afraid of? What is it that makes you run?"

She stared into my eyes as if she was confronting me, and then she spoke the one word I wasn't expecting to hear. "You."

"Me? You're afraid of me?" I said, scarcely believing what I was hearing. How the heck could she be afraid of me?

She broke our gaze and looked away, as if she couldn't tell me while she was looking at me. "I'm afraid of what you could do to me. I've never been afraid of someone's ability to hurt me before, but now I am."

"You think I'm going to hurt you?" I said, a little choked by her words.

"I think you could, if I let you," she said quietly, still not looking at me. "You have the ability to hurt me like no one else could because no one else has ever mattered before."

What she was trying to say to me suddenly all made sense. The reason she was reluctant to get involved with me. I was in some way different from all the guys she'd been with in the past. A thousand thoughts were flashing through my head, but the main one was that Maddie was telling me that I mattered to her, that I had the power to hurt her, and that scared her.

I grabbed her chin and gently pulled her head around to face me, and I could see the conflict in her eyes. I could see the vulnerability she usually hid so well, and I could also see the anger that I'd gotten her to admit to her worst fear. "Hey," I said softly, as if I was speaking to a frightened animal. "I will never intentionally hurt you. You mean the world to me, even though I am a stupid ass at times. I thought you knew that."

"Yeah. In a friend's kind of way," she said, her eyes brimming with the tears she could no longer hold back.

"No," I said, firmly. "In an everything kind of way."

Then she did something she'd never done before. She buried her face in my chest and she held onto me with everything she had. This was nothing like the flirty kisses we'd been sharing up to that point. It felt with that embrace she was pouring all her emotions into me, all her fears, all her anxieties about us. I wrapped my arms around her and held her just as tightly, because I wanted to show her I could be strong for her, that I would support her and not let her down.

We stayed like that for what felt like several minutes, and I was desperate to kiss her, but suddenly we were interrupted by a knock on the door, and Maddie jumped away from me like a startled deer. She stared at me. "You should answer that."

I shook my head. "I was planning on ignoring it, actually."

"No," she said with a frown. "You should answer it. It might be something important." Then she turned her back on me and I felt bereft of her touch.

Reluctantly stomping off to answer the door, I flung it open to find the smiling face of Ryan Carmichael, clutching one of his famous cake boxes. It had to be the only time in existence I wasn't happy to see Ryan and one of his desserts.

"Hi Reece," he said in that breezy manner. "I thought you might be kicking your heels tonight, so I brought us round something to share over coffee."

I stood back wordlessly and let him in the door. I couldn't say what I wanted to say because he was my friend and that would have been rude. Since Sam had hooked up with Kate. I'd seen a lot less of him aside from our group friend's nights, which was understandable. It was as if Ryan had stepped in to bridge the gap, and although we were pretty different in a lot of ways, he was still a good friend. And he always fed me.

He breezed into the kitchen and caught sight of Maddie spooning the remainder of the stew into a plastic container. "Maddie!" he said, with a look of surprise. "I didn't know you were here."

"Hmm. Well, mister here has been sick over the weekend, so I brought him some decent food to eat. He only has crap in his freezer."

Ryan looked at me with a worried expression. "You've been sick? Why the heck didn't you call me. I would have come over."

I didn't want to tell him I'd actually been camped out in Maddie's beautiful big bed. "It was nothing. Just one of those stupid viruses."

"He's been running a fever and he's exhausted," Maddie chipped in, in that bossy manner of hers I was beginning to love.

Ryan went into full doctor mode, feeling my forehead with the back of his hand and checking my pulse. I pulled my hand away from him roughly. "I'm fine Ryan. I'm getting better now."

He frowned at me. "Maddie's right about the crap in your freezer. You should look after yourself better, Reece. You work punishing hours; it is not possible to feed your body the way you do."

Maddie was smiling to herself. "I told him that," she muttered, before turning to me. "Okay. I've put the rest of the stew into this container. Make sure you put it in the fridge when it cools down, so you have dinner for tomorrow. Do *not* eat any of the vile contents of your freezer. Some of it has so many additives. I'm surprised you don't glow in the dark. Remember, corn dogs do not actually count as food."

I watched in dismay as she grabbed her bag and her jacket. "You're not going, are you?"

"I have to put the animals to bed," she said. "I'll talk to you tomorrow."

She hugged Ryan before giving me a quick peck on the cheek and then she was gone, leaving me staring at the door open-mouthed. I turned back to my friend to see he'd taken the lid off my stew and was examining it. "That was so nice of Maddie. This smells superb," he said, eyeing it up with hungry eyes. "Do you think she'd give me the recipe?"

"Hey, that's my stew!" I said, grumpily. "She brought it round for me because I'm sick. If you're hungry, I'll get you something out of the freezer."

"Reece, I was just saying it smells good. I wasn't going to eat it. Calm down. Have some cake."

"Sorry," I mumbled, feeling stupid as I watched him take the lid off the cake box to reveal what looked like a chocolate layer cake. "God, that looks fucking amazing," I said, walking over to get some plates out of the cabinet. "Beer won't go with that. I guess we need some coffee. Maddie put some on earlier."

I watched as Ryan cut two huge slabs of cake before he handed one to me and we went to devour them on my couch. We both closed our eyes as we savored the first bite, because it was the cake equivalent of nirvana. "How do you find the time to do all this?" I asked. "Maddie's the same. She seems to pull meals out of her freezer at the drop of a hat. All I have in my fridge is some questionable cheese and two flats of beer."

Ryan sucked his fork as if he was determined to get every last bit of chocolate that had solidified on it. "She's super organized. She preps all her meals at the weekend. Didn't you know that?"

I shook my head. Ryan obviously knew stuff about Maddie that I had no clue about. All I knew was that she loved animals, she had a filthy mouth when aggravated, and she looked sensational in those denim shorts she wore in the summer. I also knew I planned to bury my face in her beautiful breasts as soon as I possibly could. What I didn't know was any of the nitty-gritty, the everyday stuff, and I'd known Maddie a lot longer than Ryan had.

"What else do you know about her?" I asked casually.

He looked thoughtful. "I know lots of food-related stuff because that's what I'm interested in. She's a great cook and she learned most of what she knows from Nonna because she spent most of her summer holidays with her to get away from her brothers," he said, referring to Maddie's grandmother, who was well known to all of us. "Apparently Nonna makes a mean lasagna and a tiramisu to die for. Maddie won't give me the recipe for either of those things because she said then she'd have to kill me, which apparently is a Moreno tradition." He swallowed another mouthful of cake before he continued. "Despite appearances to the contrary, she's also unspeakably kind and would help anyone." He hesitated for a long moment before he delivered his zinger. "I also know she's in love with you and if you don't do something about it soon, you'll lose her."

I stared at him with my mouth open, which probably wasn't a pretty sight after I'd consumed all that chocolate cake; it was probably like looking inside a concrete mixer full of dirt. "No she's not!" I said incredulously.

He shook his head and laughed. "I'll tell you, my friend, if I had a woman who looked at me the way she looks at you, I wouldn't be dragging my feet. I'd be putting a ring on her finger."

I was silent for a moment because what Ryan had said shocked me. It never occurred to me that Maddie might be in love with me, but that led me to another question. Was I also in love with her? I wasn't a guy who wore his heart on his sleeve like Sam. God, when he'd hooked up with Kate, he'd been spouting off like a fucking poet. And then there was Ryan, always bemoaning the fact that he just wanted a nice girl to love him for who he was, so he could fill that house of his with a million kids. Now that I thought about it, I couldn't honestly say I'd ever been in love with anyone in the past, but the way I felt about Maddie was different. What if it *was* love? What the heck was I going to do about that?

I sighed heavily and put my head back on the couch, closing my eyes. God, this all felt so complicated.

"Are you okay?" Ryan said, evidently concerned. "Are you feeling unwell again? Perhaps I should check your blood pressure. I've got my bag in the car."

"I'm fine," I assured him. "It's probably just indigestion."

"I think you need to get some rest," he told me. "Why don't you take yourself off for an early night?"

"But it's only 8 o'clock!" I protested.

He ignored me and packed up the remains of the cake, which he clearly wasn't going to leave for me, before he headed for the door. He turned to me before he left. "Now, don't forget about Saturday, will you?"

I stared at him blankly because I had no clue what he was talking about, but I obviously should by the look he was giving me. "Can you give me a small clue?" I said pathetically.

"For Pete's sake, Reece. You're the best man!" he spluttered.

I suddenly panicked. "Oh, God! The wedding's not on Saturday, is it? I had it written down as the first weekend in April. Have they changed their minds?"

He laughed. "No! We're having a wedding planning meeting. We're all going to The Celestial to look at the venue and talk about food and music and things like that. Don't you remember?"

Now that he'd mentioned it, there was something vaguely familiar about what he was saying. "Yeah, of course I remember," I said, realizing I was completely failing in my quest to be the best, best man. "What time are we meeting again?"

He was grinning because he knew I'd completely forgotten about it. "Eleven at The Celestial. Why don't you pick Maddie up and score some points?"

I had to conceal a smirk because, little did he know, scoring points is exactly what I'd been doing with Maddie. "Yeah, that's a good idea," I said, closing the door behind him.

As much as I enjoyed Ryan's company, I was grateful for the silence so I could try to get my head around what was rapidly becoming a complicated situation. I frowned as I tried to unravel the tangled ball of thoughts that had taken up residence in my rather woolly brain. If Maddie was in love with me, that explained a heck of a lot. She'd told me she didn't want to lose our friendship, and tonight she'd told me I was the only person who could hurt her. Yeah, that made sense to me, because if you were in love with someone, the thought of losing them would be devastating.

I tried to put myself in her shoes and thought about how I would feel if we messed up and ended our friendship. It wasn't something I'd even allowed myself to think about in the past because I wasn't that kind of guy. I kind of took each day as it came and never really dissected things in the way that other people did. I just didn't see the point in worrying about stuff that might never happen.

I closed my eyes and tried to imagine my life without Maddie in it, and something shocking happened. It was as if my heart was on an elevator on the thirtieth floor and someone had just cut the cables and it was plummeting to the basement at speed. I clutched my chest and felt physically sick. "Holy shit!" I muttered to myself. No wonder I never did the touchy-feely thing. It was fucking awful. I resolved not to do that again in a hurry.

At least it told me something and that was that I had to move things forward with Maddie. The taking things slowly tactic was clearly not working. She seemed more conflicted than ever, and, if I didn't take charge of the situation, she was going to slip through my fingers.

I resolved to set up another date for the weekend. I wanted it to be a romantic occasion that would give me a better opportunity to win her round. Clearly, Saturday wasn't going to be an option because, for some reason, Sam and Kate needed everyone's opinion about the nitty-gritty of their wedding planning. I hoped they weren't expecting too much input from me because I didn't really have much experience selecting tablecloths.

I decided that Sunday would be the day when I put Operation Chipmunk into action. I was just thinking about what might make a romantic date when my phone rang. Seeing it was my mother, I sighed heavily, knowing that this wouldn't be a brief conversation. I hadn't spoken to her since Christmas, so she was probably phoning to ream me out about that.

"Hi, Mom!" I said, as cheerily as I could. I grabbed my laptop off the table so I could multitask and do some romantic date research while I was talking to her.

"Hello, Reece, how are you? I thought you might be sick as I haven't heard from you for so long. I was beginning to get worried," she said, not sounding worried at all, but instead decidedly miffed that I hadn't called her.

I saw this as my get-out-of-jail card free and immediately jumped on it. "Yeah, I have been sick, actually. I think I had a touch of the flu."

My ploy obviously worked because she went off into full momma bear mode. "Oh, Reece. Why ever didn't you call me? I would have driven up and looked after you. You've got no one there to cook for you and make sure you're okay. Did you go and see Ryan and get checked out?"

She knew both Ryan and Sam because I had taken them with me when I'd had to make my obligatory family visits and I hadn't wanted to go on my own. She loved both of them, of course, and went on about what nice young men they were, clearly implying I was the opposite. "It's okay, Mom. Ryan came around tonight. I'm getting over it now, I think."

"Well, that's good, because I was hoping you would come for lunch on Sunday. Robbie's coming up from Denver for the weekend with Deirdre and Emma."

My heart sank. The thought of spending Sunday with my holier than thou twin brother instead of snuggling up with Maddie filled me with dread. My brother and I were actually identical twins, but that's where the similarities stopped. In truth, we were like oil and water, and it was really hard for me to be civil when I was around him. His wife Deidre was a nice enough person, but what made it bearable was that I'd get to see my three-year-old niece, Emma. She and I were big buddies, and I took great joy spoiling her with lots of candy and teaching her pranks to play on my brother, much to his annoyance.

My mother sensed my hesitation. "Reece. I know you two don't exactly hit it off, but family is family, after all."

I could see that there was no way I was going to wriggle out of this, and my Sunday with Maddie was ruined. Or was it? "Can I bring a friend?" I asked casually.

"Of course, dear. You know how much we like your friends. Such lovely young men."

I had no intention of telling her I wasn't bringing a lovely young man. Nope, I intended to bring a lovely young woman. I'd never taken a girl home before, and I couldn't wait to see my parent's reaction when I strolled up with Maddie in tow. It would be worth it just to see their faces.

"How's Dad?" I said, changing the subject before she could press me further about which friend I would be bringing.

"Well, you know. Some days are better than others. He gets very frustrated by it all."

My dad had suffered a stroke a couple of years back and had been left a lot less mobile than he'd like to be. His speech wasn't really affected, but I got the feeling his moods were, because he hadn't been himself since. He'd never been the most patient man, but this seemed to have made him worse.

"I'm sure he'll be happy to see Emma," I told her.

"Yes, that will cheer him up. Grandchildren are great for that."

The implication underlying that statement was hard to discern, but I knew it was there. She thought I would not be increasing her grand kiddo brood any time soon. Nope, I was definitely the dark twin. The one who got in trouble at school, the one who spoke his mind in no uncertain terms, the one who was unlikely to settle down and have a family. Essentially, I was the antithesis of my goody-two-shoes brother, who'd studied theology and become a church pastor, marrying at twenty-four and giving my parents a pretty little granddaughter to dote over.

There was a crash in the background, and my mother was suddenly keen to get off the phone. "I have to go, Reece. I think your father's just broken something again. Lunch will be at one. Now don't be late, love, will you?" And with that, she was gone without so much as a goodbye. Poor Dad. I wondered what he'd broken this time. The stroke had left him a bit clumsy and when he broke stuff, he got into a right old state. I was pretty sure they were in for a rough evening one way or another.

Chapter 12
Maddie

On Tuesday morning, I was embroiled in analyzing a set of financial statements for one of my bigger clients, and my eyes were crossing. I loved this type of work because I found it a lot more interesting than the day-to-day nitty-gritty, but I needed focus, and I wasn't sure that I was applying myself in the way I should.

Pushing my paperwork to one side, I got up out of my chair and stretched, crossing over to the window to look out on the street below. It was one of those cold blustery days, and only a few of the hardiest townspeople were out and about. Sideways snow and sub-zero temperatures meant that the most sensible folks were sitting by their fires with a hot cup of tea and no intention of leaving the house. If ever there was a day to hunker down, this was it.

I contemplated the fact that I could work from home on the days I didn't have clients in the office, but I knew from experience that didn't always go well. I lacked the discipline needed to work from home successfully, and there were far too many distractions to keep me from my work. When I'd tried it in the past, I always ended up spending far too much time with my animals and achieved very little, so unless I was completely snowed in, I made the effort to come to the office every day. Besides, it was a pleasant environment to work in, and I smiled contentedly at the sight of my cozy gas fireplace that was blasting away in the antique mantel.

Knowing it wasn't a day I would want to go out and get coffee, I'd brought cream from home so I could make my own, and I settled down in front of the fire to take a break for ten minutes. Curling up my feet in the comfy chair, I knew I would have to be careful not to fall asleep as I had done on previous occasions when I got too comfortable.

I was just taking the first sip of my coffee when there was a knock on the door, and I huffed impatiently, not wanting to leave my cozy spot. "Who is it?" I called.

"It's Liam, from Heaven Scent Florists. I have a delivery for you," a young male voice replied.

Confused as to why I would be getting a delivery from the florist, I jumped to my feet, almost spilling my coffee, and flung open my door to find a teenager obscured by the biggest bouquet of pale pink roses I'd ever seen. "Are those for me?" I squeaked, completely stunned.

He read a piece of paper he was holding in his hand and then looked at my business name on the door. "Yup, delivery for Ms. Maddie Moreno."

I muttered my thanks, relieving him of the huge bouquet and placing it carefully on my desk, feverishly looking for a card to see who sent them. It wasn't even close to my birthday, and none of my brothers had pissed me off sufficiently to warrant a display of this magnitude, so I was bewildered as to who might have sent them.

I located a small, white envelope and tore it open to read the enclosed card:

Dear Chippy,

Just wanted to thank you for looking after me through that bout of man flu.

Probably would have died without you.

With love,

Your overdramatic friend

XOX

"Reece," I murmured pushing my face into the bouquet and inhaling the scent of the flowers. I was left reeling slightly that he had sent me such a beautiful gift and I was stunned by his thoughtfulness.

Realizing I had nothing to put them in, I was keen to get them in water so they wouldn't wilt, so I emptied out one of my small metal trash cans and filled it will water from the bathroom. It was a beautiful gesture, and I needed to thank him, so I quickly picked up my phone to call him.

I listened as his receptionist, Janet, answered the phone in her usual friendly manner. "Hi, Janet. It's Maddie Moreno. Could I speak to Dr. Mackey please?"

"Oh. Hi, Maddie. How are all those animals of yours? Keeping you busy?" she said.

"Yeah, always lots to do," I responded, impatient to speak with Reece.

"He was in with a patient, but I'll just see if he's free." She put me on hold, and I listened to a loop of public service announcements that were programmed into their answering service, telling me about the importance of flea and tick protection for cats and dogs.

After a while, he came to the phone. "Maddie! How are you?"

Hearing his voice made me feel stupidly gooey, and I was glad he wasn't there to see the heat in my cheeks. He definitely had the voice for phone sex, and I tried to pull my mind out of the gutter and back to the reason I'd called him. "Thank you so much for the flowers. They're absolutely beautiful!" I said, unable to prevent my voice from sounding a little giddy.

"Flowers? What flowers?" he said, innocently.

"Don't be an ass!" I snapped. "You know damn well what flowers. You're the only person with the nerve to call me Chippy."

His warm laugh filled me with a longing to see his face again. He was only two streets away, but the distance felt too much. We were both working, and we were both busy, but I would have given anything to be with him at that moment. Of course, I had no intention of telling him that, so I kept the conversation light.

"Are you feeling better today?" I asked.

"Yup, thanks to you. I'm feeling a lot better and I'm looking forward to the rest of that stew tonight. Not sure what I'm going to do for the rest of the week, though. I think I need you with me permanently."

His voice had taken on that husky, teasing quality that was so familiar and always seemed to render me tongue-tied, or worse still, speechless. I ignored the implication of his last sentence and just said, "Well, I'm glad you're feeling better. You had me worried for a while."

"So, I guess we have wedding planning on Saturday," he said with a laugh.

"Did you remember, or did Ryan tell you?" I asked, glad to be moving away from unfamiliar territory.

I heard him draw breath. "Ryan told me, but don't let Sam know. I really wanted to do a good job of this."

I grinned. "Your secret's safe with me. Eleven at The Celestial. Shall I pick you up for a change?"

He hesitated. "Okay. I was going to offer, but I don't mind being driven. Maybe there will be some free liquor samples."

I rolled my eyes, even though he couldn't see. "Yeah. We're more likely to be picking out napkin colors and looking at table settings."

"Oh, lord," he said. "I may nod off during this. I have a very short attention span, especially for stuff like this."

I giggled. "I'll make sure you stay awake."

"Hmm. I can think of many ways you could do that," he said, his voice dropping a tone.

"And none of them appropriate," I added. "Anyway, I have to go. Thanks again for the flowers, Reece. I love them," I said quietly.

"That's all that matters," he said. "But don't go yet. I had something I wanted to ask you. I have to visit my family on Sunday, and I wondered if you'd come with me. My brother will be there, and it'll be a complete bore-fest, but having you there will make it more bearable. What do you think?"

"Really? You want me to meet your family?" I said with wide eyes.

"Yeah. Well, I know all your family and you should meet mine. Sam and Ryan have been with me before, but I'd like to take you. I like to torture all my friends fairly. There should be no favoritism."

I laughed. "Reece, I am very used to difficult family gatherings. It'll be a breeze. Is your brother older or younger than you?"

"I thought you knew," he said. "He's my twin. My identical twin."

"Nooo!" I gasped. "You mean there's someone who looks like you walking around this earth? That's weird."

He was silent for a moment, as if he was thinking. "It's hard to explain. He looks like me, but he doesn't. It's like you've taken me, cut my hair into a kind of moronic basin cut and put me in socks and sandals, and voila! You have my brother Robbie."

"I can't wait to meet him!" I said with enthusiasm. "He sounds intriguing."

"Don't get too excited. You might be disappointed. Okay, I'll fill you in on the family dynamics on the way there on Sunday. Do you want to keep it a secret from the others?"

I thought about the reaction we would get if our friends knew Reece would be taking me to meet his parents, particularly Kate and Scarlett. "Yeah. I think that's safest. Unless you want Kate and Scarlett trying to arrange our wedding at the same time."

"Hmm, I catch your drift. Okay, I'll see you just before eleven on Saturday. Don't forget to pick me up, will you?"

He rang off, and I stared at my flowers, grinning like an idiot. I knew it was foolish to read too much into it, but I couldn't help but feel that maybe we were moving in the right direction. I had been a little surprised that he wanted me to meet his family, but he'd framed it as a "friends" kind of thing, so I didn't want to overthink it. Knowing Reece, he was taking me along to counteract the boredom, and there were obviously some interesting dynamics I needed to be aware of.

I put the trash can of flowers on my desk with the intent of returning to my work, but then I heard the unmistakable sound of Kate's heels on my stairs, and I flew into a panic. If she saw the size of the bouquet Reece had sent me, she'd be all over it like a bloodhound. I grabbed the trash can and ran to my small stationery closet, depositing the flowers on the floor and quickly closing the door as I heard her knock. I ran back to my desk and mopped up the small puddle of water I'd created with a tissue before calling her in.

"Wow. It's freezing out there!" she said. "I just came across the street and I'm already frozen. It's nice and warm in here though." She looked at me with a frown. "It might be too warm. Your face is quite red."

I had to conceal a smirk because my red face was more likely caused by my sprint to the stationery closet to conceal my flowers. "Yeah, I've had my gas fire cranked up all morning. I get cold just sitting around."

I watched as she sniffed the air. "It smells really nice in here. Like a flowery kind of smell. Are you wearing perfume?"

I shook my head. "Oh, it's probably my new shampoo," I said, quickly, lowering my head so she wouldn't see my expression.

"Speaking of flowers, I wondered if you would come over to the florist with me."

I screwed up my nose. "Today? Like now?"

She looked embarrassed. "Well, yeah. I've just been worrying about all the things we need to do, and I wanted to get the flowers sorted out, or at least get some idea of what might be available before we go to The Celestial on Saturday."

"Okay," I sighed, grabbing my purse from under my desk. "But we are going in your car. I don't care how close it is."

"Thanks, babe," she said with a grin. "I knew you'd say that, and the car's parked right outside. You won't even get the teeniest bit cold."

I bundled myself up and locked up my office and we headed for her car to take the two-minute drive to Heaven Scent Florists, which was on the corner of Second Street. It was a pretty little store, painted in dark green with large windows. In the summer, flowers sat outside in large metal buckets for people to select from, but at this time of the year, the delicate blooms were kept indoors, away from the fierce elements.

The old-fashioned bell on the door jingled as we walked in, and I allowed Kate to go ahead of me. I spotted Graham, the owner of the store, immediately. He shot me a cheeky wink, and I had a feeling I knew what was coming next.

"Maddie!" he said excitedly. "Did you get your..."

He stopped in his tracks because from behind Kate's back, I was scowling at him in an intimidating way whilst giving him the throat slit, you're dead signal. He seemed to catch on real quick, because he collected himself before finishing his sentence. "Did you get your hair cut? It looks very nice."

Kate spun around and looked at me, totally confused. "Maddie hasn't had her hair cut for months."

"My mistake," he said cheerfully. "Now, I guess you're here about your wedding flowers. Come out the back and look through my photographs of different bouquets and arrangements and you can tell me what kind of flowers you're thinking of. Pink roses are rather nice," he added pointedly, giving me another cheeky wink.

Kate looked between the two of us as if there was something going on, even though Graham was old enough to be my father. "You go look at Graham's book," I told her. "I just need to have a quick word with him about his upcoming audit."

He got her settled in his workroom and followed me back out the front into the store. I got close to him and narrowed my eyes. "You are the most indiscreet man I have ever met. Don't people in your trade have some kind of code of honor?"

He smiled serenely. "Am I to assume by your reaction that no one else knows about this budding relationship between you and Dr. Mackey?"

"There is no budding relationship," I hissed. "We are friends. He was sick, and I helped him out. End of story. Now can we please focus on the bride and not escalate this nonstory about Reece and me into the latest piece of town gossip, because if this gets out, I will know exactly where it came from, and your upcoming audit will be unnecessarily painful and expensive."

I was trying my best to be menacing, but I wasn't sure I was succeeding because Graham's smile was growing wider by the minute. He was evidently thrilled to be armed with a secret and didn't seem at all bothered by my threats about his audit, probably because he knew I was too professional to follow through with them.

"Weddings are good for business," he said with a smile. "Perhaps there will be another wedding in the not-too-distant future."

"If you're not careful, there might be a funeral," I said with a growl.

He smiled with hamster cheeks and turned on his heel, walking back to the workroom. Kate looked up from the book of photos she had been perusing. "Everything okay?" she asked.

"Everything is wonderful," Graham said with enthusiasm. "Now, what are you thinking for your bouquet?"

Chapter 13

Reece

Maddie had picked me up just before eleven on Saturday, and it surprised me how excited I was to see her again. I tried to play it cool as I climbed in beside her, but truthfully, all I wanted to do was press her into the seat and kiss her into oblivion. Perhaps even pull her onto my lap. In reality, I did none of those things and instead gave her a friendly grin.

"Ready to be bored out of your mind?" she said cheerfully. "Now, if they ask for your opinion about anything important, just be ambivalent, otherwise they'll end up with polka dot tablecloths and a German oompah band for the entertainment."

"Hey, I'll have you know I have excellent taste," I said, trying to sound offended but failing miserably.

"Reece, I've seen your house," she said pulling away. "You honestly couldn't coordinate a 5-year-olds birthday party. You'd have no idea that unicorns and ninja turtles don't go together."

"They don't?"

It was actually only a five-minute ride, and I guess I could have walked, but then I would have missed out on an opportunity of riding with Maddie, and I wasn't going to turn that down.

I noticed that the rest of our friends were already in the huge foyer of The Celestial as we strolled through the doors. I guessed that Ryan probably brought Scarlett, and she looked like she had come from the bakery because she was still wearing her apron.

I looked at her in confusion. "Who's watching your bakery while you're here?" I asked her.

"Oh, I just put a sign on the door that said, *Gone out for half an hour or so. Back soon.* It's pretty cold today, so I wasn't exactly rushed off my feet."

An elegant woman in a navy suit approached our group and chatted briefly with Kate and Sam before she stared at me with a look of recognition. I supposed I should know her from somewhere, but I just couldn't place her.

"Oh, Dr. Mackey. How lovely to see you again," she said with a seductive smile. She turned to the rest of the group. "He's such a kind vet. He takes such good care of my kitty."

I think it was only Ryan who could keep a straight face at that comment, and I seriously thought Scarlett was going to say something because she had that look in her eye, but Ryan was glaring at her with that dad look he was so good at. Maddie, on the other hand, was strangely silent beside me for a few moments as we followed the woman into the ballroom.

"So, you've been looking after her pussy, Dr. Mackey," she hissed out of the side of her mouth.

I knew I could probably wind her up with this, so I went with it. "She has a very nice pussy," I said. "Are you jealous?"

Maddie turned to me with an expression that was a cross between a sneer and a grimace, but she said nothing.

"Of course," I continued. "I could look after your pussy, if you'd let me."

"My pussy is exclusive," she said hotly. "I don't let just anyone look after it. Unlike some people," she said, frowning at the poor woman.

I could see this teasing was going to blow up in my face if I wasn't careful. "Mads," I said, gently. "I don't know who she is. I obviously looked after her cat, but I've forgotten her. I've never seen her socially."

"I don't give a shit what you've done with her pussy," she muttered. "Why don't you go and play in the traffic and give us all a break?"

I sniggered at her sudden outburst. This was the Maddie I knew, always blowing hot and cold, and I could never resist slapping the bull. "Your barely concealed aggression is making me hard," I told her.

She glanced down at my crotch and looked away with a smile. "Funny, I didn't notice. There appears to be nothing there."

"You will notice when you're bouncing on my dick," I said out the side of my mouth

"Filthy pig!" she hissed, elbowing me so sharply in the ribs, I cried out.

"Ow!" I yelled.

Everyone else in the party spun around in surprise, including the woman with the pussy whose name I couldn't remember. I pointed at Maddie. "She's attacking me again."

"He's being vulgar," she spluttered in her defense.

Everyone turned back, so I continued to provoke her. "I should take you outside and spank you for that."

Her look was classic Maddie, and I don't know how I didn't laugh as she turned to me, barely able to conceal her fury. "Try it and you're dead meat, Mackey. I will hide parts of your body all over Angel Peaks. In fact, I will feed parts of you to Dave."

"He's a vegetarian," I said, pulling her closer and whispering in her ear, which caused her to shiver a little.

"He would happily turn omnivore to do me a favor," she said. "Eating you would be the equivalent of biting your ass, only more satisfying."

I bit my lip and put my head down to conceal my mirth, because this was Maddie at her finest, and it was far more interesting than table linens. My shoulders were shaking silently with laughter as I tried to hold it in, but I was failing miserably and making squeaky noises. Suddenly, she shoved my shoulder and snorted with laughter, causing everyone to turn around again. We were like the two naughty kids at the back of the classroom.

Kate just looked at us and shook her head with a smile. "Just ignore them, everyone. They're obviously having one of their moments." She turned to the nameless pussy woman. "It'll be okay. They've promised to behave at the wedding." The woman nodded with a forced smile, as if she wasn't convinced, and I hoped I hadn't lost a client with my immature behavior.

Maddie had been right about the boredom factor. As much as I tried to be interested in how the tables were going to be arranged and why Uncle Fred couldn't sit next to Aunty Sue, I found it hard to stay alert. I perked up a bit when someone mentioned food, but then Ryan and Scarlett became all artistic and got into a creative disagreement about appetizers, and I completely lost the plot.

I realized it was already past noon and my stomach gurgled loudly. "Maddie," I whispered.

"You don't need to tell me you're hungry. I heard," she said.

"Did you bring anything to eat?" I asked, hopefully.

"What do you think I am? Snack woman? No, I did not bring anything to eat. Where would I be hiding food? In my purse?" she said, holding up her small bag that obviously contained nothing edible.

"I need to eat," I said, firmly. "I've not been well."

Maddie heaved an impatient sigh and then announced to the group. "I have to find Reece a sandwich or he's going to start eating the furniture. We'll be back as soon as we can. You just keep deciding about the centerpieces."

Scarlett looked sympathetic. "Sorry, Reece. I knew I should have brought those stale muffins for you. You're the only person I know who actually eats them. Apart from Maddie's brothers of course. They eat any old crap as well."

We ended up in a small café tucked away in one of the side areas of the hotel, as Maddie thought we shouldn't actually leave the building. It was an elegant little space with tall arched windows and comfortable leather furniture – a big step up from Heavenly Java.

My mouth watered as I perused the selection of sandwiches in the glass cabinet, and I ended up buying an enormous sub filled with sliced beef and salad. My appetite had certainly returned with a vengeance, and I had every intention of going back for one of their sweet treats once I was done.

Maddie was a lot more restrained and just settled for a mega latte.

"I'm not trying to be a brat," I said, concerned about what she thought of my behavior.

"I know. You're just bored and hungry; I understand," she said as we flopped down into two leather easy chairs facing a round table.

"You do?"

"Of course. I have three annoying brothers who are constantly hungry. I get it; you need to eat. Besides, I needed a coffee. You just made for an excellent diversion."

I took a huge mouthful of my sandwich and munched contentedly, happy to be getting some food inside me. "I'm obviously crap at this wedding stuff," I said. "I guess it's just not my thing."

She shook her head. "To be honest, it's not my thing either, but it means a lot to Sam and Kate, so at least try to look interested."

"I know," I said, trying to put on a remorseful expression. "So, you wouldn't be interested in a big, fancy wedding then?" I asked.

She pulled a face. "God, no. Not at all. But hey, I respect those people that do. I know this is a big deal for Sam and Kate and they want it to be special, but there are other ways of making your wedding day special."

Her answer intrigued me, and I immediately wanted to know more. "Like what?"

She took a big sip of her coffee and wriggled her butt back into her chair, evidently getting comfortable. "A couple of years ago, I went to a friend's wedding. They got married at home on their acreage with a big white tent and hay bales. They said their vows to the sound of their rooster crowing, which made everyone laugh. It just all seemed so much more personal than this." She waved her hand around the elegant décor of the hotel. "This means nothing to me," she added. "My home, on the other hand, is everything."

I was a little taken aback. I thought most women wanted a fancy wedding, but it was occurring to me I didn't know Maddie as well as I thought I did, and definitely not as well as I would like to. The desire to move things forward was stronger than ever, but I was working on that.

She seemed lost in her thoughts, and I stared across at her. The sun was hitting her from one of the big arched windows and casting rainbows across her face, which I thought was wholly appropriate. She was like a beautiful kaleidoscope of emotions, and just like a kaleidoscope, you never quite knew what you were going to get with Maddie. Sometimes she was predictable and other times she surprised you with a myriad of unexpected thoughts and reactions. But she was always beautiful, and watching her lost in her own thoughts made my heart pound heavily in my chest.

She looked up at me self-consciously, as if I'd been able to read her thoughts, and I watched a flush of pink rise to her cheeks. I would have given anything to know what she was thinking at that moment, and from her reaction, I had a sneaky suspicion it involved me. "Whatcha thinking, Chippy?" I asked, knowing full well she wouldn't tell me.

She heaved a heavy sigh. "Nothing. I was just thinking we should be getting back. Have you finished filling your stomach?"

"Nope. I need dessert." I said stubbornly and grinned as she rolled her eyes dramatically. "If you keep rolling your eyes like that, they'll fall out eventually. It's a well-known scientific fact," I told her.

"Sounds like a steaming pile of Mackey bullshit to me," she muttered, looking at her watch. "Come on, just grab what you want to eat, and we'll go back to the group. You and I are supposed to be major players in this wedding and I'm just sitting here watching you stuff your face. I don't feel I'm offering enough support, and neither are you."

"Okay," I said with a sigh. "But you'll have to take me to Scarlett's afterward so I can eat her leftovers."

Chapter 14
Maddie

The day we were due to go to Reece's parents' place was beautiful. The windstorm we'd had earlier in the week had blown through, and we were left with a crisp sunny day for our drive to his folks' house. They lived about twenty minutes north of Havenridge in a small town called Amberidge.

Reece had picked me up just after ten, and he spent the journey filling me in on where they lived and the family dynamics.

Well accustomed to proper visiting etiquette, I had made an apple pie to take with us together with a ceramic pot of hyacinth bulbs that were just starting to bud. Reece had looked at them, slightly bewildered, as I packed them carefully in the back of the car. "Is that in case I get hungry on the way?" he said hopefully.

"No, you oaf. Those are gifts for your parents. Haven't you brought anything for them?"

He shook his head and looked at me as if I was from a different planet. "No. Should I have brought something? I don't normally."

I shook my head and sighed. "I'll tell you what. You give your mom the hyacinths and I'll give her the pie."

He narrowed his eyes. "She'll be suspicious. I never take her anything usually."

"She'll be thrilled," I said, insistently.

I learned more about Reece and his family on that journey than I'd ever learned in the whole three years I'd known him. I wasn't sure if it was because his family wasn't that important to him, or whether he just didn't like talking about them. For whatever reason, he'd never felt the need to tell me he had an identical twin who he'd never really gotten along with.

"He was the snitch when we were growing up," he said with disdain. "It was like I was the dark twin; the one who was getting into trouble for something. He never had my back; not once. In fact, I think he took pleasure in getting me into deep shit."

"Oh Reece," I said. "What you're describing happens in ninety-five percent of all families, mine included. This image of the Waltons that some people have is a myth."

He shook his head with a determined look. "Nope. This was not normal. There's definitely something slightly evil about him."

I laughed. "But you told me he's a church pastor. He can't be evil."

"You wait till you meet him. You'll see what I mean. Evil," he muttered.

"Tell me about your parents," I said, turning down the heat on the car seat as I was starting to get a little overheated.

He told me that his dad had been a bank manager until he retired, and his mom was an elementary teacher. They'd lived in the same house all their married life, and his dad had had a stroke a couple of years ago.

"He's not been the same since," he told me. "He was never a really happy guy, but since the stroke, he's been worse. Like really grumpy."

"It's probably hard for him to deal with," I said. I was feeling concerned. I'd been happy when Reece had invited me along for lunch, but what he was describing didn't sound like a game of happy families. I consoled myself with the fact that more often than not, someone in my house was waging a war on someone else, so it probably wasn't much different. Having said that, we always had each other's backs, and if one of us was in a bind, we worked together to fix each other's problems. The relationship he was describing with his brother didn't sound like that at all.

"My parents are a bit formal," he said with a thoughtful look.

"What do you mean by formal?" I asked him.

"Well, with your folks, I feel welcome anytime. It's like there's an open invite. It's not like that with my family. You'd never just pop round." I stayed silent for a while because I had the feeling he wanted to say more. "Don't get me wrong, they're a steady family. Just not the warm and fuzzy variety."

I grabbed his hand. "Hey, we can't all be warm and fuzzy. You're talking to a cactus girl here, according to my brothers. Apparently, you can't hug a cactus. We're too spiky."

He smiled across at me with an untypical warmth. There was no hint of the familiar teasing in his eyes as he said, "You're not a cactus girl. Even if you like to think you are." He took my hand that was resting on his and drew it to his mouth, planting the gentlest of kisses on it. It was an innocent gesture, but it felt like the touch of his lips had turned my blood to molten lava. If he could do this to me with a gentle kiss, I knew he would be capable of reducing me to ashes.

I wanted to snatch my hand away like I normally would, but I couldn't do it, so instead I just stared at him, momentarily trapped by his gravitational pull. Had we not been driving to his parent's house for lunch, it could easily have turned into something else. But we were, and the moment dissipated into the air like smoke from a campfire.

We were silent for the rest of the journey, both of us seemingly consumed by our own thoughts, but I stirred as we passed the sign for Amberidge. I hadn't been to the town for many years, but in some ways, it was similar to Angel Peaks, with the exception that it lacked the tourist industry from the ski hill, which meant that the population stayed relatively constant throughout the year.

As we drove through the main town area, I thought about Reece growing up in a place like this, and I wondered if his upbringing had been a little like mine in a way. We were both small-town people, and we'd stuck with living in a small town rather than gravitating to the big city lights, as some people did.

We left the main shopping strip and drove through what looked like a wealthy residential area. Large established houses sat on big lots, and I imagined these were some of the original houses built for the more affluent townspeople.

Eventually we came to a beautiful white colonial house with painted siding and pale blue shutters bordering the symmetrical windows. There was a pillared portico that sheltered the huge front door, and I could see there were a couple of cars already parked in the sweeping driveway.

Reece pulled his Jeep up behind a large station wagon. "That's my brother's car," he said with a grimace. I felt inexplicably nervous, although I wasn't sure why. Had I been visiting anyone else's family like Scarlett's or even Ryan's, I wouldn't think twice about it, but for some reason, I felt like I needed to make a good impression.

We climbed out of the car, and I handed the bowl with the hyacinths to Reece. "Give these to your mom," I said, carefully reaching in for my apple pie.

As I straightened up, I noticed the mischief in his eyes, and I waited for what was coming. "By the way, Mads. They may be a little surprised to see you."

My heart sank. "What do you mean, they'll be surprised?" I squeaked. "Didn't you tell them I was coming?"

"Oh, I told them I was bringing a friend. They probably think I'm bringing Sam or Ryan. I've never brought a girl home before. It'll be a riot to see everyone's faces!" He was brimming over with hilarity and, had I not been clutching my pie, I would have swiped him around the ear. In fact, it crossed my mind to smoosh the pie in his face, but that would have been a waste of good food.

"Well, holy shit," I muttered. "I'm the surprise."

"Hey, it'll be fun," he assured me. "You're the most beautiful surprise ever."

He immediately disarmed me with his compliment, and my breath hitched a little in surprise, which made him chuckle. "Come on, Chippy," he said. "Let's go meet the troops."

The front door was locked, which struck me as a little odd, as ours was always open when we were expecting guests. Reece carefully balanced the potted hyacinths in one hand while he rang the doorbell with the other. Meanwhile, I pasted on what I considered to be a friendly smile. I think he sensed my discomfort and was enjoying it far too much. He leaned into me while we were waiting and whispered into my hair, "You look gorgeous, by the way."

I jumped away from him as I saw a woman approach the door to open it. She was taller than me, with graying auburn hair pulled back into an elegant bun. I immediately noticed she was dressed a bit more formally than I would expect for a family lunch in a burgundy skirt suit topped with an apron. I looked down at my own clothes, concerned I was underdressed. I was wearing what I considered to be a nice shirt over a pair of dark wash jeans, which I thought would be perfectly acceptable for an informal lunch, but now I wasn't so sure.

As she opened the door, I watched her expression change multiple times before it settled on a warm smile. "Reece, dear. How lovely to see you! And who do we have here?"

Reece bent down and kissed his mom on the cheek before turning to me. "Mom, this is Maddie Moreno. She's one of my dearest friends."

"I'm very pleased to meet you, Mrs. Mackey," I said, sticking out my hand and feeling like an adolescent idiot. "I brought you an apple pie. I hope you don't mind. You don't have to eat it if you don't want to." I realized I was babbling and closed my mouth quickly.

Reece's mom smiled kindly. "Please call me Pam. It was very kind of you to bring this, dear. Very kind indeed. I'm sure it will get eaten."

Reece snorted behind me. "Heck, yeah. If no one else eats it, I certainly will. Maddie's a great cook." I elbowed him and nodded at the hyacinths, because he seemed to have forgotten he was supposed to give them to his mom.

"Oh, yeah. These are for you," he said, trying to hand them over but realizing she was still clutching my pie. "I'll just put them in the kitchen for you, shall I?"

His mom actually looked quite emotional about her son giving her a gift, and I would hazard a guess it didn't happen very often. "They're lovely, dear. Thank you," she said with a beaming smile.

I waited self-consciously in the hallway while Reece and his mom took our gifts into the kitchen. I could hear the sound of voices coming from another room, but I didn't feel confident enough to just breeze in and introduce myself. I felt like a fish out of water, flapping around on the sandy beach and gasping for air.

Suddenly a little girl with long auburn hair came down the staircase and barrelled down the hallway. She stopped in front of me and fixed me with a big grin. "Hi! I'm Emma. What's your name?"

I crouched down to get down to her level and stuck out my hand for her to shake. "My name's Maddie."

"D'you wanna be my friend?" she said with an engaging smile. Kids never failed to impress me with their openness and their ability to accept people.

"I'd like that," I said, but just then Emma was obviously distracted by the person she saw coming out of the kitchen.

"Uncle Weece, Uncle Weece!" she shrieked, and flew toward him, jumping into his arms.

"Ems!" he yelled, spinning her around. "Check my pocket, Ems," he told her. "There might be something hiding in there."

Her eyes sparkled with glee. "Candy?" she said, struggling to feel in his jacket pocket and squealing with delight when she discovered a mega bag of gummy bears.

"Now, Reece. Don't wind her up," his mother said quietly from behind him. "You know how Robbie doesn't like it."

"Yeah, I know," he said, grinning.

Emma appeared beside me and grabbed my hand. "Uncle Weece, this is my new friend, Maddie. I found her here and now she's my friend."

He laughed. "Well, that's funny. Because she's my friend too."

Poor Emma looked totally confused as to how that could be. "I came here with your uncle," I told her gently. She nodded as if she understood, but I wasn't sure that she did.

Grabbing my hand, she led me through a door and pulled me into a large, brightly lit living room. Everyone stopped talking, and I felt everyone's eyes drilling into me like I was some kind of oddity. I really hoped I was wearing my friendliest smile and not some look of wild terror, which may have been more appropriate.

"I found a new friend outside," Emma announced.

Reece stepped forward and put his arm around my shoulder. "Everyone, this is my friend Maddie," he said to the assembled group. "Maddie, this is my dad," he said, indicating an older version of himself, who was seated in a high-backed chair. He looked a little grumpy, but he raised a hand in silent salute.

"This is my sister-in-law, Deidre," he continued, pointing at a pretty woman with long brunette hair who appeared to be about my age. She looked a lot friendlier than his dad and shot me a lovely smile.

"And this is my brother Robbie," he finally said.

Robbie got up out of his seat to approach me, and I was concerned my chin might hit the floor because standing in front of me was Reece. Except it wasn't Reece. It was Reece in a navy-blue suit that would have been more fitting for someone twenty years older. It was Reece with a terrible haircut that looked like it had been carried out by the local seniors' club after one too many margaritas. The whole effect was frankly addling my brain, and I was scrambling to get my words out.

I didn't need to worry because Robbie seemed happy to take over the conversation. Grabbing my outstretched hand, he smiled widely. "Well, well. We weren't expecting this, were we?" I wasn't really sure who he was addressing. Maybe it was the royal "we"? Whatever it was, it was a weird thing to say.

"I'm Robbie. I'm a pastor," he told me, which also seemed weird. Wouldn't it have been more appropriate to say something like, "I'm Reece's brother?"

"Maddie Moreno," I said, finally finding my voice. "I'm pleased to meet you all."

Everyone was shifting around, making room for me on the couch, and Emma was fussing because she wanted to sit with me, but then Reece's dad spoke up in a gruff voice. "No, no. I want her to sit next to me. Get her a chair. Emma, you sit with your Uncle Reece."

Reece raised his eyebrows in surprise but grabbed an easy chair and manhandled it next to where his dad was sitting. I sat down in my assigned seat, feeling a bit like I was at a job interview, well aware that all eyes were on me.

I smiled nervously at Reece's dad, and he smiled back. "I'm John," he said. "And I'm really interested in learning all about you." Yup, I was right. It was a job interview, although I wasn't sure what position I was applying for.

He seemed interested when I told him all about my business. I guess as an ex-bank manager he might have felt we had a similar background, and he told me all about his job. I got the impression that he missed it, although he didn't say as much.

"Do you live close to Reece?" he asked.

"No, I live five minutes outside of town. I have one of the original homesteads with a small acreage. I bought it a couple of years ago."

He pursed his lips and nodded. "Property owner, huh? My sons could learn a thing or two from you. Thirty years old and both of them still renting," he shook his head and waved his hand around the room. "Been in this house for thirty-five years."

I was aware that Robbie was looking across at us with what looked like disapproval. "Yes, but property ownership isn't for everyone, Pa. Some of us think philanthropy is more important than material wealth."

Oh shit, I thought. *I'm in the middle of a family dispute about homeownership.* "It's not for everyone, for sure," I said brightly. "But it was the right move for me, and I've never regretted it."

Reece looked up from where he was playing a board game with Emma on the floor. "Yeah, she owns it outright as well. No mortgage for Maddie."

I felt the color rise in my cheeks. "I was lucky," I mumbled.

"No, Maddie. You worked damn hard. Sure, your family helped you, but you saved the money yourself," he said.

I watched as Emma touched Reece's hand and whispered. "You mustn't say *damn*, Uncle Weece. It's a bad word."

His eyes crinkled up at the corners. "Sorry, sweetie. Good job I've got you to keep me on the straight and narrow."

"Yup," she said, bobbing her little head up and down.

Chapter 15
Reece

Maddie seemed to be a hit with my dad, and little wonder really. She'd done everything he thought people should aspire to do, and she'd achieved it at the tender age of twenty-six. When she wanted something, she went after it. She was always quick to acknowledge the help she'd had along the way from her family, but that didn't obviate the fact she'd worked two jobs from the age of thirteen to achieve her goals.

I knew the story behind her house, but my dad didn't, and I thought he'd get a kick out of it, so I pressed her on it. "Tell Dad how you got your house, Mads. It's a really cool story."

She looked a little embarrassed, but my dad told her he wanted to hear it. I knew she didn't like to brag, but I was pretty proud of her, and I wanted to show her off, particularly to my ass ache brother.

"I wanted that house since I was ten years old," she said with a wistful look in her eyes. She told everyone how she first saw it when she was riding her bike one summer and how she knew immediately she wanted it. She went home and told her dad she wanted to buy a house, but he didn't laugh at her. Instead, he asked her to tell him all about it.

"Then he looked at me and said, *houses cost a lot of money, Maddie. If you want that house, you're going to have to work for it.*"

And she had. As soon as she'd been old enough, she'd got a paper route and helped her dad out doing whatever she could, cleaning houses, yard work, and then later she'd worked bar jobs. Even at college, she'd worked two jobs. She'd kept in touch with the elderly couple who'd owned the house and had even done odd jobs for them as they'd begun to find caring for the place harder and harder.

"I could see the place slipping more and more into disrepair," she told my dad. "But I couldn't do anything. I just had to bide my time and help them as much as I could. I knew how hard it would be for them to leave, but it was just too much for them in the end."

My dad nodded, as if he understood completely. At that moment, it occurred to me that he probably felt the same way. I know since his stroke they'd had to get people in to do the stuff that he would normally do, and I suddenly realized how hard that must have been for him.

"In the end, they had to go into a care home," she said sadly. "But I went to see them and told them I was going to buy their house and restore it. They were really pleased to think I would be living in it."

"So, you bought it from them," my dad said.

She laughed. "It wasn't that easy. Nothing ever is. It went to auction, so I had to go and bid on it. I'd never done that kind of thing before and I was really nervous, but my brothers went with me and glared at anyone who was bidding against me."

My dad thought that was hilarious and he laughed out loud. I couldn't actually remember the last time I'd seen him genuinely laugh like that. It was definitely not since he'd had the stroke. Maybe it was because she didn't really know him, but Maddie was different around him than other people were. We all tiptoed around him not wanting to upset him, but she just treated him like she treated everyone else. Perhaps he was tired of being treated like he was breakable.

"Once I'd bought it, we all went to see it again, and I was really upset when I realized just how bad it was," she said. "I just couldn't see how I could make a home out of it, but my dad could see it. So could my brothers. They knew it would be great." I watched as she reached into her bag and scrabbled around for her phone. "I want to show you some photos of how it was," she told him.

She turned her phone to him, and he frowned. "It's a bit small. I can't really see it properly."

Suddenly I had a brainwave. "She's got an iPhone. We should be able to run the photos through your TV. Let's see if we can get it running."

We all walked through to the family room, including Deidre and Emma, although I noticed Robbie stayed behind in the other room, evidently not interested enough or too jealous to take part. With a joint effort, we got her phone connected to the TV, and she showed her photos. I'd never seen them before, so I sat down with my dad on the couch in the family room, fascinated by the pictures that were flashing up in front of us. It was clear that Maddie had not been a silent partner in this renovation, and it looked like she'd been as fully involved as the rest of her family. There were pictures of Maddie wielding a wrecking hammer and another of her trying to hold up a board of sheetrock on her head as they were reinstalling a ceiling. Then there were candid shots of her goofing around with her brothers, and some with her parents. She chatted animatedly through the entire process, waving her arms around and laughing as she saw photos she hadn't seen for a long time.

We were finally looking through the shots of the finished product, and I grinned as she showed shots of her bedroom where I had spent two days camped out, and her big tub where I'd stretched out in the throes of my fever.

Suddenly, the photos changed, and she gave a little cry of shock. "Oh, I didn't know these were in this folder."

At first, I couldn't make out what I was looking at, but then I realized it was a picture of me in Maddie's paddock with her donkey, Richard. It had been taken quite a while ago, certainly before she had Dave, and also before she and I became close friends. What was really interesting was that I had no idea she'd taken it, and in the shot, I was focused on Richard, crouched down in the paddock, talking to him. Dad was obviously pleased to see a photo of me at work. "That's a great shot," he said with enthusiasm. "Do you have any more?"

Maddie looked distinctly uncomfortable, and I couldn't really work out why. "Yes, I have a couple," she said quietly. "I was trying to get some good shots of Richard."

She continued to click through some similar shots until she came to a close-up shot of just my face. She'd zoomed in so it was just my head and shoulders, and I was smiling. "That's a nice one of Reece," she said in a strained voice.

My dad seemed thrilled. "That's a great shot, Maddie. Can you let me have a copy? We don't have any decent photos of Reece. He always seems to be pulling a face."

She nodded. "Of course. I'll send you a copy. That's all the interesting photos," she said, shutting her phone.

I noticed she wasn't looking at me, and she definitely had a heightened color about her. It suddenly dawned on me what the problem was. She'd taken those photos of me without my knowledge, and she'd kept them on her phone. The last one was particularly candid, and it was almost as if she'd cropped it so only my face was in the shot. These photos were at least two years old, long before I knew she had any kind of interest in me. All at once what Ryan had said to me about the way she looked at me in secret moments started to make sense.

My dad was talking to Deidre and Emma, and no one else was paying any attention to either of us, so I waited for her to raise her head and look at me. When she finally did, I flashed her a teasing smile and mouthed just one word, "busted," and I could tell by her blush she knew exactly what I meant. She'd been caught not just ogling me, but also photographing me in one of those secret moments.

My heart was racing because I'd seen a glimpse into Maddie's feelings for me, and if I could have gone to her and held her, I would have done. But I couldn't do that, so I had to leave her wrestling with whatever it was she was experiencing. Thankfully, my mom chose that moment to save the day and came in to announce that dinner was ready, so Maddie flew into helpful mode, insisting that she help my mom bring stuff in from the kitchen and fussing that she hadn't helped with the meal.

Mom had made an amazing baked ham with a ton of side dishes and the table was heaving with food, but I was dreading what was coming next as my brother spoke up. "Who would like to say grace? Reece, how about you?" he said, staring at me with that innocent look. He knew I didn't share his religious beliefs, but he continued to put me on the spot in this way and I groaned inwardly, looking down at my hands. I was just about to tell him I'd rather not, which always led to some heated discussion, when Maddie grabbed my hand and interrupted.

"Oh, Reece. Do you mind if I say grace? I don't get the chance very often at home because my dad likes to do it."

I looked at her, stunned. It was as if she'd registered my discomfort and jumped in to help me out. "Sure," I said. "You go right ahead."

"I'm going to do it in Italian if that's okay," she told everyone. "That's how we do it in our family."

We all bowed our heads, and she spoke a few words before looking up with a smile.

"That was lovely, dear," my mom said. "What did it mean?"

"Hmm. The literal translation is, *Lord, bless us and these gifts that we're about to receive from your generosity.*"

Robbie sat quietly, looking annoyed. He'd missed an opportunity to embarrass me, and he was clearly stewing about it. I was pretty sure he would try to get me back later, but for now, all was calm. He turned to Maddie. "Are your family church people, Maddie?"

Everyone was helping themselves to food at this point, and she was busy transferring some ham to her plate. "My dad was raised as Catholic, and my mom goes to several different churches. She likes the variety," she said with a smile. "They never pushed religion on us, and I think that's important. Everyone has a right to feel what they want to feel about God's existence, don't you think? Religion isn't a prerequisite for living a good life."

She gave him a hard stare, and it was a look I'd seen before. She was doing her best to be polite, but it was a look that said, *don't mess with me.* It was very obvious to me, even if it wasn't to everyone else.

I think Robbie must have clued in on it because he looked a little taken aback. "Well, as a pastor, it's my job to help people find God, so I'm not sure I agree with you on that one."

Her face tightened into a tight line. "Everyone has a right to believe or not to believe. The more you try to push religion on people, the more they will turn away. Maybe that's why so many churches are empty these days."

"You're quite right," my dad said from beside her. "You can't force what's not there."

I thought for a moment we were going to get one of Robbie's lectures that would last for the rest of the meal, but I watched as Deirdre calmly squeezed his hand, as if she was telling him to keep it under his hat. Deidre was a quiet and fairly passive person, but I got the impression she had more power in the relationship than anyone knew.

He looked up from his meal. "So, what are your feelings on philanthropy then, Maddie? Surely you think that's important. As a pastor, I go out of my way to help out wherever I can. I work in the local soup kitchen, visit the homeless on the streets, visit people in hospital..." He continued to list all the amazing things he did as we all ate uncomfortably.

Maddie ignored him for a moment and turned to my mom. "This meal is delicious Pam. I don't know what you did to the carrots, but they are amazing. You'll have to let me have the recipe." I watched as my mom glowed under her compliment, and then she turned back to Robbie. "True philanthropy is the stuff that goes on under the surface. The things that no one knows about. Take Reece for example."

Robbie snorted incredulously. "Reece? What has Reece ever done for anyone apart from himself."

Maddie was sitting beside me, and I could practically feel her vibrating. It was like there was a hum of energy coming off her, and I hoped to God she wasn't going to explode. "It's okay, Mads," I said quietly.

I watched as she breathed in deeply, as if she was grounding herself, probably thinking calming thoughts. "You obviously don't know your brother very well," she said quietly. "Reece gives more back to our community than anyone will ever know. The thing is, he doesn't do things for people because he needs the recognition. He just sees someone in need and helps out silently because that's who he is."

Everyone was looking at her as if they wanted her to continue, because clearly no one knew what she was talking about. "A couple of years ago, one of our seniors took her cat to see Reece because he was sick. It turned out he had diabetes, and he needed a lot of care and daily injections. Long story short, she couldn't afford it and she thought she would have to have him euthanized. That cat was all she had."

Maddie was breathing deeply, and I knew by the way she was talking she was trying to keep her emotions in check. It always affected her like this when she was talking about animals, and I gave her hand a squeeze under the table to let her know I was there.

"Reece told the woman that his care would be paid for from a special foundation that funded people who couldn't afford to pay for their vet bills, so in the end, she was able to keep him, and he got the meds he needed."

Robbie looked confused. "Well, that's a very nice story, but how does it demonstrate Reece's philanthropy?"

She looked him straight in the eye. "There was no foundation. Just the bank of Reece. He paid for the treatment out of his own pocket, as he has done for countless animals. And that's just the tip of the iceberg."

Everyone was quiet for a while, and then my dad spoke. "That's pretty amazing, son. I'm sure not many vets would do that."

I shrugged my shoulders, embarrassed that she had spoken about me in that way, but also a little overwhelmed that she had my back quite so fiercely. Thankfully, my mom broke the uncomfortable silence. "Okay, who would like some dessert?"

"Me, me!" shouted Emma.

IN OUR HOUSE, IT WAS a tradition that the men cleared up and washed the dishes after dinner, and today was no exception. We all crowded into the kitchen, and my mom came to supervise and hand out the jobs, while Maddie and Deidre sat on the floor with Emma to play Candyland.

Mom was like a field marshal and pretty soon we were all organized with our various jobs, ready to fight the battle of the sink. "I just want to show Reece something," she said, pulling me to one side. "He'll be back in a moment."

I followed her out of the kitchen, not sure what she could possibly have to show me, as she led me upstairs to one of the spare bedrooms. Since Dad had his stroke, they'd taken to sleeping in a downstairs room, which was easier for him, but it meant the upstairs was largely unused. Robbie and his family were obviously staying for the weekend, but I wondered how long my parents would keep this rambling family home. I knew for sure it would be a tremendous loss to them when they had to move to something smaller, but I guess it was inevitable.

She led me into one of the guest rooms, which looked as pristine as I always remembered it. "Sit down," she told me, pointing to the bed as she went off to one of the dressers. I sat on the edge of the bed, wondering what the heck was going on, and watched her return with a small black box, which she placed in my hand. "I want you to have this," she said, her voice full of emotion.

I opened the tiny box and inside was a beautiful sapphire and diamond ring that shone in the light. I looked at it bewildered for a moment because I wasn't sure why she was giving it to me.

"That was your grandmother's engagement ring," she said. "When she died, she left it to me and told me to give it to you when the time was right."

"Me?" I said, puzzled at all this. "Why me?"

My mom smiled affectionately. "Well, I think she thought you might need it one day."

I continued to stare at the ring and looked up at my mom and shook my head, still not really getting it.

Mom sighed with a smile. "You know, Robbie always had his ducks in a row, even as a young child. Not so much you. Your ducks were always all over the place, running in traffic and causing mayhem."

I winced. "I know. I must have been such a pain for you. Always getting into trouble. Always causing problems."

She laughed. "Life was certainly interesting." She paused for a moment and then she said, "You have a lovely young woman downstairs who you say is a friend. Are you maybe hoping she'll be more than a friend?"

I shrugged my shoulders and nodded. "I guess."

"Well, don't guess for too long, Reece. She clearly thinks the world of you. One day, you might need that ring. Keep it safe." She took my hand and curled my fingers around the box. "Now, come and finish your job or your brother will be complaining."

Chapter 16
Maddie

A week after we'd visited Reece's parents, I arranged to meet him at the office of The Angel Peaks Gazette so we could put a few things straight with the editor, Harry Connors. There was no way we were going to have a repeat performance of last year's shit show, when Harry turned up with an out-of-town news crew, complete with Kate's rockstar ex-boyfriend Rory Laverne, and caused all kinds of chaos.

I knew how much she hated the recognition that came with her modeling career, and that she had been hoping for an anonymous wedding without the added stress of press reporters and photographers. As much as she denied it, there were still people interested in her, particularly after her connection with Rory. Reece and I had been charged with the task of persuading Harry that he would not be turning up at the church with a mob of baying paparazzi. We were in effect the heavy mob.

I shivered in the icy wind as I waited for him to appear, wondering if I should just go in ahead of him. Just as I was about to turn and walk into the office alone, I spied him coming down the street, all legs and sex appeal, and I shivered a little more, although this time it wasn't from the cold.

"Hey, Mads," he said with that sexy smile, and he bent to kiss me gently on the cheek.

Well, at least we've progressed from hair ruffling, I thought as he followed me into the building. Whenever I had cause to go into The Gazette's offices, I always pondered at how empty it seemed. Once upon a time, the office would have been a hive of activity, but with the advent of technology and online news services, small-town papers like this were a dying breed. Really, there was just Harry and his sidekick Lucy, who I watched now as she banged away aggressively at her laptop.

She looked up from under her dark bangs and sighed. "You two here to see Harry?" she said. I nodded, and she extended her hand, pointing to the back of the office. "Well, you know where he is. Just go back," she said, before returning to her apparently vexing work.

I looked around the empty building that somehow reminded me of the newspaper office from the Superman comic strip, The Daily Planet, except not as big and definitely not as exciting. I almost expected Lucy to morph into Lois Lane and dash off after an important story, but I knew that, in reality, nothing could be further from the truth. No, The Gazette dealt with lost dogs and local events like the annual Angel Fair, and sadly, we were in no danger of Clark Kent crashing through the wall as his alter ego.

Harry's office was sequestered behind a closed glass door with peeling letters that announced his job title. I knew he had come to Angel Peaks from one of the bigger publications in Denver, and I never got the impression he was very happy about his move here. I'm not sure whether he upset someone in Denver or if they just downsized, but this was definitely a demotion.

Reece knocked on his door with vigor, and Harry shouted us into his inner sanctum, which was in fact a very sad and jaded-looking workspace. "Well, well," he said with a smarmy smile. "They've sent the cavalry. Am I in trouble again?"

Reece flopped down in one of Harry's aged leather chairs without being invited. "We are here to make sure you don't get into trouble, Harry," he said.

I took a seat next to Reece and pulled some paperwork out of my leather messenger bag, slapping it on the desk in front of me.

Harry looked at it in mock surprise. "My, my, Ms. Moreno. That looks ominous. Is it my marching orders?"

I ignored his attempt at humor and adopted my frosty business persona. "As you have probably heard, Kate and Sam are going to be married on the first Saturday in April."

Harry nodded with that same sickly smile. "Yes, I had heard that rumor. Well, isn't that lovely? I like to think I had a hand in bringing that situation to fruition."

As much as I'd resolved to keep my cool, that comment made me see red, and I shot up out of my chair. "You!" I pointed my finger with barely contained fury. "You almost killed Sam. You're damned lucky he didn't sue you after what happened."

Reece gently tugged on my hand to encourage me to sit back down. "Easy, Mads," he whispered. "Remember what we discussed?" I reluctantly plopped back down in my seat and gave Harry my best daggers look.

He did at least have the good grace to look a little sheepish. "Look. I deeply regret what happened to Mr. Garrett, but that was really none of my doing. I didn't force Ms. McKenzie to go into that derelict building, and I certainly didn't persuade Mr. Garrett to follow her. I was just following a lucrative lead."

Now it was Reece's turn to get mad. "Your fucking mob of vultures chased her down, and she was terrified." Reece was quieter than me with his fury, but a lot more menacing.

This time, Harry looked distinctly uncomfortable. "Yes, well, that's all behind us now, and there's a happy ending, so no harm done, eh?"

"That is the purpose of this contract," I said, waving the paperwork at him. "If there's not a happy ending for our friends, you will be sued, and I mean that."

"Whatever do you mean?" he said, a light sweat appearing on his brow.

Reece continued for me. "We understand that there may be a certain media interest in Kate's wedding to Sam, but they don't want it to turn into a circus. This is their day, and they want it to be low-key and relaxed. They are prepared to give you a couple of shots outside the church, but that is it. You will not enter the church during the ceremony, and you will not try to attend the reception. You will take your shots and you will go."

"So, I won't hold my breath waiting for my invitation," he said coldly.

I ignored his little barb and carried on regardless. "This contract states which publications Sam and Kate will agree to you selling the photos to. If you make a financial gain from selling any of the photos, twenty-five percent will be donated to a charity of their choice. You will not sell their photos to any of the gossip mags or dirt sheets and Rory Laverne will not be contacted about this. It's all laid out in the contract. I suggest you read it and sign it."

"And if I choose not to?" he said with a surly expression.

"If you choose not to, our wonderful local police department will be on hand to remove you on the day of the wedding. You didn't make any friends with the last stunt you pulled. The people of Angel Peaks are very protective of their own," I told him.

"Look, Harry," Reece chipped in. "We're trying to do you a favor here. This way you get to make a bit of money and Sam and Kate aren't harassed on the most important day of their lives. It's a win all round, isn't it?"

Harry steepled his fingers in front of his face with a thoughtful expression. "Well, leave it with me and I'll certainly give it some thought. Might just run it past my legal team just to make sure it's legit."

I stood up from my chair and grabbed my bag from the floor. "It's legit, believe me. I'll be back later in the week to collect the signed copy."

Considering the meeting over, I stalked out of the office and headed for the door, closely pursued by Reece. "Hey, hold on, Maddie. Do you want to grab some lunch?"

"Yeah, that would be great," I said. "Being pissed off gives me an appetite."

We decided to go back to the small café inside The Celestial because it was a little more private and Reece was hoping for a repeat order of the enormous beef sub he'd eaten last time. We grabbed the same table we'd had on our last visit, and I settled myself down into the cozy chair, allowing myself to calm down a little.

I hadn't walked into Harry's office intending to get riled up, but something about that man put my hackles up. The server brought over our food, and I devoured my grilled cheese.

"You okay, Chippy?" Reece asked, as he wrestled his sub together so he could take a bite.

"I'm getting there," I said. "I'll feel a lot better when I've eaten."

"It's a special weekend this week," he said with a wink.

I knew it was Valentine's Day on Saturday, but I'd been consciously avoiding even thinking about it. I wasn't really sure where I stood with Reece, and all our friends had plans. Sam and Kate were heading off to Havenridge to stay in the hotel where they got stranded the night the road was closed. Scarlett had persuaded Ryan to accompany her to a speed dating night in the senior center, which I already knew was going to be a complete disaster. There was no way Ryan would find anyone he liked on a speed dating night. It would take him a lot longer than that. And as for Scarlett; well, I was pretty sure she would talk so fast to try to get so much in that no one would understand her. My bet was they would end up going home together and Ryan would warm up a tray of something delicious to console themselves about the fact that they both had the worst dating track record in history.

I decided to play it cool. "What's special about it?" I said as innocently as I could muster.

He laughed. "You know damn well it's Valentine's. You can hardly avoid it with all the hearts decorating the stores, and Scarlett's been mega excited for weeks because she makes a killing on Valentine's with all her heart-shaped cookies and treats."

I shrugged my shoulder and continued to munch away at my sandwich, not really knowing what to say.

"So, I've arranged a little surprise," he said, looking quite excited.

I perked up, because it was suddenly sounding promising. "You have? Is it more dog sledding?"

He shook his head. "Nope. It's better than dog sledding. Can you get away overnight? Do you have someone to look after your animals?"

"Overnight?" I squeaked, realizing my voice had shot up two octaves.

I noticed his eyes were twinkling with amusement. Or maybe it was something else. "Yes, overnight. I'll pick you up on Saturday afternoon and bring you back on Sunday afternoon. Will that work?"

"Are we staying in a hotel? What should I pack? Is it formal?" Questions were spilling out of my mouth in a barrage of rapid-fire.

"Hey, slow down," he laughed. "No, we aren't staying in a hotel. It will be much cozier than a hotel. It's definitely not formal and you can pack whatever you feel comfortable in."

"Oh God, we're not camping, are we?" I said, suddenly concerned. "Reece, it's the middle of February. We'll freeze."

"No, we are not camping. I promise you walls and a roof and even an inside bathroom. Does that make you feel better? But don't try to get any more information out of me because my lips are sealed." He pretended to zip up his lips and throw away the key.

"Okay. I'll get Ben to look after the animals. That'll work," I said, more to myself than him. "Do you want me to bring anything? Food or anything like that?"

He shook his head. "Nope. I'm going to arrange everything," he said with confidence.

"Okay," I said quietly. "Okay."

"Then you'll come?" he said expectantly, as if my answer was in doubt.

"Yes," I said. "Definitely!"

Chapter 17

Reece

I felt antsy for the rest of the week. Usually, I loved my work and the week goes fast, but this week it felt like I was walking through treacle, because I knew this was the weekend I was planning to seal the deal with Maddie. We were going to move out of the friends' zone and into something much more interesting, and I was determined for it to go perfectly.

I'd booked an amazing little log cabin on Airbnb that I knew she would love. It was secluded, so she wouldn't have to worry about anyone seeing us or recognizing us and, above all else, it was romantic. For Valentine's weekend, Maddie deserved nothing less.

To be honest, I knew very little about romance. I was a pragmatic kind of person and romance didn't really figure on my scorecard, but I was determined to change all of that for my little chipmunk. She was worth it.

I pulled into her yard at three on Saturday afternoon, convinced I had everything planned to a tee and confident that nothing was going to go wrong. I pulled right up to her front door rather than parking up by the paddock, since I didn't want to run the gauntlet with Dave blowing his trumpet and the goats fainting all over the place.

She came out of her door before I could knock, looking casually beautiful with her soft blonde curls around her shoulders. She was clutching a soft-sided duffle bag and looking a little anxious as I approached her. I can't say I blamed her because I felt pretty tense myself.

"Hey, Mads. Let me take your bag," I said, grabbing it out of her hands and stowing it in the back of my Jeep. I walked around to the passenger side with her, determined to be a gentleman by holding the door open for her, but we both grabbed for the handle at the same time and our hands collided. She giggled nervously, and I wrapped my hand around hers as she gripped the handle. "Let's break the ice with a kiss," I whispered into her hair.

She turned and stroked my face with her gloved hand, and I bent my head to take her mouth in mine. Neither of us was playing anymore, and it was not an exploratory kind of kiss. The fooling around had stopped, and it felt like we both knew we'd moved beyond that. I felt consumed by the sweetness of her lips and the warmth of her body pressed up against mine, and I felt validated in my decision to arrange this weekend away. She was ready to open up to me; it had taken a long time, but she was ready, and the very thought was making my head spin.

I dropped my forehead to hers, breathing heavily. "Oh, Maddie. What you do to me," I murmured.

"Are we ready?" she said, softly, her question conveying a lot more than just practicalities.

"Yeah, we're ready," I said, opening the door for her to climb in.

The cabin was located in a tiny mountain community midway between Angel Peaks and Havenridge. It was mostly composed of small holiday homes owned by people who liked to get out into the backcountry for snowshoeing and trail walking.

It was a pretty drive and Maddie was quiet on the way, although she held onto my hand, which was unheard of and a very welcome display of affection. I looked across at her from time to time and drank in her pink cheeks and her pretty curls, a little in awe that she would soon be mine.

Out of the corner of my eye, I could tell she was taking stolen glances at me as well, and I hoped she was feeling the same sense of building anticipation that I was because for me it was the best feeling ever, and I wanted her to feel that too.

After we left the road and started to climb, she became more animated. I think she'd worked out where we were going, and she looked at each little cabin we passed and made a comment about how cute it was or what she liked about it.

Finally, we reached our destination. The cabin I'd rented was at the end of an unmade road, quite secluded and a long way from the other properties.

She turned to me with excited eyes. "Are we here?"

"Yup, this is it. *Stargazers Cabin*," I told her. The name was appropriate for what I had in mind later, but I wasn't about to tell her that.

She jumped out and took in the adorable little single-story log cabin and I could tell she liked it straight away. "Oh, Reece. It's beautiful," she whispered, almost in awe of the place. The heavens had smiled on me because the weather was perfect, and the place was sparkling in the sunlight like a little jewel.

She turned to me with a huge smile. "I love it!"

I inwardly sighed in relief. Although I had a sneaky suspicion she would like it, I'd never arranged this kind of thing before, and it had been pretty stressful pulling it all together. It was totally worth it to see the look of excitement on her face, and I made a mental note to do this kind of thing often.

We approached the big wooden front door, and I checked on my phone for the key code that would let us in. The warmth of the place hit us as soon as we walked in, and I realized it not only had heated floors but also a south-westerly aspect, which meant the afternoon sun had been streaming through the enormous windows all afternoon.

It was a small and cozy layout with an open-plan living space and two bedrooms off to the side. Despite its size, the cabin was fitted out beautifully, and I think both Ryan and Scarlett would have approved of the kitchen. The warmth of the logs and the stone fireplace gave it a real woodsy vibe, but the most stunning feature was the view out of the floor-to-ceiling windows in the great room. Because we were at quite an elevation, we looked out over the valley where all the trees were dressed in a layer of fresh snow. It was breathtaking and not lost on Maddie, who was staring out of the windows, seemingly in her own little world.

I came up behind her and wrapped my arms around her, resting my chin on her head, confident that she would be okay with it. "Happy Valentine's, Mads," I said. "Do you like it?"

As she turned, I swear there was a glimmer of tears in her eyes. "Like it? It's the most beautiful surprise ever. No one's ever done anything like this for me before. Ever."

Of course they hadn't, because from what I could tell, most of Maddie's boyfriends had been total jerks who hadn't deserved her. I had to be careful with my thoughts because I'd been a jerk in the past as well, but I was determined to put my ass-like behavior behind me. She clung to me for a while with her head buried in her chest, as if she needed a moment to get her head together. I was happy to give her that moment because she was in my arms and that was where I wanted her to be.

She broke away with a sigh, and I took the opportunity to get things moving along. "Okay, I need to get some stuff from the Jeep, and then we could have a quick snowshoe walk before we lose the light. What do you think?"

She nodded with a smile. "Sounds great. But I can help you get the stuff from the car. I'm pretty strong, you know," she said, flexing her muscles for me.

"Oh, I have no doubt about that," I said, hoping she was going to demonstrate some of that for me later.

I heard her give a little cry of surprise. "Oh, look! The owners left us some wine and chocolates."

I walked over to the kitchen island, and sure enough, there was a nice bottle of red wine and a heart-shaped box of chocolates together with a note that they hoped we had a good weekend. I had other treats in the car as well, so we certainly wouldn't be short of food or alcohol.

We put our boots back on and trooped out to the Jeep to grab our things. I grabbed the large cooler that contained our dinner and our breakfast, along with a few other things, and Maddie grabbed both overnight bags. "Just drop them in one of the rooms right now," I told her.

We hadn't discussed sleeping arrangements, but I'd deliberately booked a place with two bedrooms because there was no way I wanted her to feel pressured into anything. I was still running with my original game plan of letting her take the lead, and the bedroom layout gave her an out if she felt she needed one. I'd gotten this far with her; I didn't want to blow it at this stage. I knew I was in this for the long stretch, not just one night of fun.

I didn't want Maddie to have to cook, so I'd chatted up the chef at Cherubs, the restaurant in town, and he'd prepared a meal for me and put it into foil trays, complete with instructions on oven temperatures and cooking time, because he knew I was a complete neanderthal in the kitchen. As I unpacked everything and put it into the fridge, Maddie looked duly impressed.

"Wow! You've really pulled out all the stops," she said with a grin.

"Yup. Every single one of them," I said. "Okay. You ready for snowshoeing?"

We bundled into our winter clothes and got into our snowshoes. I'd brought ski poles as well because I didn't know what the terrain was like or how deep the snow would be. The owners had left a really useful map of a loop we could take, so we were all set.

We headed out into the snowy landscape and Maddie had obviously found her tongue because she talked incessantly, her words coming out in an excited rush. You didn't see Maddie like this very often. She was great at sarcasm and quick retorts, but this seemed like a much more natural side of her; almost childlike. She was really quite enchanting, and I allowed her to chatter on, not wanting to disturb her flow.

She was striding out in front of me, clearly very skilled at walking in snowshoes, when she paused and put her fingers to her lips, although I hadn't actually been talking. I came up beside her to see what had caused her to stop and there, in front of us about five yards away on the trail, was a beautiful buck mule deer with a full set of velvet-covered antlers.

Maddie stood mesmerized for a few seconds, and then she silently shed her gloves and fumbled around in her pocket for her phone to take a photo. "He's so beautiful," she murmured, almost inaudibly. She wrestled her phone free from her pocket and snapped away. The flash that came on automatically startled the deer for a moment, but he didn't run. He stared directly at us, probably contemplating what to do. I hoped he wasn't planning on using those pretty impressive antlers, and I was thinking about how I would get Maddie behind my back if he decided to attack.

Thankfully, he seemed to realize we weren't a threat and after a few minutes, he stalked off into the woods and Maddie sighed. "Aww. That was magical. Wasn't it?"

She turned to me, her eyes lit with a sense of wonderment. I'd seen it in her eyes before when she was interacting with her own animals, but now in this outdoor environment where everything seemed to sparkle in the sunshine, her natural beauty took my breath away.

"I'll tell you what's magical," I said, my voice sounding huskier than usual. "You're fucking magical." I dropped my ski poles to the ground and held her face in my hands, sinking in for a kiss but wanting so much more. *Not yet*, I told myself. *Not yet*.

"Hmm," she sighed, in what I hoped was appreciation. "You're pretty magical yourself, Dr. Mackey."

I laughed. "If you're going to compliment me, I feel I should record you to playback at a later date, when you think I'm not so magical."

She batted me playfully on the arm and the moment was lost, but not for long, I thought to myself, not for long.

Chapter 18
Maddie

I was finding it hard to wrap my head around the effort Reece had put into this weekend. I'd never really thought of him as a romantic kind of person. He was far too practical for that, but this was a different side of Reece, one I'd not really seen before. I'd seen glimpses of it for sure, but he was always careful enough to conceal them under a veil of sarcasm and wit. It was only in the last few weeks he'd dropped his cover a little and let me catch glimpses of something that painted a different picture.

We got back from our walk ravenous, and Reece wanted to prepare dinner for me. He showed me what he'd brought from Cherubs, and it looked mouth-wateringly yummy.

"I'm not going to let you do everything while I sit on my ass and drink wine," I told him.

He pulled a face. "Why not? Look at everything you did for me last week."

"That was different; you were sick. Okay, let's get dinner sorted out before one of us eats the other one," I said, and by the sounds that were coming from Reece's stomach, that wasn't too far-fetched.

"All that fresh air made me hungry," he said with a laugh, pulling the foil containers from the fridge.

Despite his protests, I muscled my way into the kitchen, and we read the instructions on the containers. "This stuff is pre-cooked, so we need to make sure we reheat it properly," I told him. "Food poisoning is not romantic."

He winced. "Tell me about it. I've had food poisoning before."

"Oh no, bad seafood?" I asked while trying to figure out the stove.

He shook his head. "Nah. Just something unrecognizable out of my freezer."

I hit him with a dishcloth. "Reece! You are going to kill yourself one day with that stuff. They could use it for germ warfare. You need to let me go through it and replace it with good stuff."

"Bossy ass," he whispered into my hair, causing a shiver to go up my spine.

"Not bossy," I said, trying to ignore the sensations resonating in my core. "I just have good organizational skills." I paused for a minute. "Does it bother you?"

He looked confused. "Does what bother me? The contents of my freezer?"

"No. My bossiness. My brothers always told me I was bossy." I turned the dials on the stove to the temperature I needed and was pleased when the red light came on to show me it was heating up.

He was behind me while I was fiddling with the food, and he wrapped his arms around me in a cocoon of warmth. "Nothing about you bothers me, Maddie," he murmured. "Except seeing you naked, of course, but that bothers me in a whole different kind of way."

"Yeah. You got the whole peep show that day, didn't you?" I said, sliding the trays into the oven, glad that I could blame my pink cheeks on the heat that was blasting out. "Okay, we should give that at least thirty minutes," I said, turning around to face him.

His face was not teasing, but there was a definite fire in his eyes. Perhaps he was recalling the shower room incident when he hadn't been able to do anything about the way he felt. Now he could; and so could I.

"Hmm. Thirty minutes. What could we do with thirty minutes I wonder?" he said with a husky tone to his voice.

"Did you bring any board games?" I asked.

He smiled. "Nope. No board games."

I decided to go the flirtatious route because it was fun and that was who we really were. We both knew what was going to happen that night. "Reece. I know what you're thinking, and thirty minutes won't even get us started. There's no point in starting something we won't finish for hours, is there?"

He used his arms to cage me to the countertop. "Oh, Maddie. Are you teasing?"

I stroked my finger around his face and thought about how god-damn beautiful he was. "Not teasing. Promising."

He put his head back and groaned. "And what am I supposed to do with this erection in the meantime?"

"You'll be eating soon, and then you'll forget all about it for a while. Okay, pour me a glass of wine, and maybe we can sit by the fire while we're waiting for dinner to be ready."

He grabbed the bottle of wine, keeping one arm at my side, seemingly reluctant to give up completely. I could feel his hardness pressed up against me, and it was all I could do not to grab him because he felt amazing. But I wanted our first time to be perfect. This was Reece, and Reece mattered to me like no one else had in the past. I didn't want a quick fumble under the sheets. I wanted everything.

We went to sit on the couch in front of the impressive stone fireplace with our wine, and Reece put on some sultry jazz music that he obviously had ready. He sat at the end of the couch, and I cuddled up into him, pulling my feet up. "Hmm. This is lovely," I said. "You are definitely acing it in the romance stakes."

"Good," he said with a smile. "That was the plan."

I poked him in the ribs. "So, there was a plan, was there?"

He tried to hold in a giggle. "Yup. I called it Operation Chipmunk."

I laughed as well because Operation Chipmunk was an unlikely name for a night of seduction. "Operation Chipmunk. How romantic," I said, through my giggles.

"Hey, don't knock it. I planned it out like a military operation."

I rubbed his arm. "Hmm. So, what was your next move in this military operation then?"

"It's classified," he said, with his finger to his lips. "I could tell you, but then I'd have to ravish you."

"Oh, I don't think anyone has ever ravished me before. It sounds interesting. I might be down for a spot of ravishing." I was enjoying the way this conversation was going. It was like our usual banter, only much more interesting because it was a lot flirtier. We sat in silence for a good while, each of us apparently consumed by our own thoughts before the oven pinged, telling us that dinner was ready. "Oh, saved by the bell," I said. "I guess the ravishing will have to wait a little longer."

"Lucky for you," he said, as I pulled him up out of the couch.

Dinner smelled divine, and when I opened the stove, I was happy to see the sauces were bubbling, which was a good sign it was heated through thoroughly. I plated our food onto warm plates while Reece busied himself laying the table and lighting some candles he'd brought with him. Finally, he dimmed the lights, and we sat down with our meal.

He topped up our wine glasses before lifting his for a toast. "Happy Valentine's Maddie. The first of many." His words touched me, and we clinked our glasses together before attacking our food, which looked amazing. I told him it was better than anything I could have made, but he dismissed that by telling me my beef stew was even better than his mom's, which I thought was quite the compliment. I knew from experience that guys had a thing about their mom's cooking.

Our conversation was unstrained and easy, with lots of joking and laughter. Two old friends enjoying dinner together before moving on to dessert, and I wasn't thinking about the chocolate. I resolved not to drink too much wine, so I sipped away at my one glass, making it last and refusing top-ups.

Once dinner was over and we'd cleared up. Reece put on his jacket and boots. "Are you leaving?" I said with a grin.

"No, I just have to do something outside, and then we're both going out. I have a surprise."

I placed my hand on my heart as I watched him disappear out the front door. He seemed so excited by all the things he'd planned, and he'd clearly put a lot of thought into it. And it had all been for me; everything he'd thought about had been with me in mind, and I couldn't remember anyone ever going through this much trouble to make me happy. A lump caught in my throat, and I cursed myself inwardly. This was not the time to be getting all emotional.

Pretty soon he appeared back through the door, banging snow from his boots. "Okay, I just have to grab a few things and then we'll be all set."

I watched as he collected some items from the cooler he'd brought in earlier. I was intrigued by the little foil packages. "What are those?" I asked.

He grinned like a ten-year-old kid. "I've lit a fire and we're going to make s'mores. Come on. Let's turn out as many lights as we can. You'll see why in a minute."

I pulled on my coat and boots and we both wandered outside carrying the supplies. I gasped when I saw the little fire he'd made next to a bench that held a couple of blankets.

"Okay, sit down and look up," he instructed. "This is why it's called Stargazers Cabin."

I looked up into the sky and gasped in amazement. The sky was filled with a blanket of beautiful stars. I could see now why he wanted to turn out as many lights as he could. "That's spectacular," I whispered.

"I know," he whispered. "And I knew you'd appreciate it. You love this kind of thing, don't you?"

I nodded and reached for him. "You brought the stars for me, Reece. I can't believe it." I held onto him for a long time because I wanted him to see just how much I appreciated everything he'd done.

Finally, he pulled away. "Okay, let's not cremate the S'mores. Charcoal S'mores aren't good."

He pulled them out with a gloved hand and carefully unwrapped them, letting them cool a little before we ate them. "Oh, they're so good," I moaned, as the chocolate and marshmallow melted in my mouth.

"I know, right?" he said, clearly thrilled that his surprise had panned out, and he hadn't burned anything. "And the best thing is that I still have chocolate sauce leftover." He shot me an exaggerated wink, and I tried my best to look shocked.

"I can't think what you'll need that for," I said, trying not to smile. I looked across at the beautiful man beside me and my heart did a flip. He had a tiny streak of chocolate that had dripped from his lips onto his chin, and I ran my tongue across my own lips, thinking about all the things I could do with that solitary drip of chocolate. Whenever I was this close to Reece, it felt like someone had lit a fire inside me. The single glass of wine I'd had was enough to fuel that desire, and I boldly leaned forward and, using the very tip of my tongue, licked the chocolate off, starting at his chin and working up to his lips.

When I reached his lips, I whispered into them, close enough to cause vibrations. "You missed a bit."

With a small groan, he pulled me closer to him and devoured my lips with his own. With his tongue diving into my mouth, he tasted sweet and provocative, and I felt I couldn't get close enough to him.

Moving over, I straddled his lap, so I was facing him, and he growled in approval.

Pulling away, he looked into my eyes, and I could see a fire in him I'd never seen before. This was a man teetering on the edge of control, and it was as hot as hell. When he spoke, his voice was husky and full of longing. "I think I've done enough star gazing for the night. How about you?"

I nodded without speaking because I knew my voice would betray the depth of my feelings, and I wasn't ready to show just how deeply I'd fallen for him. I slid from his lap, and he dealt with the fire before we headed into the cabin wrapped in each other's arms.

Once we'd shed our outdoor clothes, he drew me over to the fireplace and he lay down on the couch, pulling me towards him. I snuggled into his chest, and he whispered into my hair. "It feels like all my dreams are coming true tonight."

"Mine too," I told him. I suddenly remembered I'd brought him a gift and now seemed like a good time to let him have it. I looked up at him. "Would you give me a moment? I got you a Valentine's gift, and I want to get it for you."

"Now?" he said with amusement. "You want to get it now?"

I nodded. "Oh yes. You'll understand why when you see it."

Chapter 19
Maddie

He released me reluctantly, and I headed into the bedroom where I'd dropped my duffle. After quickly brushing my teeth and fussing with my hair, I dove into my bag and pulled out what I was looking for. It was the black silk baby doll and thong that Scarlett and Kate had bought me the day we went to Havenridge. At the time, I couldn't see myself ever wearing it. Thongs weren't generally my thing, and it wasn't the kind of thing I'd wear to clean out the animals, but tonight was the perfect night for it.

With shaking hands, I stripped off my jeans and sweater and pulled on the sexy lingerie. I'd tried it on at home already, but now it wasn't just me that was going to see it. I examined myself critically in the full-length mirror on the wall and suddenly my confidence fell away. The camisole top was quite sheer, and my breasts were clearly visible through the fabric. When I turned around, my ass was also on show. I stood there wishing my legs were longer and everything else was a little less round. I wasn't sure I was the right shape for this kind of underwear, and I told myself it would have looked better on someone like Kate, who was tall and slender, or even Scarlett, with her petite, doll-like frame.

I stood there for some time, turning around and biting my lip with worry, when there was a gentle knock on the door. "Maddie are you okay?" he asked.

"Yeah. You can come in if you like, I suppose," I said. My bravado had departed like a thief in the night, and I was left feeling insecure and more than a little embarrassed.

He walked through the door and clapped his hand over his mouth. "Is this my gift?" he said, almost inaudibly.

"Well, yeah. But now I have it on, I think I look... stupid."

He strode over and held onto both my hands, looking me up and down. I felt like a bug under the microscope as he slowly drank me in. "Turn around for me," he said huskily. I reluctantly did what he asked. "Holy Christ," he murmured.

"I know," I said, sadly. "It's just not me, is it?"

"I think I need to sit down for a second," he said, pulling me toward the edge of the bed. I watched him anxiously as he took a couple of deep breaths and then he spoke. "Okay, that's better. You know you really should give a man some warning if you're going to wear something like that because I nearly punched a hole in the front of my damn jeans."

I giggled and relaxed a little. "So, you think it's okay?" I asked. "I'm just not sure I have the right shape for this kind of thing."

"Stand up, Mads," he said, quietly. "Right here in front of me." I did as he asked and stood in front of him as he sat on the bed, looking down at my feet. "I'm puzzled, Maddie, and this isn't the first time. Tell me what you see when you look in the mirror."

"My legs are too short, my boobs are too big, and my ass would fill the back of your Jeep," I said, a little sullenly.

"That's really weird," he replied. "Because I see this beautiful, sexy woman who affects me so deeply, I find it hard to stand. No one's ever done that to me before, Mads. Ever."

I looked up at him and my eyes met his. "Really? I never thought you were interested."

He pulled me around and sat me on his lap, lifting my chin. "I have always been interested. But you weren't ready. Are you ready now?"

"I've always wanted you, Reece. We just got into this strange friends thing, and I didn't think you saw me that way. I thought I was just a drinking buddy."

He snorted. "If I wanted a drinking buddy, I'd pick Sam or Ryan or even one of your brothers. It was the only way you'd let me near you. Maybe it was the only way you felt safe, all those insults and fooling around."

I'd wasted so much time with Reece, but I was determined I would not waste any more time. "I'm ready now," I told him. "I'm so ready."

He smiled that slow, sexy smile that I loved so much. I knew full well he had probably reached the edge of his restraint because, sitting on his lap, I could feel the hardness of his erection on my bare ass. He kissed me gently before he said. "By the way, Mads. Best fucking gift ever! My mom used to buy me underwear as a gift and I used to complain, but it was never like this, and it didn't have you in it."

"You have too many clothes on," I told him, and I started to unbutton his shirt. He stood up to help me get it out of his jeans and then I hastily stripped off his t-shirt. "Oh," I gasped, as the black fabric peeled away to reveal a slender and muscular abdomen. "Oh my God," I murmured, and ran my fingers over the outline of his abs.

"Please tell me that's a good, *oh my God*," he said with a smile.

"How have I kept my hands off you all these years?" I muttered, unbuttoning his jeans and carefully pulling down the zipper over his erection.

"I don't know," he said. "But it feels like it might have been some particularly nefarious form of torture."

"Not just for you. For me too. The number of times I've just wanted to grab you and wrestle you to the ground," I told him, kneeling and pulling down his jeans and coming face to face with a very turned-on Reece in a pair of straining black boxer briefs. "Well, hello. Look who I've found. And he looks pleased to see me."

"Come up here," he said with a husky growl. "I need to touch you."

I rose to my feet and was a little taken aback by the latent desire etched on his face. If I was ever in any doubt that Reece wanted me, the look on his face now made it all very clear. "But I haven't finished undressing you," I protested with a pout. "I was just getting to the best bit."

"Don't care. It's my turn," he said gruffly. "Okay, about this gift of mine. Is it actually the underwear, or is it what's contained in the underwear?"

I put my arms around his neck and whispered seductively in his ear. "I don't think it would fit you Reece, so I guess it's all of it. It's all yours; always has been."

That seemed to affect him because he wrapped his arms around me in a tight embrace and clung to me as if he needed a minute. I stroked his hair and gently nibbled the side of his neck, making him moan in pleasure.

"Let's take it off, Mads," he said. "You look beautiful in it, and we can play with it later, but I'm desperate to see you naked again. You can't even begin to imagine how many times I've relived finding you in that shower room." He pulled at the bottom of the camisole, and I put my arms up over my head so he could peel it off in one motion.

"Oh, God. They're just as beautiful as I remember," he said, staring at my breasts. "Can I touch? Please." The last word came out as a plea.

"Of course," I said softly. "You have my permission to touch everything. I already told you, Reece. It's all yours."

"Thank you," he mouthed, as if I were giving him an amazing gift. I don't know what I expected from Reece as a lover, but I was only realizing now how respectful he was. I wondered if it was because we were already friends and already had that close connection. It didn't feel weird between us at all, which I had always been afraid of. It felt more like a natural progression, the progression from friends to lovers.

"Lay on the bed, Mads," he said. I noticed he hadn't bothered removing my thong, but he seemed too bewitched with my boobs right now, which was fine by me. He stroked one breast with gentle reverence, and his delicate touches made me moan with pleasure. "Hmm. Sensitive. Somehow I knew they would be," he said, almost to himself. Without warning, he lowered his head and took one nipple into his mouth, applying the lightest of suction. The sensation was so intense I almost bucked right off the bed. He placed one hand firmly on my stomach. "Steady there, Mads," he said with a cheeky grin. "Seems like you like that."

"Hmm. Lovely," I said, sounding scarcely coherent. He'd barely started, and he'd already managed to reduce me to jelly. I was afraid I would be a gibbering wreck by morning.

He continued with his ministrations, his movements slow and gentle. He stroked his fingers down my stomach to the top of my panties, grazing the top of them in a teasing motion, before he stroked his fingers over my mound.

"Reece," I said, the word coming out like a hiss of air.

"Okay. These are fun, but they're coming off," he said with a determined look. He peeled them off with his thumbs and sighed in appreciation. "You're beautiful here too," he said, grazing his fingers over me. "And so wet." He ran his finger lower, and I moaned softly. "I have a sneaky suspicion you taste better than chocolate sauce," he said, lowering his head and latching onto the sensitive bundle of nerves.

His technique was slow and lazy, but at the same time it was insistent, and if oral sex featured in the Olympics, Reece Mackey would have an unfair advantage. I could feel that ball of energy building deep within me, working its way up my spine, until I suddenly exploded into a powerful orgasm.

"Oh, my God. Reece!" I cried out, reaching for him.

"It's okay, Mads. I'm here, but I'm not done with you yet. Not by a long shot." He grinned up at my bewilderment from between my legs as he gently slid a long finger inside me, exploring and teasing, playing with my sensitivities until I thought I would go out of my mind. I hadn't been with a man before who took this much time to please a woman. I felt treasured and cared for in a way I never had in the past. This was different. But then this was Reece, and in some way, I knew things would be different with him.

He massaged a particularly sensitive spot deep inside me, and my body pulsated around him as the second orgasm hit me, no less powerful than the first.

I didn't want him down at my feet for a moment longer. I needed him inside me, and I beckoned him insistently with my hand. "Please come up here now, Reece," I pleaded. "I need to feel you inside me right now."

I heard him chuckle. "Even bossy in bed, heh?"

We were now eye to eye, and I put my finger on his nose. "Not bossy. I just know what I need," I said breathlessly. "And what I need is you. And why the fuck are you still wearing underwear? How did that happen?"

He laughed as I knelt up to finish the job I'd started earlier, and I peeled off his boxer briefs to reveal him in all his glory. Stripped bare and laying back on the bed with his arms behind his head, I stared at him with a mixture of anticipation and envy. He had to be the most beautiful man I'd ever seen, and I ran my fingers over him gently, still in my post-orgasmic state of euphoria.

Bending down, I took him in my mouth and felt him shudder a little as he gave out a low groan. "That's fucking amazing, Maddie, but you have to stop. I want to come inside you. Let's save that for later."

I looked at him questioningly. "Did you bring condoms? Because I have some if you don't."

He gave me a wry smile. "Did I bring condoms, she asks," he said, giggling. "Yes, Maddie. I brought a lot of condoms."

"Then let me have one Dr. Mackey, so I can put it on," I said, holding out my hand.

He held out a foil pouch and then pulled it away at the last minute, faking me out. "Can I rely on you to put it on properly?"

I rolled my eyes, making him laugh. "Yes, Reece. I put them on bananas in tenth grade, didn't you?"

He handed it over with a grin, and I tore the foil pouch before sheathing him. Then I prowled back up the bed to him. "How do you want me?" I whispered.

"I want you everywhere, in every damn position known to man," he growled. "But right now, let's start with me on top, because I've been dreaming about that."

"Me too," I said, shuffling under him.

"Christ, Maddie. The very thought that you've been dreaming about me doing this to you makes me so hard." He was hovering above me, and I stroked his beautiful face. The kidding had stopped, and his face had grown serious. It was the moment we'd both been waiting for, for so long without realizing it. As he positioned himself and sank into me, he held my gaze and his eyes never left mine. It was intense and emotional, and I almost felt like I wanted to cry because it felt so damn good and so damn right.

He inched his way in slowly and he drew in a breath. I think he was desperately trying to hold on to control, but it was slipping away from him. "You okay?" he said, his voice thick with desire.

I adjusted my hips so he could sink a little deeper into me, because I wanted to feel him all the way, feel that ultimate stretch and know that there was nothing between us except the rush of the blood in our veins.

"I need you deeper, Reece," I murmured. "I need you so deep inside me I won't know where you end, and I begin."

That seemed to push him over the edge because suddenly he started to thrust faster and harder and I groaned with pleasure, wrapping my legs around his back. "I'm holding off here, Mads," he said breathlessly. "I want you to come again."

"I'm close," I said, pushing my hips up into him and adjusting the angle. That must have done it, because I came with a loud cry as colors danced in front of my eyes.

He put his head back and came just as loudly, his face contorted into a look of unrestrained pleasure. "Maddie, Maddie, Maddie," he crooned, as if the very sound of my name comforted him in the intensity of the moment.

He collapsed down beside me, panting and holding me tightly as if he was afraid I would get up and leave. "I need to deal with this condom," he said with a sigh. "Don't go away."

I giggled. "We're in the middle of nowhere, Reece. Where would I go?"

"You might steal my Jeep as a joke," he said, swinging his legs out of the bed.

"No," I murmured. "I have no intention of going anywhere. I'm right where I want to be."

Chapter 20

Reece

It was the middle of the night and there was barely any light in the room, apart from a small wall-mounted night light. I could just make out Maddie's face as she slept silently beside me. We'd both collapsed into bed after a very soapy and naughty shower and fallen asleep almost immediately. But now, at the time of night when your thoughts often invade your slumber, I was awake and staring at the woman I thought I would never have.

My heart felt light but heavy at the same time as I stared down at her face. She was everything I dreamed she would be, and with every sway of her hips and every sassy retort, I was falling deeper and deeper under her spell. I wanted a real relationship with her. One that was out in the open where everyone knew she was mine and I was hers. I wanted to walk down the street in Angel Peaks hand in hand, go out to restaurants, cuddle at our friends' nights, do all the things that couples did, but I knew that even now that she was still hesitant.

She'd asked me something last night before she'd fallen asleep. "Do you think friends can be lovers?" she's said sleepily as she'd cozied down under the sheets. "Sure," I'd said. "I think friends can be lovers and lovers can be friends." I'd wanted to press her on it and tell her I wanted to be much more than just friends and lovers. I wanted to be everything to her, and that thought had hit me hard because it was not something I'd wanted in the past with anyone. I wanted a life with her in her little house with all her animals. Christ, I'd even put up with Dave if I could have Maddie in my bed every night. I just wasn't sure that was what she wanted. I felt a genuine connection with her, and I could tell she was deeply affected by me, but at the end of the day, she was a very independent woman. Maybe what I wanted was just a step too far for her.

I thought about the ring my mom had given me the weekend I took Maddie home with me. She'd known then that Maddie was pretty special, and that's why she'd given it to me. I could see it on Maddie's finger, sparkling in the sunlight. I could imagine that house full of kids and animals, and Maddie and I joking and laughing the way we always did. For once in my life, I was looking to the future, but what about her? What did she see in her future? I was almost afraid to ask.

She stirred in her sleep and rolled over, opening her eyes and looking up at me. "Reece," she whispered. The sound of my name on her lips was the sweetest sound in existence.

"Hey, Mads," I said, stroking her face. "You okay?"

"I want you," she said in a husky voice, reaching her arms up for me. I allowed myself to be consumed by her touch once again, pushing my concerns to one side for now.

⌐

WE WERE LATE OUT OF bed the next morning for obvious reasons, and I could see that having Maddie in my bed could be a major distraction. We even found a use for the chocolate sauce, so neither of us was hungry early, and we ended up having more of a brunch. She refused to let me cook, which was probably very wise, but at least she was happy with the selection of food I'd brought.

I watched her cooking up a storm in the kitchen as I got the coffee going and she sang away happily to herself. "Not The Pina Colada Song today?" I asked.

She grinned. "No. That's Dave's song. I only sing that for him."

"What do you mean it's Dave's song?" I said incredulously, pouring out the coffee.

"It's a magic trick," she said, putting a huge Spanish omelet on my plate. "His previous owner told me about it. Whenever he's anxious, you just have to sing The Pina Colada Song. It calms him right down. Works like a charm. Even Ben knows it."

We sat down at the table, and she was looking very pleased with herself, and I knew why. "So, you're telling me he bit my ass because you failed to sing The Pina Colada Song to him?"

She took a mouthful of her omelet and groaned happily, clearly satisfied with her cooking efforts. "No, Reece. *You* failed to sing the song, so he bit your ass. Not my fault."

"But you never told me," I spluttered.

"I know," she said, and then she started to laugh, and the sound of her laughter went straight to my groin.

God, at this rate my dick's going to drop off, I thought to myself, considering the number of times we'd had sex in the past twenty-four hours.

I started on my omelet and had to agree with Maddie. It was damn good. I don't know how she got everything to taste so good, but it was clearly a knack she had. "I think that's criminal negligence, Ms. Moreno," I said in a stern voice. "You failed to provide me with an important piece of safety information and because of that, I was injured on the job."

She snorted. "Bullshit," she said. "If I'd told you, you have to sing The Pina Colada song when you're treating Dave, what would you have done?"

I thought about that for a moment while I drank my coffee. "I probably would have thought you were winding me up."

"Exactly. So what was the point? It was inevitable you were going to get your ass bitten. But next time you'll know. See?"

"I don't know the words. Or the tune." I grumbled.

"No problem. I'll teach you," she said happily. "You don't need to know all of it. Just the important bits." And then she proceeded to sing what she considered to be the important bits that would prevent a Dave-related attack.

I chuckled as I finished the rest of my breakfast and cleared up the plates. "You know, a lot of people told me you were crazy when I arrived in Angel Peaks, and I'm beginning to think they were right."

She frowned. "I was pretty horrible to you when you arrived. I feel bad about that now. I usually end up feeling bad when I'm like that. You must have thought I was a terrible person." She looked regretful about the whole situation.

"Strangely enough, no," I said. "You had quite the opposite effect. I saw you coming toward me with your hands on your hips, eyes flashing, and my dick stood to attention."

She thought that was funny and laughed. "How can you be turned on by that? It wasn't the last time I was wretched to you. I'm sorry, Reece," she said quietly.

I walked over to her and crouched down, holding her face in my hands. "Hey. Stop beating yourself up. I think ninety percent of the time I was to blame. I just can't help pushing your buttons, Maddie. You're delicious when you're angry."

"You might not always feel that way," she said with a sad expression. "It wears thin with most people eventually, even my own family."

I stroked her beautiful soft curls and raised her chin so she was looking at me. "Do you know what you remind me of? You're like a summer storm, Maddie. Spectacular and sometimes unexpected, but you blow over real fast. I know you don't mean it."

She looked at me with wide eyes. "No one's ever described my anger issues so beautifully before." And then she wrapped her arms around me and buried her face in my neck, and it was all I could do not to take her back to bed. But I knew we had to be out by noon and that was fast approaching.

IT WAS A QUIET RIDE back, with both of us a little subdued. It had been an amazing weekend, but now it was over, and I think both of us were wondering where we would go from here. I had meant to ask her before we left the cabin, but we got busy packing up, and then she had wanted to thank me properly for the weekend, so we'd returned to bed for a quickie, which I would never turn down.

She clung to my hand on the journey with her head resting on my arm as if she didn't want to lose the physical closeness we'd built over the weekend. I knew we needed to broach the subject, so I plucked up courage and dived in with both feet.

"Mads. What happens now?" I asked.

She looked at me, seemingly confused for a moment. "What do you mean?"

"I mean with us. What happens with us?"

She was quiet for a moment and then she said, "What do you want to happen?"

I thought my actions had made that clear, but I was happy to clarify for her. "I want you and me to be in a real relationship. I want to walk down Main Street with my arms wrapped around you and have the whole town talking about us. I want to make out with you in your office at lunchtime. I want to have you sitting on my lap on our friends' nights with you snuggled up to my chest."

"I want that too," she whispered, giving me a glimmer of hope, but somehow, I knew there was more to come. "But I want to keep it a secret until after the wedding. It's only six weeks away.

"Can I ask why?" I said, a little choked.

"Because when it gets out that you and I are together, there will be an enormous fuss for a while, from the seniors' center right down to the ice cream store. You know what small-town living is like, and I've lived in Angel Peaks all my life. I just want the focus to be on Sam and Kate for now, with no distractions. It's their big day." She looked across at me with a look of regret, because she knew it wasn't what I wanted to hear.

I pulled over to the side of the road because I wanted her to know I meant business. "Maddie. I'm not talking friends with benefits here. I'm talking about us being together properly, as a couple. Do you understand?"

She nodded. "Reece, I want to be with you. I just want it to be at the right time."

"I just want you to know that after this damn wedding, I'm announcing it to the world. In fact, I'll take out a full-page ad in the Angel Peaks Gazette. That'll make Harry Connors happy."

She stroked my arm. "It'll be fun sneaking around and trying not to get caught. You'll see. The time will go super fast."

I wasn't convinced, but I could see it was all I was getting for now.

Chapter 21

Maddie

On the Monday after Reece and I returned from the cabin, I was due to have a girls' night with Scarlett and Kate. I was hoping they would be so caught up in their own weekends that they wouldn't be too concerned about what I had been up to, because I was pretty sure my face would be beet red if they started asking me about what I'd done over the weekend.

Just thinking about what Reece and I had been doing made me all hot and needy, and I constantly felt the need to phone him for a booty call. Before he'd left on Sunday, he'd announced that he wanted-ed to sleep with me every night, but I'd persuaded him that that might not always be practical or possible. Despite that, I'd found my-self handing over a spare key to my place, which he'd wrapped his hand around with a smile as if I'd given him a piece of gold.

I warned him he would have to be careful and not park the Jeep in the yard, in case I had unexpected visitors. We even worked out an emergency drill in case someone showed up while he was there which involved him crawling into the closet under my roof space to hide. He seemed game for it all and it was quite fun really. I also told him he would need to warn me when he was coming over since I kept a baseball bat under my bed in case of intruders and I didn't want to inadvertently knock him out by mistake.

For some reason, girls' night ended up being in Scarlett's tiny apartment above the bakery. I think because she had to work the next day and get up unspeakably early, she liked to be at home so she could just tumble into bed when we left.

Scarlett's darling little apartment above the bakery was no bigger than a shoebox really, but it was just so Scarlett. Kate and I arrived to-gether, and we squeezed into the tiny living space which did double duty as a kitchen, eating area, and bedroom. As usual half-finished paintings were strewn around, and her windowsills were lined with paint pots and palettes. It would have been a cute little space to live if she didn't try to cram so much into it. She desperately needed a studio space to do her painting, but I knew how tight her finances were, so that wasn't going to happen anytime soon.

I noticed she was wearing a new hat tonight instead of her regular pirate hat or knitted Viking helmet. It was really intricate with what looked like crocheted tendrils of hair spilling down over her shoulders. "Nice chapeau," I told her. "But I can't quite make out what it is."

Scarlett giggled and turned around, and I could see from the back there was actually a knitted octopus on her head and what I thought were tendrils of hair were actually tentacles. "What do you think?" she said with a grin. "It was really expensive, but I had to have it. It's unique."

I walked around her and examined it. "Well, in that case, it's just like you. It's certainly a work of art."

"I know, right? Unique," she said again. She seemed a little wound up, and I wondered if she'd consumed too much coffee again. If there was one thing Scarlett didn't need it was a stimulant.

Kate and I sat together on the small couch and Scarlett pulled up a wicker chair after she'd poured three glasses of wine. "Okay!" she said rubbing her hands together. "I thought we could have a fun debrief on Valentine's. Who wants to go first?"

We all looked at each other, and I shook my head. "Don't look at me. I didn't do anything interesting."

Scarlett had a big grin on her face, and I knew something was coming. "Well, that's strange, because Ben told me you were away for the weekend. So, who exactly are you banging Maddie?"

"I'm not banging anyone," I spluttered, trying to think on my feet. "If you must know, I went away for a spa weekend because I didn't want to spend Valentine's on my own."

"Oh," Kate said, looking interested. "Which one did you go to?"

I was desperately trying to think of any of the spa hotels in the area, but I was drawing a blank. I realized I would have to make one up. "Oh, it's a brand new one. Only opened up a few weeks ago. It's called.... Happy Feet," I said inwardly cringing because it was the worst possible name I could have come up with.

Scarlett almost spat her wine across the table. "Happy Feet?" she said, shrieking with laughter. "Who the fuck calls a spa Happy Feet? Does it employ penguins as aestheticians?"

"Well, obviously they specialize in feet," I said huffily. "Feet massages, reflexology, pedicures, all that kind of thing."

"Oh, let's see your feet then," Kate chipped in. "They must be looking amazing if you spent the whole weekend there."

"I'd rather not show you," I said, feeling my face burning. "I have a toenail fungus, and it's pretty disgusting."

Kate and Scarlett were looking at each other with their lips sucked in, trying not to laugh. I was so busted, but I was not backing down, and I rapidly tried to change the subject. "What about you Kate? How did your weekend of love go?" It was a great tactic because she immediately went all gooey, love hearts appearing in her eyes.

"It was amazing," she sighed. "Sam booked the honeymoon suite. I thought we were going to be staying in the room we stayed in before, but he wanted it to be really special."

I snorted. "You're not even married yet. Aren't you supposed to save the honeymoon for after the wedding?"

"No harm in getting a bit of practice in," she said with a coy smile. "We *practiced* all weekend," she added, putting added emphasis on the word *practiced*.

"God, I'm so jealous," Scarlett said, scowling. "I've had no sex for ages and you two are getting it all. It's not fair."

I opened my mouth to protest, but she jabbed her finger at me. "I know you're banging someone, Maddie Moreno, and I'm going to find out who it is. Is it Pete from the repair shop who fixed your brakes? Gord from the ice cream store? Lenny from the arcade? Who is it?"

"Scarlett, all those guys are over forty. I'm not that desperate. I told you where I was. If you choose not to believe me, that's up to you." My voice had shot up an octave, which was never a good sign. I was feeling cornered and whenever that happened, I usually lashed out with my tongue. Kate knew that and she diplomatically intervened before things escalated and I blew a gasket.

"Scarlett, leave her alone. She's entitled to a private life, just like the rest of us. Why don't you tell us about your weekend?"

Scarlett played with her octopus tentacles thoughtfully. "Well, as you know, Ryan and I went to the Angel Peaks annual speed dating event."

"I've never been to one of those things," I said. "How does it work?"

Scarlett got into her subject with enthusiasm. "It's really cool. There's a room full of people and you rotate around the tables, spending five minutes with each person. At the end of the evening, you give the organizer a sheet of paper with the people you liked. and if they liked you too, there's a match and you get contact details."

"Sounds great," Kate said. "Was it successful?"

Scarlett pulled a face. "Not exactly." We both looked at her for more information, and she took a minute to collect her thoughts. "First off, they held it at the Evergreen Seniors' Center, so you know what that means."

"There was lots of yummy food?" I suggested.

She shook her head. "Most of the participants were over seventy. I had one very sweet octogenarian propose marriage to me in the first two minutes."

"So, the participants were a little mature," Kate said, suppressing a giggle.

"Very," she said. "But Ryan did manage to snaffle a recipe for an amazing lemon cake, so the evening wasn't a complete disaster."

Kate and I were both laughing and trying not to spill our wine. "What happened next?" I asked.

"Ryan was depressed, so we went back to his place, and he made the lemon cake, and we ate it and watched My Fair Lady."

"This just keeps getting better," I said. "Is there any relevance to the fact you watched My Fair Lady?"

Scarlett nodded animatedly while she tucked into a large bag of Doritos. "Yes! Ryan loves musicals. Didn't you know? I voted for Mamma Mia, but he said only My Fair Lady would get him out of his funk."

"And did it?" Kate asked.

"I don't know. I fell asleep during *On the Street Where you Live*, and he threw a blanket over me. I woke up the next morning in his big armchair."

Kate sighed with a sad expression. "Poor Ryan. Are you sure it wouldn't work between you two, Scarlett?"

I looked across at Scarlett with an orange Dorito stain around her mouth, wearing her octopus hat, and it surprised me that Kate even had to ask that question. Ryan wanted a very particular kind of woman. Someone he could care for but that would put up with his slightly OCD tendencies. She would have to be sweet and kind, just like him, and she would have to be happy to go the whole traditional route of marriage and a family because at the end of the day, that was what Ryan wanted.

"I think we have a mission, ladies," I said, grabbing a notepad and pen from my purse. "We need to find Ryan a wife. One who's not Scarlett."

We spent the rest of the evening brainstorming local women who might be suitable for Ryan, but we drew a blank. I could see we would have to cast our net further afield if we were going to find someone. One thing was for sure, they didn't live in Angel Peaks right now.

〜

WE WOUND UP OUR EVENING just after nine so that Scarlett could get to bed, and I drove home through a February snowstorm. I parked my car closer to the house than I normally would, so it would be easier to get out in the morning, but I realized if it kept snowing this hard, I would have to drag out my small tractor in the morning and clear it before I could get to work.

When I got in the door, I saw a pair of large boots sitting on my doormat and recognized them as belonging to Reece, and my heart rate immediately kicked up several notches. Walking into my living room, the fire was burning away nicely, and he'd clearly added a few logs, so it was really toasty, but he wasn't there. I locked my front door and went in search of him.

"Reece. Where are you?" I called, but there was no answer. I checked all the downstairs rooms, but he wasn't in any of them, so I ascended the stairs with a smirk. My bet was he was going to be naked in my bed, and just the thought of that was sending electrical charges through my already hyped-up body.

I stared into the empty bedroom bemused and wondered if he was hiding somewhere intending to jump out on me and scare me, which was definitely his style. Then, I heard splashing sounds coming from the bathroom and I realized where he was. The cheeky bastard was in my big tub.

I tiptoed down the hallway and threw open the door to the sight of Reece boldly spread out in my bathtub and obviously pleased to see me. "Oh!" I said, unable to take my eyes off the impressive sight. "Making yourself at home?"

"Hmm. See something you're interested in?" he said with a slow, sexy smile. "Why don't you come and join me?"

I inadvertently licked my lips and he chuckled. "I don't think there's room," I said, trying to keep my voice cool and even.

"There's plenty of room," he said. "I'll draw some more hot water. Take your clothes off. I've been waiting for you."

"You have?" I said, pulling my sweater over my head.

"Yeah. Like all fucking day."

Chapter 22
Maddie

Over the next few weeks, Reece and I got into a routine that seemed to work for both of us. Sometimes he would come for dinner and stay the whole evening, which he loved, or other times he would sneak into my bed at 11 p.m., after we'd both come home from whatever event we were attending.

It was unlike anything I'd ever had in my life, and I was surprised at how easily we fell into what could be construed as a relationship. Of course, we still had to sneak around, but we were both determined that we would come out in the open after the wedding.

I had lulled myself into this perfect little dream world, playing house with Reece, having sex with Reece every night, talking with Reece, laughing with Reece; it was like all my dreams had come true and I was lapping it up like a cat laps up cream.

I was also super busy helping Kate with wedding planning and, as the big day drew closer, she naturally became more and more wrapped up in everything. She wasn't exactly Bridezilla, but there were certain moments of near hysteria when things didn't go according to plan that I'd never seen in her before.

It wasn't going to be a huge wedding since neither of them had much in the way of family. Sam hadn't seen his mother for many years and, although Kate tried to persuade him to ask her to come, he'd flatly refused. I think it still burned with him that she hadn't protected him when his dad had been so abusive, and I can't say I blamed him.

Despite not having big families, they were still having around seventy guests, and the inevitable disasters happened, just like all weddings. Graham didn't think he was going to be able to get the exact flowers that Kate had chosen, as it was so early in the season.

Being in a small town meant there was less choice when something went wrong, and my head spun with everything.

It made me all the more determined to never have this kind of wedding, and I dreamed of an outdoor wedding at my own little house with my nearest and dearest, surrounded by my animals. When I was feeling self-indulgent, I allowed myself to daydream that Reece was the man waiting for me at the end of the haybale aisle, and I had to give myself a stern talking to on more than one occasion. I had no idea what kind of future he wanted or whether he even saw a future with me because we'd never discussed it. Sure, we were close, but then I think we'd always been close, even before the sex had started. But close didn't equate to forever, and I had to keep reminding myself that.

Ten days before the wedding, I was sitting in my office waiting for my 10 a.m. client, feeling decidedly nauseous. I hadn't felt like breakfast that morning and now it seemed like I had terrible heartburn. I really hoped I wasn't coming down with something, and I wandered down to my private bathroom down the hallway from my office. I kept it locked, because I didn't like sharing my bathroom space with all and sundry and I rooted through the vanity looking for some antacids that I was pretty sure I kept there.

My hand swept over a box of tampons and the sudden realization of something I was normally so vigilant about swept over me like a wave of horror. Forgetting all about my heartburn, I rushed back to my office to grab my phone and look at my calendar. I started having sex with Reece on February 14th and my period should have come at the beginning of March. Today was March 25th, which meant I was over three weeks late.

I flopped into my leather chair, trying to make sense of all this. How could I have missed something like this? I always knew when my periods were due, and I was as regular as clockwork. The truth was, I'd been so wrapped up in my little bubble of contentment with the man of my dreams that it hadn't even occurred to me.

I tried to tell myself that it might not be the worst scenario. Perhaps having sex several times a day delayed your period. I'd never seen that much action in my entire life, so it could just be that it was a shock to my system. Yeah, that was probably it, I thought, trying to think calming thoughts. I knew I couldn't be pregnant because we'd been diligent about using condoms and those things were pretty fail-proof. Or were they? Perhaps the chocolate sauce play hadn't been such a good idea.

I don't know how I got through my 10 a.m. appointment with Bill from the local hardware store. He must have thought I'd completely lost my marbles, and in the end, I apologized and told him I wasn't feeling too good. He was super sweet and even offered to drive me home, but I had something I needed to do, so I rescheduled his appointment and headed to the local pharmacy.

The problem with small-town living was that there was no such thing as anonymity. I remember how painful it was for me to walk into this very store and buy my first pack of condoms, and now here I was coming back to buy a pregnancy test. The ironic thing was that it was the same person behind the counter as when I'd gone in for those condoms all those years ago. Delia Hibbert, the sweet, white-haired pharmacist.

She smiled as she saw me approach. "Hello Maddie, dear. How are you? How's your mom and all those brothers of yours?"

I was in no mood to pass an hour of social niceties and the store was currently empty, so I made a few quick curt responses and got straight to the point. "Delia, I need a pregnancy test. For a friend."

Delia was totally professional, bless her heart, and her face showed no reaction at all. "Of course, dear," she said, reaching up to grab a box behind the counter. "Now, these are quite accurate these days, but tell your friend to get to the doctor and have a blood test as well. That's the best way."

I nodded. "Thanks, Delia. I'll be sure to tell her."

I paid and watched as she carefully popped the test into a plain white bag before she handed it over. "Now, you take care, Maddie. And don't forget. Your friend needs to see a doctor."

I thanked her and rushed back to the office. I needed to put my mind at rest, and I wasn't prepared to delay this for a second longer than necessary. My office was the only one on the third floor and it had a glass door to my area that could be locked, so I quickly secured the lock, put up my closed sign, and headed for the bathroom.

With shaking hands, I broke open the package and read the instructions. Then I read them again because it made little sense the first time. I duly peed on the stick and looked at my watch. Three minutes! How could it possibly take three minutes when I felt like my whole life was about to implode?

I remembered one of Ben's tricks for when he had to wait for something. He was notoriously bad at waiting, so he used to count things. I looked around for something to count and started to count the ceramic tiles on the floor: twenty. That wasn't long enough, so I unrolled the toilet paper and counted the number of sheets. It was a new roll, so that took much longer. Two hundred and ten sheets later, and I was left with a pile of unrolled toilet paper that I would have to dispose of, but that didn't matter because when I checked my watch, I saw the three minutes were up.

I was wracked with nerves as I picked up the little stick, thinking about how finding out about a pregnancy was supposed to feel different than this. It was supposed to be a happy, joyous occasion, not something fraught with anxiety.

I stared down at the little window and took in the two lines and the word "pregnant." Holy shit! I was pregnant. I dropped down onto the toilet with a thud, my head in my hands and my heart in my throat.

Walking back to my office in a blur, I sat on the armchair next to the gas fireplace and tried to sort out the mess of thoughts and feelings in my mind. I placed my hand reverently on my stomach and tried to take in the fact that there was a tiny human being growing away in there; half of me and half of Reece all wrapped up in a beautiful little bundle. It wasn't that I didn't want kids; I absolutely wanted them, lots of them in fact. In weaker moments, I'd imagined chubby little legs in rubber boots running around my acreage and playing with the animals.

The problem was that I had no idea what Reece wanted. He always seemed such a carefree spirit, I wasn't sure that a family was on his list of things he wanted in life. I'd seen him interact with his niece Emma, and he was really good with her, but being an uncle was way different from being a dad. One thing was for sure, I wasn't going to force this on him. If we were going to be together, it would be because we wanted to be, not because of some sense of obligation.

I spoke to our baby, because it was suddenly all becoming real in my mind, and I needed to make that connection. Gentle rubbing my belly I said, "It'll be okay, little bean. Mommy's going to take good care of you, and you will be so loved." Tears that I hadn't even been aware had been forming spilled out of my eyes and ran down my cheeks.

I sat for a while in quiet contemplation and then I thought of my mom. She had raised four children at a young age, and she had been fine. Admittedly, she had the support of my dad, but I had a whole army of family and friends who I knew had my back. Whatever Reece wanted, I was not alone. Everything would be okay. The problem was I'd fallen in love with Reece Mackey, and I desperately wanted him to want this too. I knew I would have to tell him, but I wasn't

ready to do that just yet. I needed some time to adjust and get used
to the idea, and I needed to see my mom.

It was lunchtime, and she was used to various members of her
family descending on her in search of food. I still had my key, so I
let myself into our familiar family home and breathed a sigh of relief.
My mom and dad had built a haven for us in this place. It was full of
memories of laughter and fighting, huge family meals, and even the
odd quiet moment. I don't know how she'd managed to raise four
such strong-minded kids without losing it, but she was always calm,
and she was the safe place we all could come home to.

"Hi Mom," I called, guessing I'd find her in the kitchen.

"Maddie?" she said, surprise in her voice. "I wasn't expecting to
see you today."

I wandered into our spacious family kitchen and the smell of
freshly baked cookies wafted into my nostrils. My mom was always
able to feed an army at the drop of a hat, and I was grateful that I'd at
least inherited that skill from her. Her freezer was packed with meals
and yummy treats, and she gleefully fed anyone who walked through
her door, from her own family all the way down to the mailman.

"There you are, love," she said with a warm smile, drying her
hands on a dishtowel. She approached me and wrapped me in one of
her warm hugs, which made my heart thud sadly. Pulling back, she
inspected my face as she always did. "You okay, love? You look a little
pale."

"I'm fine," I said, pulling away. "I think I'm just a bit tired. Do
you have any soup?"

My mom grinned, thrilled to have somebody to feed. "Yes. I have
minestrone and freshly baked biscuits. Will that do you? Come sit at
the table, we'll eat together."

I took a seat at the enormous kitchen table that had gotten a little
bashed over the years. This table had seen a lot of action; cars had
been driven over it, science experiments had exploded on it, and oc-

casionally brothers' heads had been bashed on it. This table could tell a lot of stories. I swept my hand over it now, reliving some of the family meals we'd shared there.

She placed two steaming bowls of hot soup on the table before returning to fetch a tray of cheese biscuits warm from the oven. She took a seat opposite me and smiled. "So, what's new? Do you have anything new to tell me?"

I shrugged my shoulders and blew on my hot soup, not quite ready to share my news and not even knowing where to start. No one knew about my relationship with Reece, and now I was pregnant with his baby. It was going to come as a shock to everyone. I knew whatever happened, my family would be supportive, and I was pretty sure she would welcome a grandchild; she dropped hints often enough. I just didn't know where to start.

I ate silently for a while, enjoying the comfort that could be derived from some excellent home cooking, then I broke the silence. "You were pretty young when you had Matteo, weren't you?"

She laughed. "Yes. I was twenty-two. Your dad and I had only been married for six months before I fell pregnant, and we were living in a tiny apartment on the other side of town. It was before we bought this place."

"That must have been tough," I said, buttering a warm, crumbly biscuit.

She looked thoughtful for a moment. "I wouldn't say tough exactly. I mean, Matteo was huge, and we outgrew that apartment pretty fast. That's when we bought this place, but it was like a building site for quite a few years while your dad renovated it. He was busy working and trying to build his business, while also working on this place at the same time, and I kept popping out babies."

I laughed. "It must have been chaos."

"At times it was. But there was always a lot of love in this family. That's what carries you through this stuff, Maddie. It's love. Nothing else matters, really." She smiled and grabbed my hand and I looked up, desperate to share my deepest secret with her, but then I heard heavy footsteps and it could only mean one thing. One of my brothers was home.

"Mom, it's me!" My brother Ben called from the hallway.

"Come on in, love. Your sister's here for lunch." My mom said.

"I hope she hasn't eaten everything," he replied, breezing into the kitchen.

He planted a light kiss on my mom's cheek before clasping his arms around me from behind and kissing the top of my head. "How are you, Mads? Did you notice I taught Henry a new expletive the last time I stayed?"

"How the hell would I notice?" I growled. "Every word he uses is an expletive."

"Oh, did you stay at Maddie's recently?" My mom said, and I realized she hadn't known I'd gone away for the weekend with Reece.

"Yeah, I needed to get away for the weekend," I said as casually as possible.

"I think she was seeing a man," Ben said, with an exaggerated wink.

"Mind your damn business!" I snapped.

"Whoa! Well, I guess that answered that question. It was a man," he said with a smirk.

"Why does it have to be a man? Maybe I just needed a weekend away. I am entitled to a private life, you know." I knew I was getting more irate than I should have, but my brain wasn't exactly firing on all four cylinders.

"Okay, you two," my mom said, with that soothing voice of hers. "Let's just cool it down a bit. Of course you're entitled to a private life, Maddie, and it's very good of Ben to look after your animals when you go away."

"Yeah, except he corrupts my parrot and empties my freezer," I grumbled.

Mom rubbed her hands together. "Okay, who wants dessert?"

Ben cheered as if he hadn't seen food for a month, and my mom trundled off happily to collect a tray of muffins. He looked at me seriously. "You okay Mads? You seem a bit off."

I sighed and leaned my head against his arm. Out of all my brothers, Ben and I were the closest. "Yeah, I'm fine. Sorry, Ben, I didn't mean to snap. I'm just a bit down."

He extended his arm and wrapped it around my shoulder. "Why don't you go and see Nonna, then? She always manages to sort you out. You always used to go and see her when you had your knickers in a knot."

I laughed at his expression. "My knickers are not in a knot, but that's a good idea. I haven't seen her for ages. Maybe I'll go for the weekend."

"I guess you want me to look after your animals again then?" he said.

I nodded. "You're the best, Ben. Feel free to empty my freezer, but please teach Henry something nice for a change."

"Perhaps a nice song," he said with a grin.

"Putting swear words to music does not constitute a nice song," I said drily.

My mom returned with the muffins and smiled when she saw Ben with his arm around me. "Maddie's going to see Nonna for the weekend," he told her.

She nodded approvingly. "That's a great idea. She'll be thrilled to see you."

Chapter 23
Maddie

Being Friday, Ryan was hosting one of our regular friends' nights and, since the wedding was the following week, it would be the last friends' night when all of us were unmarried. The next one we held, Sam and Kate would be back from their honeymoon and would be a married couple. It was a sobering thought; they would be married, and I was pregnant. It felt like the entire fabric of my life was changing, and I felt unsettled in a way I never had.

One thing was clear in my mind and that was I was going to be okay. If Reece decided he didn't want to be with me and the baby on a permanent basis, I would be heartbroken, but I was in a much better situation than many single moms because I had a huge support system.

Ben's idea about visiting Nonna had been an excellent one. Nonna had been my North Star when times were tough. During my teen years, I'd spent many weeks of my summer holidays on her farm, learning about animals and riding her horse, Elvis, bareback. She was a straight talker and guaranteed to never give you any bullshit, but she was also unspeakably kind, and I think she knew how hard it was for me to find my place in the world growing up with three brothers.

I'd already decided I would leave early the next morning, and I just needed to get through friends' night. Of course, I also needed an excuse to prevent Reece from coming over and spending the night. Not that I didn't want to see him. I just wanted the chance to talk things through with Nonna and get my head straight, because I knew when I told him about the baby, he may call things off, and I had to be strong enough to accept that. There was no doubt in my mind that I was in love with him, but I knew I might have to let him go. And as heartbreaking as that was, it was a reality, and it was one I might have to deal with.

Friday was always a busy day for Reece, since he often had surgeries, so I knew he would be a little late to Ryan's place. I was the first to arrive, and I parked my truck in Ryan's driveway and carefully carried the pot of chili that I'd made up to his front door. He swung it open with a wide smile, clearly thrilled to be entertaining. "Maddie!" he said enthusiastically. and kissed me warmly on the cheek before helping me with the chili. "Mmm. This smells great," he said. "You're the first one. Come on in and make yourself comfortable."

Ryan's beautiful and expensive house on the golf course had been built by my dad a few years ago, and Ryan had purchased it as soon as he moved to Angel Peaks, feeling the need to put down roots as soon as possible.

I walked into his great room and sighed because he had an unusual sense of style for a man living on his own. Pale slip-covered couches surrounded an enormous coffee table, and a few antique pieces were dotted around. The house boasted five bedrooms, and I knew Ryan would dearly love to fill them with kids. I didn't think men got broody like that, but Ryan definitely had a deep craving for family life. He was one of life's carers; a doctor, a great cook, and a true friend. I instinctively rubbed my tummy and thought how things would be different if Ryan were the father of "little bean", as I was calling the baby. He would be over the moon and would probably turn into an overprotective dad overnight. But I wasn't in love with Ryan. I was in love with Reece.

I was interrupted from my musings by the sound of Scarlett's voice as she greeted Ryan with enthusiasm. "Oh, nice hat," I heard Ryan say, wondering which one of her creations she was sporting tonight.

As she bounced into the great room, I was reminded a little of Tigger from Winnie the Pooh. Her irrepressible energy and joie de vivre were impressive, and I wondered if she ever got depressed about anything. I couldn't see it somehow as she approached me with a huge grin and octopus headgear. Scarlett was one of life's eternal optimists and if life ever gave her lemons, I'm pretty sure she made champagne.

"Maddie!" she yelled. "Have you opened the wine yet?"

I rubbed my stomach. "No, I'm not drinking tonight. I'm driving to Nonna's tomorrow morning, and I need to keep a clear head."

She grimaced. "Oh, you poor thing. You have to stay sober."

I laughed. "I know, but I'll make up for it with those treats you brought," I said, pointing to the box in her hand.

"Yeah," she said wickedly. "Let's hide them from Reece and scoff them all ourselves."

"Fat chance of that," I said. "He can sniff out food at a hundred yards, I think."

The doorbell rang again, and Kate and Sam entered with lots of excited chatter. "Here comes the bride!" Scarlett said with a grin. "Best you don't eat too many of these treats or you won't be fitting into that dress of yours."

A terrible thought occurred to me as I looked down at my stomach. I had no idea how quickly a baby bump appeared, but I hoped to God it wouldn't be before next Saturday or Kate would kill me. I was no longer the hot girl of honor; I was the knocked-up girl of honor.

There was a final ring of the doorbell and my stomach flipped because I knew who it was. "I'll get it," I told Ryan. "You're busy in the kitchen."

I took a breath before opening the door, and there he was, as gorgeous as he had been when he left me in bed that morning, wearing the same sexy smirk that affected me all the way down to my toes. "Hi, Mads," he said in a whisper. "Do you think they'd miss us if we disappeared off to one of Ryan's many bedrooms for half an hour?"

I took his arm and led him in. "I think they would definitely miss us. Come on in. Did you have a busy day?"

"Yeah," he murmured. "And I missed you like crazy." He squeezed my ass as we walked down the hallway, and I batted his hand away as he chuckled.

I pulled him back before we entered the great room. "Reece, I'm going to be away for the weekend. I have to go to Nonna's and Ben's coming over to stay tonight, so we won't see each other until Monday."

He frowned. "That's a bit sudden, isn't it? You didn't mention it this morning."

I tried to think fast. "I didn't know I was going until today. When I went to see my mom, she said Nonna wanted to see me. I would have called you, but I didn't want to disturb you in surgery."

He nodded, but he didn't look happy. "Okay. I guess it'll have to be Monday then." The smirk returned to his face before he said, "But you'll have some catching up to do. Three days away from you is too much."

I smiled and rubbed his arm, regretful that I couldn't just sit down with him and tell him my news, confident in the fact that he would be thrilled about it. "Come on," I said. "We don't want the others getting suspicious."

I walked in ahead of him. "Hide those treats," I told Scarlett. "And fast. I think he's hungry."

She poked her tongue out at Reece and dramatically dashed into the kitchen with her boxes. "You won't stop me, little redhead," he called after her. "The treats call to me, and I have to answer the call."

Despite my anxiety, it was a fun evening. My chili was a hit and Ryan had made far too much food as usual. I was glad I wasn't drinking because it gave me a chance to look around the room and really observe my friends. Kate was sitting comfortably on Sam's lap with her head on his chest, lost in her own thoughts. Ryan and Scarlett were discussing the relative merits of two of Ryan's appetizers, and Reece was sitting quietly with a beer, looking happy but tired.

I realized it wasn't only the last night we would all be single. It also might be the last night we assembled like this as friends. I had no way of knowing what Reece's reaction to the pregnancy would be, and it might be hard to be friends if he wanted no part of it.

We'd reached a lull in the conversation and Scarlett jumped up, keen to make an announcement. She dashed out to the kitchen and retrieved the white box she'd brought with her. "In honor of this momentous occasion of losing two single friends and gaining two boring ones, I have made a special treat." Placing the box on the table, she opened it to reveal a whole stack of iced cookies decorated with a ball and chain. "Ball and chain cookies!" she shrieked. "How appropriate is that?"

Everyone laughed, but then Sam chipped in, "Marriage to this woman is not a ball and chain. It's a fucking miracle and believe me, it will come to each and everyone one of you when you find the right person." Kate nuzzled his neck, and I thought they were going to start making out in front of us.

"It won't happen to me," Scarlett said. "I'm unmarriageable material."

"More like unmanageable," Reece quipped.

"That's not true," Ryan protested. "I'm sure there's a man out there who's brave enough to warm to your rather unique qualities."

We all laughed at Ryan's tactful description of Scarlett's weirdness, and then Kate spoke, "Okay, let's make a bet about who is going to be next down the aisle."

"Are we putting money on this to make it interesting?" Sam asked.

"That won't work," Reece said. "Because if we all bet on the same person, who gets the money?"

"I'm having first dibs on Maddie," Scarlett yelled, clearly getting into the spirit of things.

"That's not fair," Kate protested. "I was going to vote for Maddie."

"Yeah, she'll probably going to marry that damn llama of hers," Reece said with a grin. "Dave and Maddie. Together, forever."

I laughed. "Hey! I think Dave would make a wonderful life partner for someone. He's loyal and he would keep you warm at night."

"I'd rather marry Henry," Reece said. "He's fucking hilarious, and he doesn't bite."

The room was erupting into chaos, with everyone suggesting unlikely partners for each other, until Reece spoke above the noise. "Well, you can forget about me. I won't be settling down anytime soon, if ever. Nope. I'm just not the settling down kind."

I suddenly felt as if someone had punched all the air out of me. It was a very Reece thing to say, and I don't know why I was shocked, but I could feel the tears pricking in my eyes. Any thoughts that he would want to settle down with me and our baby suddenly dissipated like fog on a winter's morning.

I was careful to keep my amused smile etched on my face, and while the hubbub continued, I wandered into the kitchen and got myself a glass of water. After a couple of minutes, Ryan came out as well. "You okay, Maddie?" he said with a concerned look.

"To be honest, I've had a headache all day," I told him. "I think I'm going to slip away, but I don't want the others to know, so please don't mention it."

"But they'll notice you're gone," he said.

I looked over at my group of friends and noticed someone had got a raucous board game out and they were all gathered around the table. "Not for a while," I said with a smile. "Thanks for hosting, Ryan. It was amazing, as usual."

He went to lead me to the door, but I shook my head. "No, you stay here. Then no one will know." I gave him a quick peck on the cheek and let myself out as quietly as possible.

I climbed into my truck and allowed the tears to flow. "Don't worry, little bean," I told the baby. "We're going to be just fine." Somehow I managed to drive home in one piece, and I was a little calmer when I walked into the house.

Knowing immediately what I had to do, I picked up my phone and called Ben. "Hey, Ben. Do you think you could come over tonight? I've decided to go to Nonna's now."

There was a stunned silence. "Now? For fuck's sake why? Have you even checked the weather? It's dark Maddie, leave it until the morning."

I tried to gulp back a sob. "Ben. I have to go tonight." I said firmly.

I heard him heave a sigh. "Okay, I'll be there at around ten. I have a key, so you don't need to wait. Maddie, are you okay?"

"Not really," I said. "I'll tell you when I get back. Thanks, Ben. I love you."

"Love you too, Mads. Take care on the roads for God's sake."

No sooner had I rung off from Ben when my phone buzzed with a text, and I knew immediately who it was.

Reece: Where the hell are you? Why did you leave?

Maddie: Change of plan. I have to go to Nonna's tonight. I'll see you on Monday.

I switched off my phone and threw it in my bag before heading out into the snowy night.

Chapter 24
Maddie

I knew that this was absolute madness to make this journey at night at this time of the year, but I don't think I was thinking that clearly when I threw my hastily packed bag into the back of my truck. Nonna's farm was an hour south of Havenridge and, although the road to Havenridge was usually clear, it got a bit sketchy after that. I just had to hope that the snowplows had been out and cleared the road. My truck was four-wheel drive and good in most conditions, but it wasn't a magic carpet.

I made good time to Havenridge, but I was a little concerned that the snow that had been falling lightly now seemed to be coming down a lot faster. As I turned off onto the rural road that led to Nonna's farm, I realized it hadn't been plowed for a couple of days and there was a thick layer of packed snow on the surface of the road. It was no big deal. I'd been driving these roads long enough to deal with a bit of snow, and I gritted my teeth and carried on.

The snow got heavier on the journey until I was about fifteen minutes from Nonna's house when there was a complete whiteout. Snow had blown over the edge of the road, and it was impossible to see where the pavement ended and the verge began. I crawled along at about twenty miles an hour, but it became impossible to see and I pulled off slightly to the side in despair.

There was no one on the road because no one would have been stupid enough to be out on a night like this. I was concerned that I was in a treacherous position stuck on the highway like that, and I was concerned that someone might hit me, but there was nothing I could do. I couldn't go forwards and turning around and trying to go back was useless.

I'd turned off the engine, and I shivered a little in the cold, feeling around in the back of my truck for the blanket I always kept there in the winter months. I felt completely helpless and as I sat there, I realized it wasn't just myself I'd put in danger; it was the little one I was carrying as well. "Sorry, bean," I said, with tears streaming down my face. "I've only been a mom for a day and I'm crap at it already."

Scrambling around in my bag, I tried to find my phone so I could call Nonna and try to get some help, but just as I was finding her number, I saw flashing lights behind me. I was concerned it might be a snow plow that wouldn't see me, and would push me off the road, but as the vehicle got closer, I realized it was a police car.

I watched in my mirror as an officer climbed out of the SUV and approached my truck with a flashlight. He shone it into my window and I rolled it down, coming face to face with my high school ex-boyfriend. Jed Carter.

His face broke into a wide grin. "Maddie? Maddie Moreno? What the heck are you doing out on this road in this weather?" I think it was then he noticed my tears, which probably shocked him because I was not a girl known for any kind of emotion, particularly one that might have betrayed any weaknesses. "Where were you headed?" he said gently.

"I was trying to get to Nonna's," I said, feeling stupid to have broken down like that. Jed knew Nonna. Heck, everyone knew Nonna; she was that kind of woman.

He smiled. "Well, you almost made it. It's about another ten minutes. Do you want to follow me, or do you want to ride with me, and we'll pick up your truck tomorrow?"

Riding with Jed sounded like a good option, but I didn't want to leave my truck on the road all night, so I told him I'd follow him. He drove slowly in front of me with his lights flashing, and it made it much easier to stay on the road.

It took longer than ten minutes because of the speed we were driving at, but pretty soon I saw the lights of Nonna's farm and followed Jed into the driveway. The door to her farmhouse flew open and there she was, standing there in her nightgown and robe, obviously ready for bed.

Jed was a gentleman and helped me down from the truck, probably realizing I was still a little shaky, as my grandmother stared with an amused expression. "Well, my girl, it's not the first time they've brought you home with a police escort. I thought you were coming tomorrow."

"Change of plan," I said with a weak smile.

Nonna looked at Jed. "Young man. You come on in and have some hot coffee and something to eat. You deserve at least that for saving my granddaughter."

He shook his head. "No ma'am. I think I better get back out there. Maddie might not be the only one stuck out there tonight."

We both thanked him and watched as he disappeared down the driveway with his lights still flashing. Jed was a good man, probably too good for the likes of me, I pondered. I couldn't remember why we'd split, but it was probably due to my filthy temper, which had been much worse in my teen years. I'd lost many men that way but now I might be losing the man I loved for a very different reason.

I turned to Nonna, and she held her arms out to me. "I have no idea why you're here, child," she said. "But it sure is good to see you."

We walked inside the farmhouse, which was actually a rough-hewn log cabin my grandfather had constructed some fifty years ago. They had raised their family there, including my dad, and Nonna once told me the only way she would ever leave it was in a box. When I'd bought my place, I'd finally understood that sentiment because I felt the same way.

"You're ready for bed," I said. "Sorry I came so late."

She laughed. "Oh, I'm ready for bed at eight these days. I was just watching some crappy television. Anyway, I'm pleased to see you. Sit down by the fire."

The warmth of the woodstove brought me back to life as I sat on the old, floral-patterned couch. I was so relieved to be there in one piece, I let out a long sigh. "I didn't think I was going to make it."

She stared at me with a solemn expression. "It must be something pretty serious to have you driving all the way out here at night. I know you wouldn't normally do that." And then she just sat there quietly, and I knew she wouldn't outright ask me what the problem was because that wasn't her style. Nonna got me like no one else did. I got the impression she had a similar temper in her younger years, and she saw me as a younger version of herself.

I looked up at her with tears brimming over. "I'm pregnant."

"Ahh," she said on a long beat. "Well, that is pretty important. Now I understand why you're here. Let's have some tea and then we can chat."

There were never any dramatics with Nonna. She just wandered off into her kitchen and put the kettle on to boil while she hummed quietly to herself, as if all was right with the world. I knew at once I'd come to the right person. As a confused and angry teen, I'd often come running to her. My grandpa had been alive then too. They always took me in without judgment and made me work things out for myself rather than telling me the answers.

She came back carrying a tray with two mugs and a steaming pot of tea, along with a pot of honey. "You need something to eat?" she asked.

I shook my head. "No. I ate already. A hot drink would be good, though."

I watched as she carefully poured the tea and drizzled the honey into the cups before handing it over. "So. You're carrying my great-grandchild. That's quite the thing, isn't it?"

I nodded, not really knowing what to say to that. She was right. This baby would make her a great grandmother, and it would make my parents grandparents for the first time. That *was* pretty special.

"And how are you feeling about it all? I'm guessing it wasn't planned."

"I only took the test today," I told her. "It was a shock. A real shock. We used contraception."

She laughed. "We Morenos are a fertile bunch, Maddie. Your grandpa only had to look at me, and I was pregnant. I guess it runs in the family." She was quiet for a moment. "I guess what I should have asked was, are you happy about it?"

I stirred the honey in my tea and lifted the spoon out, watching as it trickled back into the cup in a syrupy river. "I think I am happy. I mean, I've always wanted a family. It's just complicated."

"Does your mom know?"

I shook my head. "No one knows. Only you."

"Not even the father?" she asked.

"No," I said quietly.

"Hmm," she said. "He's going to need to know, Maddie, and as soon as possible. It's not fair to keep it from him." There was another long pause. "Am I allowed to know who it is? Do I know him?"

She knew Reece quite well, actually. A couple of years back her old horse, Elvis, got sick and the vet from Havenridge said he was too busy to come out and see him, so Reece had driven the three-hour round trip to help her out. He'd also met her at some of our family gatherings, and I knew how much she liked him. She called him wicked, and she wasn't far wrong.

"It's Reece Mackey. The veterinarian," I said.

I watched as a smile of recognition spread over her face. "Ah. Reece. I like Reece. Elvis likes him too."

"Well, that's all that counts," I said with a smile, and I wasn't far from the truth. Nonna was as crazy about her animals as I was, and Reece had scored major points with her in the past.

"So, you've been stepping out with Reece Mackey then," she said, pouring herself another cup of tea.

"I wouldn't exactly call it stepping out. More like sneaking around. No one knows."

Nonna looked confused. "Why? Was it just supposed to be a bit of fun?"

"Yes. No. I don't know what it was." I put my head in my hands, trying to shut out the thoughts that seemed to be spinning out of control.

"Do you love him, Maddie?" she asked quietly.

That was a question I knew I could answer with certainty. "Yes, Nonna. I love him."

She heaved a big sigh before saying. "Let's go to bed, love. You need your sleep. You've got more than yourself to think about now."

We both stood, and she wrapped me in her arms for a tight hug. She smelled the same as I always remembered. It was the Italian soap she always used that smelled of lemons and bergamot. It was a very distinctive scent, and she was the only person I knew who used it.

I made my way into my familiar bedroom and sighed contentedly. Nonna's house was full of worn memories and there was no fancy façade on show here. An old quilt that she told me she'd made when she was pregnant with my dad covered my bed. and on the dresser were photos of Nonna and my grandpa through the years.

I slipped into my llama pajamas and climbed into bed, happy to find that she'd installed an electric blanket, which hadn't been there the last time I stayed. I turned out the light and stared into the darkness, my heart full of confusion. But under all of those layers of chaos was a feeling of joy and excitement. This baby was more important to me than anything. It was a piece of Reece and me and no one could ever take that away from us, no matter what transpired in the next few days.

I rested my hand gently on my stomach. "Goodnight, bean," I whispered.

Chapter 25

Reece

I stared at the message on my phone in utter confusion. Why the hell would Maddie just take off like that? Admittedly, I'd been a bit distracted with that stupid board game, and I hadn't realized she'd actually left. We'd all had a turn and, as usual, Scarlett's turn lasted longer than it should have, so it must have been a good fifteen minutes before I'd noticed she'd gone.

Ryan had joined us at the table to take his turn, and then we all looked around for Maddie.

"Is she in the bathroom?" Kate asked.

I watched as Ryan shook his head. "No. She left actually, a little while ago. She didn't want to say anything because you were all having fun. You know Maddie. She's always thinking of others."

I inadvertently let my frustration get the better of me. "What the fuck!" I yelled. "She could have at least said goodbye."

Ryan was quiet for a moment and then he said, "I think there's something going on with her. She said she had a headache, but I got the feeling it wasn't that. She just didn't seem like herself."

Everyone was talking among themselves about what could be wrong with Maddie, and I casually grabbed my phone and shot her a text. Admittedly, I was a bit grumpy with my text, but I was totally confused at the message I got back, telling me she'd already left for Nonna's place. Why the hell would she make that drive at 8 p.m. at night when the roads were probably sketchy?

We carried on playing the game, but my heart wasn't in it; I just wanted to get home and call her, but if she was on the road already, chances were she wouldn't even answer. Coupled with that, I was worried sick about her on that road at night. I knew the road between Havenridge and Nonna's place well, and it wasn't great at the best of times, let alone in the dark. I knew Maddie was a skilled driver, and she'd driven these crappy roads since she passed her test, but it didn't dispel the sick feeling I had in the pit of my stomach.

Thankfully, after another half hour, Scarlett started to flag, as she so often did. Getting up at 5 a.m. every morning wore her down and by the end of the week, she was usually shattered. Sam and Kate said they'd hang around for a while, but I took Scarlett's departure as a cue for me to go as well.

I climbed into my Jeep and immediately tried to call Maddie, but it went straight to voicemail, which didn't surprise me. I drove home despondently, trying to think through the events of the evening and what had caused her to bolt like that.

As soon as I got in, I made myself a coffee and sat down to do some serious thinking. I tried to go through every single thing that had happened, every conversation, every gesture to find out where I'd gone wrong because, by that stage, I was convinced I'd screwed up in some way; it was the only plausible explanation for why she'd gone.

My head buzzed with the effort of piecing everything together, but more than that, my heart felt heavy in a way I'd never experienced before. I sat there wanting Maddie with my whole body, needing her, because by now she'd become as essential to me as the air that I breathed. I was in love with her. If I was being totally honest with myself, I would say that I'd been in love with her for a long time, way before our trip to the cabin, way before anything serious had happened between us.

I closed my eyes and did a visual run-through of the evening. When I'd arrived, she'd seemed fine and happy to see me. I'd squeezed her luscious ass and she had giggled, so I didn't think that was where I went wrong. We ate, there was some goofing around with Scarlett which was normal, then we consumed those weird ball and chain cookies she'd brought. Things were starting to fall into place a bit like one of those safe locks that clunked every time you got the right number.

Suddenly my eyes flew open as I realized what might have upset her. Oh, holy shit! I muttered under my breath. It was the conversation about who the next person would be to get married. I groaned as my words came back to haunt me: *"Well you can forget about me. I won't be settling down anytime soon, if ever. Nope. I'm just not the settling down kind."*

I'd said that because I knew how paranoid she was about anyone finding out about us, so I had been pretty sure she hadn't wanted me to wax lyrical about being desperate to get married. I remembered looking at her after I'd said that, and she had been smiling. Except it hadn't been a real smile, and if had I been paying attention, I would have noticed that. It was a fake smile, the kind of smile you use when you know it's the right thing to do but you're actually not feeling it at all. She'd listened to my words and believed them to be true, when they couldn't have been further from the truth. There was nothing I wanted more than to settle down with Maddie, but I wasn't even sure that was what she wanted.

We'd known each other all that time but we still didn't communicate that well. We talked about everything except how we felt about one another, both of us scared to death to admit to anything. But it was one I was going to put right because first thing tomorrow I was going to be heading to Nonna's place and telling Maddie what she meant to me. I only hoped it wasn't too late.

❧

I WAS ON THE ROAD BY 8:30 the next day, planning to arrive at Nonna's by around ten. It had snowed heavily the night before, and I was hoping they'd cleared the road to Nonna's place, although my Jeep could cope with most things. Thinking about the roads made me worry again about Maddie, and I hoped she'd reached her destination safely. I had thought about phoning her before I set out, but then I figured it would be better if I just turned up.

I plunged my hand into my jacket pocket and turned over the box that my mom had given me on our last visit. I knew I needed to make a gesture to Maddie to show her how much she meant to me, and this was the biggest gesture I could think of. There was no doubt in my mind that she was the woman for me. I would never find another woman like Maddie, even if I searched forever. I needed to get that ring on her finger and make her mine before she assigned me to the discard pile.

I silently berated myself for not having told her before, but to be fair, she was equally unforthcoming about her feelings for me. I hoped that was because she was afraid to admit it, and not because she didn't actually have any feelings for me. Either way, I would be finding out pretty soon.

The drive to Havenridge was pretty easy, and I chowed done on some donuts and coffee I'd picked up before I left Angel Peaks. As I turned off onto the rural route that led to Nonna's farm, I was shocked at how much snow had fallen. I stuck the Jeep in four-wheel drive and lowered my speed, trying not to think about Maddie negotiating this road the night before.

I was about fifteen minutes from Nonna's place when I saw the flashing lights of an emergency vehicle up ahead. I slowed down to a crawl, and my stomach turned when I saw there was a vehicle in the ditch. I couldn't tell what kind of vehicle it was because it was on its side and partially covered in fallen snow.

I pulled up behind the police vehicle and jumped out to talk to the young officer who was securing the scene. "Please tell me there's not someone in that vehicle," I said. "My friend drove this way last night. I need to know she's safe."

"No, we got the driver out safely," the officer said. "Who's your friend?"

"Maddie Moreno. She's twenty-six, small and blonde..."

"And a whole barrel full of trouble?" The officer said with a laugh.

"You know her?" I said, wondering how this guy knew Maddie.

"I sure do. We were at high school together and you don't need to worry, she's fine. I escorted her to Nonna's last night after she got stuck in a whiteout," he told me. He looked at me curiously. "I'm surprised you let her drive on a night like that."

I shook my head. "Oh, I didn't. She escaped."

With that, the officer fell apart, laughing. "Oh my God. I wish you luck my friend. She is one feisty lady."

I agreed with that sentiment and asked if he needed any help to get the truck out, but he told me he had a tow truck on the way, so I left him to it.

Pretty soon I was pulling into Nonna's yard in front of the old log cabin that I knew Maddie's grandfather had built. I noticed Maddie's truck was parked up in front of one of the barns, so it reassured me that she had indeed made it.

Nonna was a pretty special lady, and everyone who met her loved her. I'd come to see her elderly horse Elvis quite a while ago when Maddie had told me she was having problems getting a vet out to see him. She was so gracious and really grateful, and I remember her telling me quite a bit about Maddie that day. She was clearly really proud of her and, somehow, that didn't surprise me.

As I got out of the Jeep, I spotted Nonna at the door with her working clothes on, decked in a worn old coat and a pair of rubber boots. "Reece," she said with a big smile. "How lovely to see you again." She walked down the steps and greeted me with a hug. "I'm guessing you're here to see my granddaughter."

"I am," I said. "Is that okay?"

She laughed. "Of course it's okay. She's inside. You just go straight on in. You've had quite the drive. There's coffee on and some muffins if you're hungry."

I smiled. "I'm always hungry, Nonna."

"I know," she said with a grin. "You're just like my Lorenzo. He was always hungry, too." She turned to go. "I'm just going over to feed the animals and have a chat with Elvis. I'll probably be a while," she added with a wink.

I banged my boots off before I went through the old wooden door and sat on the bench in the entryway to remove them. The house felt warm, and it smelled divine, an enticing combination of coffee and fresh baking.

I saw Maddie immediately, standing awkwardly by the wood-stove. She smiled, but it wasn't her usual confident, full-face smile. It was a smile filled with uncertainty and concern. My heart jumped at the sight of her, but I was worried at this reception. I was expecting her to be mad at me for what I'd said, but I barely recognized my normally self-assured girl.

"Hey, Mads," I said quietly. "You scared the shit out of me last night, taking off like that."

"Sorry," she mumbled, looking down at her feet. "I'll fix you some coffee. Come in and sit down. There," she added, pointing to an aged, overstuffed armchair. We were clearly back to the seating arrangements. I took my assigned seat and watched as she returned carrying a tray of coffee and what looked like blueberry muffins, which she placed on the small table in front of me.

"I guess I screwed up last night," I said, keen to acknowledge my mistake. "I'm sorry if what I said upset you, but you need to know I was just trying to keep the others off our scent. I know how much you didn't want people to know about us, and if I gave them any sign I was keen to settle down, they'd have been all over it."

She nodded sadly. "I know. It did upset me at the time, but I understand why you said it. I'm just as much to blame as you. I know all this sneaking around has been hard."

"Yeah, it has." I agreed. "And not what I really want."

She looked really upset, as if her eyes were about to brim over with tears, and none of this was really adding up. She didn't seem that bothered with what I'd said the night before, so it couldn't be that that was causing her such distress. Suddenly, she looked up at me with tear-filled eyes. "Reece, I'm pregnant."

I almost dropped my coffee, so I put it carefully on the table in front of me. "Say that again," I whispered.

"I'm pregnant with our baby, but I want you to know that I have no expectations of you. If you don't want any of this, I will be absolutely fine, and the baby will be fine, and I have my family and lots of support."

Her words were coming out in a great rush of air as if she was trying to get it all out at once, and the tears she was clearly trying to keep in came spilling out down her cheeks. "Fuck the seating arrangements," I said gruffly. "I'm coming over."

I sat beside her on the couch and pulled her into my arms, and she sobbed as if her heart were breaking. I held onto her tightly, trying to take on board the bombshell news she'd just delivered and trying to get a grasp of what it all meant. The strange thing was that I felt a sense of elation, which wasn't what I was expecting.

"You want to know what I think?" I murmured into her hair. She nodded, so I continued. "I think neither of us has been honest." She looked up at me with a questioning expression, and I pushed the blonde curls from her eyes. "Hmm. I think we've both been feeling some things and not owning up to them because we're scared."

"You could be right," she said.

"We need to start being honest with each, Mads," I told her. "I'm going to ask some questions and I'd really like honest answers. Do you think you can do that?"

She was quiet for a moment before she answered. "I can be honest, if you promise to be honest, too."

I gave her my assurance I would before I continued. "Tell me how you feel about the baby," I asked her.

She found a tissue in her pocket to dry her tears and took a deep breath. "I only found out yesterday. It was an enormous shock; I just wasn't expecting it," she explained. "But now I've gotten used to the idea, I'm really happy. I always wanted a family. I just wasn't expecting it this soon."

That was the answer I wanted to hear, and I smiled. She was happy to be having our baby, and a warmth glowed deep inside me that spurred me on. "Okay. Now this one might be trickier for you to answer, I know. How do you feel about me?"

She looked up at me as if she was searching my face for something. "I'm in love with you, Reece. But I understand if you don't feel the same way. I don't want you to feel trapped."

Her tears had started again, so I took the tissue from her and dabbed at her tears. "Can I show you something?" I fished around in my pocket and pulled out the ring box that my mom had given me, opening it to show her what was inside. She stared at the ring with a puzzled expression.

"What is it?" she asked.

"It's my grandmother's engagement ring, and I brought it with me today to ask you to marry me, because I am so in love with you that I can't bear to spend another minute without you."

She touched the ring gently with her finger. "It's beautiful," she murmured, clearly mesmerized, but then her expression changed back to one of concern. "But what about the baby?"

"Our baby is a beautiful complication. I've always wanted a family too, but I never really thought I was responsible enough to pull off family life. With you by my side, I know I can. I'll be the best husband I can be, but I will be an ass at times because that's who I am. I'll also be the best dad I can be, and I know damn well you are going to make an amazing mom." I paused for a moment. "Can I put this on your finger now?" She nodded and allowed me to slip the ring on her finger. It was a little big for her tiny fingers, but nothing that a quick trip to the jeweler's wouldn't fix. "Do you like it?" I whispered.

"I love it," she said. "It's so unique."

"Just like you then," I said. "Kiss?" I held her face between my hands and gratefully took her mouth in mine. We'd been apart for one night and it had been hell. I was going to make damn sure that would never happen again. "I don't think I got a yes from you," I pointed out.

"I don't think you asked me," she said, some of her usual sass returning.

I sighed and took the ring off her finger and knelt in front of her. "Maddie Moreno, I know you're going to drive me crazy, but I love you more than you could ever imagine. Will you marry me?"

"Yes!" she said, but then her face clouded over. "Although I don't want people to think we're only getting married because I'm pregnant."

I slipped the ring on her finger, stood up, and pulled her into my arms. "Frankly, my dear, I don't give a flying fuck what people think, but if it makes you feel better, I'll take out a full-page announcement in the Gazette telling the whole town I'm madly in love with you and they all need to mind their own damn business. What do you think?"

She laughed. "I think that will make Harry Connors very happy." A mischievous expression swept over her face. "Of course, now that I'm pregnant, you know what that means, don't you?" I shook my head, not sure what she was getting at. "No more condoms," she whispered in my ear. "We can go bare."

I raised my eyebrows at her. "Well, that's a huge plus, but to be honest, they didn't fucking work anyway. I put it down to my super sperm."

"Nope. Chocolate sauce," she said.

"You're telling me chocolate sauce got you pregnant?" I said incredulously.

"Well," she said playfully. "I seem to remember when we were at the cabin you insisted on filling me with chocolate sauce and licking it out." My dick immediately sprang into action at just the very thought of that particular activity.

"So," I said huskily, nibbling down her neck. "What was the problem with licking chocolate sauce out of you?"

"The leftover chocolate probably degraded the latex," she said with a smirk.

"Hey, I'm sticking with the super sperm story," I told her.

NOW SHE WAS TRULY MINE I wanted to tell the whole world straight away, but she insisted on getting the wedding out of the way first. I knew she didn't want anything to take the shine off Kate and Sam's day, but I was impatient for people to know.

Two days before the wedding, I slipped away to see Sam and Kate at their place because I had something to ask them. Kate looked a little worried as she opened the door for me. "Reece. Is everything okay? Sam said you wanted to talk to us. It's not about the wedding, is it?

Kate had been a little freaky as the wedding date got closer, and I could see she thought there'd been some kind of last-minute disaster by the look on her face. I touched her arm and tried to reassure her. "Everything's fine, Kate."

She looked relieved and walked with me to the kitchen where Sam was making coffee. He smiled when he saw me. "Hey, Reece. What's going on?"

He poured us all some coffee and we went to sit at their kitchen table. Their house was lovely and reminded me a little of Maddie's place. It was in the old part of Angel Peaks and Sam has spent about two years restoring it. When Kate moved in with him, she'd fallen in love with the place, and it looked like they would be staying put for the duration.

I took a breath, not really knowing where to start. "I wanted to talk about Maddie," I said.

Kate immediately looked concerned. "Maddie? Oh God is she okay? Nothing's happened, has it?"

I laughed. "Kate, you really need to calm down. Maddie's fine. It's just that. Well, I seem to have fallen in love with her."

"Oh, holy crap," Sam said with a look of shock. "I wasn't expecting that." He paused for a moment. "Does she even know?"

"Yes, she knows. She definitely knows," I said with a lascivious wink.

Kate looked like things were falling into place for her. "Wait a minute. You were with her on Valentine's weekend, weren't you? She was giving us this bullshit story about being at some fancy foot spa called Happy Feet. It was the worst lie I've ever heard."

I put my hand on my heart. "Busted! Yup, we were definitely together that weekend." I realized I must have been grinning like an idiot, but I couldn't help myself. "Anyway, why I'm here is because I needed to ask your permission to make a small announcement at your wedding."

I told them my plans and they were totally on board, thrilled to be a part of our secret. Of course, I was only telling them half of the secret. The rest could wait until they came back from their honeymoon.

Chapter 26
Maddie

It was 6 a.m., and Reece was lying on the bed with a pained expression. "So, explain to me again why I have to spend the night without you."

I leaned over and kissed him. "Because as best man, you are spending the night with Sam at Ryan's place, and I am spending the night at my parent's place with Kate and Scarlett."

"It's not fair," he said sulkily, sounding like a six-year-old who had been denied candy. "I vowed I would never spend the night away from you again, and here we are a week later and you're doing this to me."

I laughed at his petulance. "Reece, it's tradition. The bride and groom cannot spend the night before their wedding together."

"Well, it's a stupid tradition and it's not happening for our wedding," he grumbled. He grabbed my hand and pulled me back to bed, pulling me in close to him with a sigh. "I'll just be glad when all this sneaking around is over, and I can move in here permanently."

"Me too," I whispered. "After tomorrow we can go official. No more sneaking around, I promise."

He nuzzled into my neck. "I love you, Mads," he whispered.

"I love you too Reece," I murmured, holding him as tightly as humanly possible. He pulled away and started to kiss down my body, and I tried to stop him. "We don't have time for that. You have to get back to your place to get ready for work and keep up the pretense for one more day."

He ignored me and kept kissing lower. "I'm just going down to say good morning to our baby," he growled.

I giggled. "I seem to remember the last time you went down to say good morning to the baby it took you over an hour, and you totally bypassed the baby."

"There were other parts I needed to say good morning to as well," he told me. "I've told you before. I'm very easily distracted.

~

IT HAD BEEN MY MOM'S idea to have Kate's last night as a single woman at our family home. I think she felt that since Kate had spent so much time there when she was growing up, it would be special for her, especially since she didn't have her own mom with her anymore. Bob, her stepdad, had already arrived, and he was staying at The Celestial, which would be really convenient for him after the wedding.

I hadn't told my mom and dad about Reece and me, and I hadn't told them about the baby. We planned to tell them the day after the wedding and I had sworn Nonna to secrecy. This weekend was all about Sam and Kate, and when they were safely on the plane to Hawaii for their honeymoon, we would tell our families and friends our good news. In fact, Reece had threatened to stand in the town square and announce it with a megaphone. He found the fact that he'd knocked up the maid of honor as part of his best man's duties wildly funny, and I could see that he intended to get plenty of mileage out of that one.

I was actually really excited about the prospect of telling people, and I couldn't wait to see the look on Scarlett's face when I told them I was not only marrying Reece, but that I was also pregnant. I figured Kate would have to wait until she came back, or I'd send her a cryptic text which would have her guessing all through her holiday. Somehow, I had the feeling that Sam would find a way to distract her, anyway.

Of course, the one disadvantage of Kate staying over was that all my brothers wanted to stay as well, so my mom was going to have a house full of rather noisy guests. As the guest of honor, Kate was allowed to choose her favorite meal for my mom to cook, and it amazed me that she went for a carb-filled pig-fest of lasagne and tiramisu.

"I thought you actually wanted to fit in your dress tomorrow," I joked.

Besides the huge tiramisu, Scarlett had brought along a couple of boxes of specially made wedding cookies, some of which were appropriate, and some of which were decidedly inappropriate. I was glad my mom was so open-minded, but then I guess she had to be with my brothers.

The three of us were all sitting around drinking tea with my mom enjoying some quiet time before the boys came home. Kate's dress was hanging in her room along with mine. As the bride, she was the lucky one who got her own room, and I would be sharing with Scarlett. I really hoped she wouldn't keep me up all night with her excited chatter. Suddenly there was a flurry of activity as a large pair of boots could be heard coming through the door, and I knew the inevitable had happened.

"Where's the bride?" my eldest brother, Matteo, shouted. "I want to kiss her before that idiot Sam Garrett gets the chance."

My mother shot out of her chair like a rocket and rushed out to the hallway to give Matteo a piece of her mind, and we all collapsed into laughter as we heard her berating him. He appeared in the doorway a few seconds later, grinning sheepishly.

"Apparently I have to apologize for my inappropriate behavior," he said, not looking at all apologetic. "But I'm still coming to kiss the bride!" he yelled and ran toward Kate as she scurried away screaming.

I looked at Scarlett and rolled my eyes. "God, only one of them is here so far and there's already chaos. This is going to be a complete shit show."

She laughed. "Aw, Maddie. It's going to be fun. Your brothers are great."

"Would you like to marry one of them?" I said hopefully. "I could let you have all three at a knock-down price."

Kate appeared back in the kitchen, red in the face. "Your brother is a monster," she said, giggling. "I'd forgotten."

Matteo came and sat at the table after he'd washed up from work, grinning like an idiot. "An evening with two beautiful women," he said. "It's going to be great."

"You shouldn't leave Scarlett out like that," I told him. "You'll hurt her feelings."

He looked confused for a minute and then he said, "I apologize. An evening with two beautiful women and my sister. There, is that better?"

"So, I guess we're having an evening with three ugly dimwits and my dad," I retorted.

Scarlett was laughing so much that tears were running down her face. "This is brilliant!" she spluttered. "Why don't I have a family like this?"

We heard the front door open, and a quieter set of footsteps. "Ugly dimwit number two approacheth," I said in a horror movie voice. My brother Josh, who was actually the most civilized out of all of them, came in and we all shrieked with laughter.

"Oh God," he said, blushing slightly. "Have you three found the alcohol already?" He wandered over to Kate and hugged her self-consciously. The two of them had shared a date a couple of years ago, but they soon discovered they had no chemistry and kept it as friends. "Hey, Kate," he said quietly. "There's still time to change your mind, you know. I'm still free."

She smiled at him sweetly. "Thanks, Josh, but I think my mind's made up."

He wandered over to my mom, who was busy at the oven, and gave her a hug. She smiled up at him and cupped his face with her hand. Mom had always had a soft spot for Josh, and I could understand why. While the rest of us were yelling and causing pandemonium, Josh could be found sitting quietly with a book. That was until someone pushed him too far, and then he could be just as ballsy as the rest of us.

I was just wondering where Ben and my dad were when I heard someone creep in through the door. Ben was obviously trying to be quiet, and I raised my eyebrows at the girls. "Here comes the third loon. I think we have a full set."

Suddenly he burst into the room dressed in a sexy fireman's uniform, complete with helmet and suspenders but no shirt.

"What the fuck are you wearing?" Matteo yelled in astonishment, and my mom spun around to give him a piece of her mind but was struck silent. In fact, everyone was staring at him with open mouths, so he took the opportunity to explain.

"It's the night before Kate's wedding," he started. Everyone nodded, mutely. "And traditionally there's entertainment." He said waggling his eyebrows suggestively. "Well, I'm the entertainment!"

"Oh, holy shit," I muttered. "Ben's going to strip."

"Yeah! Get 'em off!" Scarlett yelled with enthusiasm.

He took a bow. "Thank you, Scarlett. I knew *you* would appreciate my idea. And you'll all be pleased to know I have a really big d..."

"You stop right there, Ben Moreno!" my mom yelled, marching toward Ben with intent. "Get upstairs and put some proper clothes on."

"Aw Mom!" he complained. "I've been practicing. I'm really good at it."

"I don't care how good you are," she said, approaching him with a menacing look. "You are not taking your clothes off in front of these girls."

"Don't worry, Ma," Matteo chipped in. "Half the girls in Angel Peaks have seen Ben's tackle, and apparently it's not as big as he thinks it is."

During all this chaos, my dad had slipped in unnoticed. I saw him first, and he shot me an affectionate wink before he quietly stood beside Ben. I don't know what it was about my dad. He was a peaceful and gentle man, but he commanded immediate respect from people, including his three sons. All he had to do was look Ben up and down.

"I was just going to change, Dad," Ben said quietly before he stomped off to the stairs.

Dad looked around at the assembled group with a wide smile. "Ah, Kathryn. Tomorrow, you will be married. We are all so very proud of you."

Kate got up and gave my dad an emotional hug, and I noticed her eyes were filled with tears. I knew for sure the tears would be flowing tomorrow because it was a remarkable event that no one ever could have imagined happening. A girl who had been mercilessly bullied was marrying the boy who made her life hell. There was so much shared trauma between them that most people would have thought it insurmountable, but these were two very special people who had not only survived but had thrived, and now they were facing their future together.

With my dad marshaling events, the meal passed without too much mayhem. My brothers were always well behaved when they were eating because it was their favorite thing to do.

"You not having wine, Mads?" Ben said, passing the bottle of red down the table.

I shook my head. "Nope, as maid of honor, I need to keep a clear head for tomorrow, even if everyone else is wasted."

My parents nodded approvingly, and I felt a little guilty that they didn't know the real reason I was passing on the alcohol.

"I'm not drinking too much either," Kate said. "I don't need a big red nose for tomorrow. God, do you think Reece will make sure Sam doesn't drink too much?" she said with a concerned look.

Scarlett laughed. "We're talking about Reece here. They're probably already wasted."

Kate looked panicked. "Don't worry," I said in a soothing voice. "Ryan is there. He will make sure everything is fine. He's probably hidden all the alcohol or watered down the contents."

"Of course, you're right," she said, breathing deeply, her hand on her chest.

"Yeah! Good old Ryan!" Scarlett said, lifting her glass in a toast.

"The most boring man on the planet," Ben added with a chuckle.

I knew Scarlett wouldn't stand for that. She may not be romantically compatible with Ryan, but there was no way she would let anyone run him down. "Hey! At least he always remembers to wear underwear, unlike some people at this table."

"I'm sure I don't know what you mean," Ben said with a smirk.

"I'm talking about the time you came to fix my lights, and you were mooning at me from the top of your ladder. It was traumatizing," Scarlett said, causing everyone to shriek with laughter. The thought of Scarlett being traumatized by the sight of a guy's ass was beyond belief.

After dinner, my mom and dad tactfully retreated to their sitting room, and the rest of us descended on our huge family room. We were pretty noisy, and it felt more like a college dorm party than a bunch of mature adults.

I was itching to talk to Reece, so seeing that everyone was occupied, I sneaked off to find a quiet corner of the house to text him and ended up in our downstairs bathroom.

Hey, I texted. *Can you talk?*

Give me two seconds, he texted back.

I waited for a couple of minutes, looking around at the fading décor of the bathroom and thinking it could do with a reno. Pretty soon my phone rang, and I snatched it up.

"Hey," said a sexy voice at the end of the phone. "Missing me so much you couldn't last the evening without talking to me?"

"No," I lied. "Not at all. I just wanted to make sure you were looking after Sam and not letting him get too wasted."

He laughed that husky laugh that shot straight to my core, because he knew as well as I did that that wasn't true. "Well, if you're too scared to say it, I will," he said. "I love you and I'm missing you like crazy, and yes, Sam's fine. Ryan's watching him like a hawk. It's no fun at all."

"I love you too," I whispered.

"Are you staying in your old bedroom tonight?" he asked.

"Yeah, why?"

"Because I thought I would sneak out later and climb up the ivy at the side of your house. I want you, Mads."

I laughed. "Well, I'm sharing with Scarlett, so that's not very advisable."

"Do you think she'll be up for a threesome?" he asked.

"Reece Mackey, you're a pig!" I spluttered.

"I'm kidding," he said, obviously enjoying winding me up. "There's only you for me, Mads. It's been that way for a long time."

I held my hand on my chest and felt the tears prick in my eyes. "God, these pregnancy hormones are making me emotional," I choked out. I suddenly heard Sam shouting Reece's name in the background.

"I have to go, Maddie. I'll see you at the church. Love you," he whispered.

"I love you too, Reece. Good night."

I wandered back to my family and friends, feeling like I was floating. It might have been Kate's wedding we were preparing for, but I was feeling like my life had turned around in so many ways, and I had so much to look forward to. I was in love with an amazing guy, and he loved me. We were getting married, and in a few short months, I was going to be a mom. For now, only we knew, but pretty soon we were going to hit our friends with the mammoth secret we'd been keeping, and I couldn't wait.

Chapter 27

Reece

I stood in front of Sam and adjusted his tie because he seemed pretty incapable of doing very much. "Chill out, Sam," I told him. "You're marrying the woman of your dreams in less than an hour."

He bit his lip and looked me straight in the eye. "What if she changes her mind and doesn't show up? I wouldn't blame her after what I did to her."

I grabbed the tops of his arms and shook him slightly. "Sam, I thought we weren't going to think about that today. Kate loves you. You only have to see the way she looks at you to see that. It's so fucking obvious. She forgave you a long time ago, but you need to forgive yourself."

"He's right," Ryan said, walking into the room and adjusting his own tie. "You're a good man, Sam. Don't let what happened in the past color your future."

Sam looked emotional and put his head in his hands for a moment. "I don't deserve her. I don't deserve to be happy."

"Horseshit," I said dismissively. "Now, pull yourself together. She wants to see you smiling and relaxed when she comes down that aisle, not freaked out. Do it for her, even if you can't do it for yourself."

"Here, take this", Ryan said, approaching him with a brown bottle.

"Are you giving him drugs?" I asked. "Because if you are, I want some too."

Ryan shook his head. "It's Rescue Remedy. All natural."

"All-natural fucking mumbo jumbo," I muttered as I watched him place four drops onto Sam's tongue. "We should just all have a big whiskey. That'll sort everything out."

"No alcohol!" Ryan said sternly.

239

I looked out the window and saw the huge white limo that I'd ordered to deliver us to the church. A similar vehicle would be picking up the girls from Maddie's place, and I smiled as I thought of her. I couldn't wait to see her in her dress because I knew she was going to look amazing, despite her misgivings.

"Okay! The car's here," I announced. "Let's take a quick selfie before we leave. The last one as three single guys. In the next photo, one of us will be wearing a ball and chain."

"A manacle of love," Ryan said solemnly, causing Sam and me to explode into laughter as I took the photo.

SAM AND I STOOD AT the front of the church, waiting for Kate to arrive, and I glanced around. "Nervous?" I whispered.

"Nervous doesn't even cover it," he muttered back.

"Rescue Remedy didn't work then?" I asked him.

"Total crap," he replied, "but at least it made Ryan happy."

I couldn't remember the last time I'd been in church, but it was quite a while ago. This one was pretty, small, and filled with big windows casting sunbeams over the present occupants.

Sam was doing his best to cover his nerves with a big smile, greeting some of the guests and generally looking like the all-around good guy I knew he was, despite the fact that he was petrified Kate wouldn't show up.

Suddenly there was a flurry of activity at the door and the music changed to let us know the bride had arrived. Sam and I both looked back towards the entrance to see Kate beginning her walk down the aisle with her stepdad Bob on her arm. If you could encapsulate pride, it would be what was plastered all over Bob's face as he made that journey with his stepdaughter.

I was too distracted to really notice what Kate was wearing because I knew who was coming up behind her, and I was desperate to see her. Bob took a step to the right to move Kate closer to Sam, and then I saw her and drew in a sharp breath. My Maddie looked like something out of a dream in a dress that was a deep dusky pink. It seemed to be shot through with fire because as she moved through the sunlight, it looked like she was glowing. Her hair was caught up in an elegant updo and she was wearing a serene smile. I wanted to go to her and hold her, but I knew I couldn't, not just yet anyway. Most of all, I burned with pride from the inside out because I knew she was mine, not just friends, not just lovers, but everything.

She had been looking from side to side at the assembled guests and had given a discreet wave to her parents, but suddenly she looked directly at me and smiled a knowing kind of smile, like she was hiding a big secret. I rewarded her with a wink and had to hold down a giggle when a subtle blush rose to her cheeks. I would have given anything to know what she was going through her head, but knowing Maddie, it probably wasn't suitable for church.

My girl, my baby, my future. It was all there, wrapped up in that beautiful package. There might have been a wedding going on around us, but at that moment, I wasn't aware of it. I had to snap myself back to reality when the pastor welcomed everyone because I knew I had a job to do.

The ceremony was actually really well done, and both Sam and Kate were pretty emotional, which was understandable. I was really glad that Harry Connors stuck to his word. After he'd got the shots he wanted outside the church, he'd disappeared. I hadn't been worried because I'd had a chat with Maddie's brothers before the event and prepared them for any press invasions. Anyone trying to get past Matteo Moreno would have to be seriously insane.

After the wedding, we all swept into the driveway of The Celestial in our white limos, feeling a bit like movie stars as several of the local people gathered to get a glimpse of Kate in her wedding dress. Thankfully there was no press hanging around.

The cat woman whose name I still couldn't remember was there waiting for us, and she was obviously in charge of proceedings because she drew the wedding party into a side room while all the guests assembled in the ballroom. She handed around glasses of champagne, and I watched as my sweet Maddie shook her head and asked for an orange juice. Wanting to show a bit of parental solidarity, I put my glass back on the tray and asked for one too and was rewarded with a smirk from my sweetheart.

Sam looked at me in confused, obviously bewildered I was turning down the booze. "I need to keep a clear head for my speech," I said with a grin. "It's a great one!"

"Oh, God help us all," I heard Maddie mutter, and everyone laughed.

I looked around at my assembled friends, and my heart lurched. Sam and Kate looked relaxed and happy now the ceremony was over, and the love and joy were shining out of them. Scarlett was dressed in a miniature tuxedo with her auburn curls falling around her shoulders, whispering to Ryan, who was looking equally smart, about the details of the wedding cake, which none of us had seen yet. And then there was Maddie, who was doing her best to look coolly casual whilst sneaking me knowing looks when she thought no one was looking. I felt so much love for this group of people and was so thankful that life had thrown us together like this. We had such vastly different personalities, but they felt like family.

Cat woman came to tell us that everyone was ready for us in the ballroom and that the DJ was going to introduce us as we walked in. Ryan and Scarlett were going to be first, followed by Maddie and me, and finally, the bride and groom. We made our way to the huge double doors and two members of staff opened them in unison as everyone in the room stood and turned their eyes our way.

"Ooh, scary!" Scarlett said. "I have to get all the way over there to our table without falling over or saying anything inappropriate.

Ryan smiled down at her with affection. "I've got you, Scarlett," he said, giving her his arm. "But I take no responsibility for what comes out of your mouth. Why don't you imagine you're eating a really sticky toffee?" he added helpfully.

The DJ announced them, and they made their way in to cheers from the Moreno boys. Meanwhile, Maddie had sidled up beside me and slipped her hand through my arm. I gave her a quick smile. "You ready?" I whispered, my words conveying a lot more than just walking into a ballroom full of people.

"I'm ready, Reece," she murmured, and, as she squeezed my arm gently, my stomach flipped over. I wondered if anyone would notice if we slipped off and got a room.

"And now please give a big welcome to our hot girl of honor, Maddie Moreno, and our wonderful best man, Dr. Reece Mackey."

The crowd broke into laughter and Maddie's brother whistled loudly as we made our way toward our seats. Maddie was grinning widely. "Did you tell him to say that?"

"I didn't need to," I said. "It's obvious."

Sadly, Maddie was on one side of Kate and Sam, and I was on the other, so I wasn't able to sit with her. I took her to her seat and pulled out her chair like a gent before I made my way to my own place. Kate and Sam joined us to the loudest welcome of all, and soon we were all tucking into an amazing meal.

Pretty soon it was time for the speeches, and I rustled my papers nervously. I didn't mind talking in front of groups, but this was important, and I really wanted to make a good job of it for Kate and Sam. Bob went first and as predicted, it was pretty emotional. He obviously talked about how he wished Kate's mom, who'd passed a couple of years ago, could have been there, but mostly he talked about Kate and how lucky he was to be her stepdad. There were a lot of tears, and I hoped my speech would be a little lighter.

I had a few funny stories about Sam, which lifted the atmosphere somewhat, but mostly I told everyone what an amazing friend he'd been since I came to Angel Peaks, which he had. "Now please raise your glasses to the bride and groom," I announced. "Kate and Sam, we wish them all the love in the world."

Everyone toasted the happy couple and Sam and Kate both hugged me, clearly thrilled I hadn't said anything too embarrassing. It was time for the first dance, but I hadn't quite finished, and the DJ knew this, so he held off.

"Just before I send Kate and Sam off to the dancefloor, I have one more announcement to make," I said with a smile. "You see, some people were surprised that Sam had chosen me to be his best man. Can you believe that?" I asked everyone, to much laughter. "A certain person had serious doubts I would even get the date right," I said, shooting Maddie a mock glare, and she put her head in her hands and laughed. "But the thing is, I got lucky. I had this book," and I waved the book that Ryan had given me to show everyone. "But I also had something else. I had the maid of honor. Sorry folks, the hot girl of honor, to help me, and hasn't she done the best job today?" Maddie's brothers were on their feet cheering and whistling, but they weren't prepared for what was coming next.

"So, while Maddie and I were helping plan this wedding and trying to support Kate and Sam without completely screwing up, something weird happened. Would you come over here for a second, Maddie?" I said, smiling at her wide eyes, because she knew what I was about to do next. Her cheeks were pink as she stood up and made her way behind Sam and Kate and across to me, and as she got to me, I put my arm around her and held her close.

"So where was I?" I continued. "Oh yes, something weird happened. Didn't it Mads?" She looked up at me and nodded, probably not sure what exactly I was going to say. "Yes, folks. The hot girl of honor and the best man fell in love."

There was a stunned silence for a moment, and then the room erupted into cheers. People were on their feet clapping, and Maddie looked up at me. "You outed us!" she said in astonishment.

"I said I would after the wedding. It's okay, I got the bride and groom's permission. I couldn't wait a minute longer Mads. I love you too much." I threw the mic onto the table and took her into my arms for a passionate kiss as our friends surrounded us, all talking at once.

"What the fuck is going on?" I could hear Scarlett from somewhere beside me. "How come I didn't know about this?"

"It's the best wedding gift ever," Kate said with a huge smile.

I pulled away from Maddie just long enough to nod to the DJ, who announced the first dance, and I pulled Maddie down onto my lap, wrapping my arms around her. I knew it wouldn't be long before her entire family was there, but, as I looked up, I could see her mom with her hands clasped to her heart and a look of pure joy on her face.

Maddie leaned her head against my chest, and we watched Kate and Sam caught up in their own little personal bubble of happiness. "It looks good on them," Maddie whispered.

"What does?" I asked her.

"Love," she replied.

I gently lifted her chin and looked into her eyes. "Looks good on you too, babe. I've never seen you look this beautiful." Then I watched as the tears welled up in her eyes. "Shit. Did I say something wrong?" I said, concerned I'd upset her somehow.

She laughed and gently pushed my arm. "No. You did everything right. You just can't say sweet things like that to a pregnant woman. I am probably going to be terrible to live with for the next nine months. My emotions are already all over the place."

I grinned and waited to deliver my punchline. "Do you honestly think I'll notice?"

"Good job I love you, Reece Mackey," she said with a mock scowl.

The first dance ended, and that was our cue to join Sam and Kate on the dancefloor. I'd already asked the DJ to play a very special song for the next number and, as the first bars of Funny Valentine by Frank Sinatra started up, I took my girl in my arms to the cheers of those around us.

"Oh my God, Reece. Did you arrange this song as well?" she said, clearly stunned.

I nodded. "Well, we needed a song, and this one seemed appropriate. By the way, I've been meaning to ask you what you were thinking in the church when I winked at you. You looked like you should have been wearing tinfoil in your shoes."

I watched as a delightful blush rose to her cheeks, and she giggled. "I was thinking how hot you looked in this suit," she said, smoothing her hands down my lapels. "And I was wondering if you would consider keeping it on tonight once we get home, so that I can slowly take it off you, or maybe tear it off you in a frenzy."

"Well, there's a coincidence," I said. "Because I was thinking about how beautiful you looked in this dress and I was wondering what kind of underwear you might be wearing under a dress like this."

The look she gave me was classic Maddie. Flirty and teasing with that hint of sass, it set me on fire just like it always did. "I have no intention of telling you what kind of underwear I'm wearing under this dress," she whispered in my ear. "You're just going to have to find out for yourself."

"Can we go and rent a room now?" I said eagerly.

She laughed that husky laugh and shook her head. "Uh-uh. Your best man duties don't end until all the guests have gone, which could be much, much later tonight."

"I could go and pull the fire alarm," I suggested. "That'll get rid of them all super fast."

She shook her head. "Nope. I won't allow you to do that. You're just going to have to wait."

"Waiting isn't my strong suit," I told her, more than a little frustrated.

"Oh, I don't know about that. You waited for me for almost three years."

"Hmm, I did, didn't I?" I said, gently tucking her hair behind her ear. "The truth is, Chippy, I would have waited a lifetime for you because you were so worth the wait."

We stopped dancing and she looked at me with wide eyes that told me everything I needed to know. As she drew me in for a kiss, I was vaguely aware of some raucous cheering going on somewhere in the background, but none of that mattered right now. My friend had become my lover and my lover was going to become my wife and the mother of our child. Friends with benefits was fun, but this was so much better.

About the Author

Sophie Penhaligon was born and raised in the South West of England before moving to the Canadian Rockies, armed only with a snow shovel and bottle of Southern Comfort. She currently lives in the Pacific Northwest with her family and her rather naughty black Labrador.

Sophie enjoys writing novels about heroines she can relate to and heroes she can fall in love with, and she is a voracious reader of fun and sexy romances. She has a master's degree in education and has enjoyed a variety of interesting careers, drawing inspiration from her colourful life experiences.

Read more at https://www.sophiepenhaligon.com.

Printed in Great Britain
by Amazon

82032345R00149